THE DRAGON KING

Dragonspeaker Chronicles Book 3

PATTY JANSEN

GET FREE EBOOKS

CHAPTER 1

A **CUP OF HOT TEA** was a risky thing to carry on a boat even if this boat only rocked gently. The tea was still hot enough that the heat was spreading to the handle on the metal mug.

So Nellie held the steaming cup through the sleeve of her dress as she carried it out of the cabin onto the deck.

The riverboat had been travelling slowly since escaping the harbour of Saardam the previous afternoon, and the silent, oppressive night had made way for a pale morning.

Through the cold and misty night, the water had lapped gently against the bow, and the ship had rocked softly in the current and with the movement of the sea cows in the harness. They'd stopped briefly to allow the animals to rest, but kept going again as soon as it was light enough to see, because they were refugees and Nellie had no doubt that someone would come after them, if not to recapture the prisoners then to take back the shiny Guentherite order's riverboat they had stolen.

But, so far, the trip was peaceful, and it was assuring to think all was well with the world and that the journey out of the city would lead to safety.

The cabins were spacious and luxurious, but so many people were in the group that it was cramped on board anyway. They hadn't planned on taking quite so many people—people like Madame Sabine, who demanded her own room, or the hapless monk Brother Martinus who had been unfortunate enough to be on board when Nellie and Mina climbed onto the deck.

Nellie had bandaged Martinus' head from where she had knocked him unconscious with a broom, and apologised profusely.

At least it was relatively warm. There was a stove on the far end of the main cabin and plenty of wood to burn.

The children and a few prisoners who were unwell took the benches, which would normally be used by monks studying scripture. Some others were so tired that they slept on the deck, but Nellie had only dozed while seated leaning against the wall. It might be warm inside the cabin, but the deck was cold, and she kept sagging sideways. The cabin was full of the noise of people snoring and children talking.

On top of that, she worried about pursuers and kept an ear tuned for shouts drifting in from outside. But it had been quiet all night, and when she came to the deck with the tea, it was still quiet.

The ship was indeed very pretty. The wood was gleaming dark, the railings polished, the windows and portholes clean and covered with red curtains. The deck was scrubbed, and a strip of tar and sand ran just inside the railing so you didn't slip when walking there. The mooring ropes lay neatly coiled on the deck.

Henrik stood on top of the wheelhouse. He had his hands in his pockets and looked vigilantly over the countryside as it passed.

He noticed Nellie and smiled at her.

"Here's tea for you," she said. "Drink up before it gets cold."

"Thank you."

Nellie set the cup down and climbed up the ladder to the roof. "Anything to see?" she asked as he warmed his hands on the tea. They were big hands, too, with hair on his fingers. His nails were clean, which was always a good sign that a man looked after himself.

"It's been very quiet," he said. He sipped from the tea.

"That's good, isn't it?"

"You would think so. Although I would have expected someone to follow us."

Nellie turned around and let her gaze roam over the misty fields and the churning expanse of the river, completely empty.

Frost dusted the grass and the bare branches of the willow trees that grew by the riverbanks. With the recent rain, most of the reed beds were flooded. Patches of ice stuck to the dead stems to show that the level of the river had been even higher.

"It might take them a little while to get a ship organised, now that we've taken theirs," Nellie said. "But they'll come after us."

"You would think so," Henrik said.

"What are you saying?"

"Trouble might wait for us further up the river. They don't pursue us because they know we'll be stopped further upstream."

Could that be? "What makes you think that?"

"The Regent regularly sends patrols out to the borders. If they've gotten word to them, they'll be waiting for us."

That was a worrying thought. "How can we find out who they are and where they hide?" Henrik might know that, being a palace guard.

But he didn't. "The men who get sent out here have nothing to do with the palace guards," he said. "They're rough and unsavoury types and, most often, they're sent because they need to be taught a lesson. The Guard Commander gives them their orders, and they carry them out by any means available. If they want a post in the city —and most of them do—they have to provide 'evidence' that their orders were carried out satisfactorily. The orders often involve hunting down and killing criminals, and the evidence consists of items that the thief would never be without. Ears. Hands. Feet. That sort of thing."

Nellie shuddered. "Would they do that to a group of women and children?"

"I don't know. These are not civilised men, and we don't want to run into them. I don't know where they are. They consist of nimble teams of a few men and horses each. They travel around and go where they're needed."

Nellie knew one way of finding out if trouble lay ahead: magic. They could use water magic by checking what was going on upstream, and wind magic if the wind came from that direction.

Except none of the "witches" who were in the cabin of the ship, after having escaped being drowned for witchcraft, were real magicians in possession of any useful magic. In fact, the only person who had any magic on board the ship was a six-year-old girl.

She asked, "So what can we do?"

"I think the closer we come to Aroden, the more likely it is that we'll run into the Regent's patrols. As soon as they see this ship, they'll know we have no business being on it."

"We can dress up as monks."

"Do we have enough habits for everyone?"

Nellie didn't know. On a first inspection of the ship, she had seen some cupboards that might contain clothing, but she had been too busy to check the contents.

She said, "We can simply tell them why we're here: because we want to leave town, and the Order lent us the boat because the monks needed to pick up produce from the farm."

"I don't think that story will have any legs," Henrik said. "They'll know that not even ordinary monks get to travel on this ship, let alone people who are not monks. I don't know that Brother Martinus is going to cooperate and tell outsiders that we're real monks."

No, that was probably true.

Brother Martinus was an unfortunate complication. Apart from having a sore head, he had also quietly pointed out that he was now a prisoner of theirs. If any of the Regent's men questioned him, it was likely that he would tell the true story.

"Would the mercenaries know that the Regent has died?"

"Probably not, but telling them may not have the desired effect. If the Regent is dead, the men are free from their obligations to the city guard and whoever sent them out here as punishment. They've now got weapons, and a ship with people they can rob has just arrived."

"Really? Would they do that?"

"They're not nice men. We should avoid talking to them or getting close to them."

"And these men work for the Regent? I thought they would need to be honourable."

"In the city, yes, but out here, it's about survival."

Nellie shivered. Henrik had placed his empty cup on the roof of the cabin and continued studying the riverbanks.

If they encountered those men, what could they do to

prepare? Most people could hide below the deck, and a few of them could dress up as monks. With a bit of luck, the guards would recognise Gisele as a regular monk and would let them through.

Henrik changed the subject. "How is everyone down there?"

"Most of them are still asleep, thankfully," Nellie said.

"No more complaining?" He referred to Madame Sabine's demands about sleeping space.

"They're too tired for that."

"Today will be interesting."

"Yes." She didn't need to say any more.

After escaping from the harbour, the full implications of what they had done had dawned on her. The group of supposed witches whom they had rescued from the harbour didn't just include the people they had wanted to rescue. It included a captured monk, and the Regent Bernard's wife, Madame Sabine.

Having gone for a bath in the ice-cold water of the harbour, Madame Sabine had been too shaken to cause any trouble last night. She had even consented to taking off her clothes so that Agatha and Gertie could dry them in the galley, and she had sat quietly with the other women under the blanket, her face pale and her pretty hair dripping with dirty harbour water.

This blissful state of silence would not last forever. Soon she would start making demands.

Once they came to the village where Nellie's family lived, how would those villagers react to having this noble foreign woman imposed on them?

No, Nellie was not looking forward to that at all.

"What about our monk?" Henrik asked.

Nellie shuddered. She could still feel the thud of the broom in her hands hit the poor man's head, and could see him crumpling on the deck. By the Triune, she'd hit a *monk*. "He's been quiet too."

"Has Gisele seen him yet?"

"Briefly. I don't think they knew each other well."

The discovery that one of the monks who had served in the palace was female and not even a monk had shaken him. Henrik worked for the guards, and the guards were supposed to have picked up things like this.

Nellie suspected that in the next couple of days, Henrik's belief in the infallibility of the guards would be badly shaken. Another thing she was not looking forward to.

"That girl disturbs me," Henrik said. "It seems like she is propelled by magic. I don't know that she ever sleeps."

Gisele had admitted to Nellie that she had some sort of affinity with magic, although Nellie didn't quite understand what she had meant by being an anti-magician. The amount of knowledge about magic that was routinely ignored in Saardam disturbed her. It was why they were in a bad situation like this.

It was why no one had realised that Shepherd Wilfridus was a powerful magician.

It was why the royal family had been killed.

She said, "Gisele is not a bad person."

"Maybe not, but very strange one."

Someone else had come on deck. Or maybe the small figure with a blanket around him, seated on the roof of the main cabin, had been there all the time. He sat with his legs drawn up to his chest, huddled in the blanket, as he quietly observed the passing riverbank.

Prince Bruno looked very much like a child.

"He doesn't look like much," Henrik said, seeing Nellie look at the boy. "I thought he was fourteen."

"He is fourteen. I'm not sure where he has spent most of his life. It could be that he has been malnourished in that prison all the time. He might never even have seen any of this." She waved her hand at the scenery.

"True. Poor boy."

Nellie climbed off the cabin, leaving Henrik to his guard duty, and went onto the roof of the main cabin.

Prince Bruno turned his head when he noticed her. His eyes were dark and hollow, his face pale. His chin sported a bruise.

Nellie said to him, "You should be down on the deck, resting."

He said nothing, so she sat down next to him. She put her hand on his shoulder, but he didn't react to her touch at all, so she let it slide off. It was as if he had forgotten the times he'd sat on her lap while she'd read him stories.

After a short silence, he asked, "Where is Saarland?"

That was a strange question.

"This is Saarland." She waved her hand at the river and the riverbank and the trees and a few cows that were grazing peacefully.

"Is it very big?"

"No. Saarland is a small country, but it is quite impor- tant. We have an important port city."

And there she stopped, because these questions were strange, indeed. Why did it matter how big Saarland was?

In the previous few days, Prince Bruno had not spoken more than a few words. Admittedly, there had not been the time to sit down and talk.

She continued, "What have you been told? That it's a very big country?"

"Important," he said, as if fixating on that word. His face took on a solemn expression as he said that. It was a strange situation.

Nellie hugged herself. It was cold up here and now the breeze was coming up. The topic of the conversation was unsettling, too.

"So where are the people?" he asked.

"Most of the people live in Saardam," Nellie said.

"But what about the farms with rich houses and many crops and animals?"

"There are farms behind these levies." Although she wouldn't call them rich.

She had no idea where he was going with this discussion.

He squinted at the riverbanks, but in this part of the river they were high enough that you couldn't see over them even from the top deck of the riverboat.

Inside the cabin underneath them, people were talking—mostly children, but a woman replied. It sounded like Agatha, who would be responsible for making breakfast.

Nellie had better go down to check. "Why don't you come down to get some breakfast?" she asked Bruno. The galley was well stocked, and they had plenty of grain for making porridge.

Prince Bruno gave her a blank look.

"Are you hungry?"

That seemed to do the trick, because he rose. Nellie hadn't seen the dragon box underneath his blanket, but he picked it up and carried it with him.

He slid off the sloping roof and went in the direction of the cabin door.

Nellie was left by herself, feeling a distinct chill inside. Whatever she had hoped this young boy might do, she wasn't sure if any of it would come to fruition. His ordeal might have been too damaging and left him too strange to behave normally. Too strange to resurrect the royal family. Too strange to sit on the throne.

And that brought with it a set of disturbing memories.

Henrik's arrow had gone straight into the Regent's heart, and the man was surely dead. She hated to think the chaos it would have brought to the city. Who was going to take over from the Regent?

Nellie found Gisele and young Koby at the stern of the boat. They looked like they were having a great time, talking and laughing. They both turned around when Nellie came.

"Oh, good morning," Gisele said.

Koby smiled. "Look, Nellie, she is teaching me how to look after the sea cows."

Indeed, Gisele had been drawing a figure on the captain's note slate which showed the beams, how the beams were attached, and where to put the cows, including notes about dominant animals and where to put them, and males and females.

"Do you have any experience with this?" Nellie asked her.

"I did all of this work when I worked as ship's boy." There was no limit to the experiences of this strange woman.

And Nellie wasn't sure whether she could entirely be trusted. "Have you seen anything unusual so far?"

"It's been as quiet as death," Gisele said.

Nellie was sure she intended the ominous tone to the statement. Gisele was not afraid and didn't speak of death and misfortune in hushed tones.

"We might need to rest the cows for a while," Nellie said. "The current is strong, and they will be tired."

"If we can find a safe spot to anchor. Most of the jetties are flooded, and if I'd seen a place to rest, I would have stopped."

Yes, Gisele must be tired, having sat here through the night.

Nellie said, "I'll have a quick breakfast and then I'll come up to relieve you."

She went down from the roof through the side door of the galley.

Inside it was hot and steamy, and Agatha stood over a big pan on the stove.

"Good morning Agatha," Nellie said.

Agatha turned around and gave her a scowl.

Nellie shrank back. "Whatever is the matter?"

"That woman thinks she knows everything. Whenever we get where we're going, I want you to put her as far away from me as possible."

"Which woman?"

"The pampered noble witch."

"Madame Sabine?"

"I would drop the *Madame*. This woman behaves like a fishwife. She has no manners whatsoever. We rescued her —she can't boss us around."

"What did she say to you?"

"She's telling me how to cook, how to make a fire, how much porridge to put in, as if she knows all this stuff."

Nellie went into the main cabin, where many people had now woken up. Most of them had their clothes back, even though some of the children complained that the clothes were cold and damp.

This sure was a ragtag band of strange people thrown together.

Nellie spotted Madame Sabine seated on a bench with poor Wim, the palace taster, and another woman they had rescued last night whose name Nellie didn't know. Madame Sabine wore a man's shirt and trousers that they'd found in one of the sleeping cabins and was talking animatedly, spreading her hands as she did so.

In the noise of the cabin, Nellie couldn't hear what she was saying, except that she didn't look angry. Wim and the woman ate with vacant expressions, and Madame Sabine just talked. There was no evidence of a disagreement but, clearly, Agatha expected Nellie to do something. Ask what the disagreement with Agatha was about, perhaps?

Inside the door was a little cupboard from which Anneke and a couple of the other children were taking bowls and spoons for dinner. They stacked them in a basket and went into the galley.

Nellie helped carry steaming bowls of porridge into the cabin. She made sure Bruno got a good portion. He sat on the bench in the very corner of the cabin with the dragon box on his lap.

Little Bas sat next to him.

"Why are you keeping Boots in that box?" he asked.

"He is tired. He needs to sleep."

"Are you really a prince?"

Nellie couldn't hear Bruno's reply. She had arrived at Madame Sabine's table.

She put the bowl of porridge down, and expected some sort of protest about *I'm not going to eat that*, but none came.

Madame Sabine grabbed the bowl and spoon and started shovelling the porridge into her mouth. She still had her hair tied up behind her back and reminded Nellie of the hungry groundsmen who sometimes came into the palace kitchens.

This was sure a strange woman.

So Nellie sat down at the same table, and started eating her porridge.

Madame Sabine glanced sideways across the room at Bruno a few times. After a silence, she said, "Does he have to carry that box with him everywhere he goes?"

"He's afraid that people will steal it."

Madame Sabine met her eyes in a sharp look. "I didn't *steal* it. The church did."

"The church paid for it. My father even disagreed with it."

"Your father was an old-fashioned fool. He had all the knowledge and was too afraid to do anything with it."

"He might have had good reason."

"Reason or not, the church had no right to have the box."

Nellie raised her eyebrows. "So, were *you* going to give it back to the young prince, then?"

"That creature is too evil for a boy of his age to handle."

"Yes. Adult thieves clearly do much better."

Touché. Madame Sabine gave her an icy look.

Nellie returned an equally icy stare. A fog had lifted off Nellie's mind. All the time in the palace, they had been eating food laced with magic, and it was not until Nellie left the palace that she realised the palace banquets made people happy. All the silly things the guests did or said never mattered because everyone was numb with magic and nobody cared.

For a while, they ate in an uneasy silence.

Then Madame Sabine continued as if Nellie had said nothing, "I was just saying to Wim we should be having a rest. There is likely to be trouble further up the river, and we want the team of cows to be fresh and well fed."

What did she know about sea cows? "I have just spoken to the people upstairs, and they agree except there is no safe anchorage, and we don't want to get bogged in any of the banks. The river is high, and most of the jetties are flooded."

"Then we must go into one of the smaller side creeks."

Nellie lifted her chin. "I'll let the captain know."

Madame Sabine gave her a sarcastic look. "You're playing with me. We don't have a captain. The captain of the ship got left in the city. I know, because I saw his face as we were taking off with his ship."

Nellie picked up her empty bowl. "One ship, many captains. I'm going to give Gisele a break."

But as she crossed the crowded cabin, it occurred to Nellie that they needed someone with a strong hand to lead them, or there would be many disagreements.

And that person should not be Madame Sabine.

CHAPTER 2

AFTER SHE FINISHED her porridge, Nellie left the cabin and went back into the cold air outside. She walked along the side of the ship to the stern where Gisele and Koby were still talking. They turned around as Nellie joined them.

"Your turn for breakfast," Nellie said.

Gisele took the opportunity gladly, but before Nellie sat at the bench behind the beam where the reins were tied, Koby insisted on explaining everything about the cows and what they had done since the break of daylight.

Nellie knew most of these things, but she let Koby talk. Looking after the cows and being given a responsibility had brought out the life in Koby. For the first time since meeting her, Nellie noticed a spark in her eyes.

"Have breakfast," Nellie reminded her.

"Oh, but I like it here," she said. "Someone needs to look after the animals."

"I can look after them. You can come back, but first I want you to have breakfast. I have no idea what else will happen today, and I want you to be well fed."

Koby left, and Nellie busied herself for a while

studying how the harness was tied up and how the cows were doing.

They had slowed down and were going at a steady pace upriver, sticking to the sides where the current was not as strong.

The poor things must be tired.

She let her eyes roam over the water, looking for a place to rest for a while. The mist hung close to the tops of the riverbanks, shrouding trees in a foggy blanket, although bits of blue sky peeped through here and there.

She knew there were no houses along the river because of the regular spring floods, but still it was disturbing not to see anyone. It was as if the world had been abandoned. She thought of the first time she had fled like this, with Mistress Johanna and Prince Roald, and how, when they had walked up the riverbank, they had found burned out farmhouses where all the people had been killed.

The memories gave her the shivers.

"Back again?" a male voice said.

Nellie turned around.

Henrik came walking past the side and sat next to her on the bench.

"Aren't you cold?" she asked.

"It's better now than it was earlier this morning," he said.

Which didn't answer her question. "There is breakfast if you want."

"Maybe later."

Whatever he was waiting for, he didn't say. His eyes studied both sides of the river, constantly checking and being vigilant.

"Have you seen anything?" she asked. He unsettled her a bit because it looked as if he expected some evil to spring out from behind a willow tree at any moment.

"No, and that disturbs me."

"Why?"

"Because a few times during the night, and again just now, I've heard the horse's hooves, so I know that someone is following us, but I can't see them."

"One horse, or many horses?"

"It seems only one. At first I thought I was dreaming, or hearing sounds that I'm unfamiliar with. But there is definitely a horse somewhere on that side."

He gestured to the right, which was the side of the bank Saardam was on.

Nellie peered at the riverbank, but couldn't see anything either.

Yet it was only to be expected that someone would keep checking them out. The boat was going at a speed slow enough for a horse to keep up. The vessel was big and heavy, made of solid wood, and with more people on board than it was designed to comfortably carry.

"What do you want to do about this follower?"

"I'd shoot him if he came close enough."

Nellie remembered how he had shot the Regent and tried to shoot the Shepherd at the same time. This was a dangerous man.

"And will he come close enough?"

"If he is smart, no. I expect him to be smart. He hasn't shown his face all night."

Now Nellie understood why he didn't want to go inside. He was the only person on board the ship who had any skill with weapons.

"Do you want me to get breakfast for you?"

"That would be nice."

So Nellie made her way back to the cabin, because the sea cows looked like they were behaving themselves.

Inside the galley, Agatha was still stirring the pan.

"Have you had any breakfast?" Nellie asked her.

"Not yet, but when this is done, I'll leave the cleaning up to the kids, and I'll have a good bowl."

Agatha knew how to look after herself.

"I'd like a bowl for Henrik."

"Of course. I expected him to come in. What is he doing out there?"

"He says someone is following us, and he's waiting for them to show themselves."

"Following us?"

"On the riverbank. On a horse."

Agatha looked worried, but she took a bowl and filled it to the brim with thick steaming porridge. She gave it to Nellie. "Tell him we're working on the sugar."

Nellie carried the bowl outside where it steamed even more. "Here you are, eat it up quickly before it gets cold."

Henrik took the bowl and spoon from her with a grateful expression on his face. He sat down on the bench to eat.

For a while, Nellie watched him, and then she watched the sea cows which were still slowly swimming up the river.

"How familiar are you with this section of the river?" she asked.

He couldn't answer because his mouth was full.

She continued, "We need to rest the cows somewhere. They need to graze."

He nodded, swallowed and said, "Hopefully we'll find a safe spot around the Bend."

The Bend was a loop in the river where the water flowed strongly, flanked on one side by fertile farmland and on the eastern side by impenetrable marshland. According to rumours and stories, ghosts and other evil creatures inhabited those marshes.

Some smaller towns were also around that area. Her family lived further up the river.

Henrik had almost finished his porridge when all of a sudden he jumped up.

Nellie had been leaning on the railing and got a fright from the sudden movement.

He flung down his bowl—the spoon fell to the deck—and climbed on top of the cabin roof in a couple of agile leaps that belied a man of his age.

"What's the matter?"

Henrik looked over the surrounding countryside. He pointed. Nellie expected something about the horse, but he said, "There is a ship up the river."

Nellie peered into the mist. She thought she was seeing something, but it was difficult to tell.

Ahead in the river was a tongue of land where some willow trees grew. They were all bare and lifeless now, but the stand was quite thick, and could easily hide people, a wagon or maybe a boat.

"What are you seeing?"

He pointed again. "There are people on that side, too."

The other side of the river was more open, but Nellie still couldn't see what he was talking about. His eyes must be better than hers.

Henrik jumped off the cabin. "We must stop here."

"If the cows stop swimming, we'll drift to the riverbank."

"Could be, but there is a trap waiting for us. We must be extremely careful."

"Should we turn back?"

"No, because it's likely people will be behind us, too. Even if there aren't, these people will be suspicious and suspect we have something to hide."

True. "So what will we do?"

"We have to keep going. I suggest we go carefully, because if we come in too fast, that will cause problems, too. We should stick close to the banks so they can't surround us on all sides."

"What about the person on the horse?"

"The other bank."

But that side was low and marshy, a misty landscape with ghosts. Nellie shuddered. "What do you want me to do?"

She had no idea how he knew all these things about the people she couldn't yet see, but it was not her place to question someone with much more experience.

"Go and warn the others. Tell them to stay inside, preferably below the deck so it looks like there are only a few people on the ship. Make sure they have something to defend themselves with if we are boarded."

But Nellie was sure that if bandits or soldiers boarded the ship, all would be lost anyway.

She went back inside, taking Henrik's bowl and spoon as a matter of habit. She looked over all the people in the cabin and hated how she would disturb the peace. At least they'd had a decent breakfast.

Nellie put the bowl and spoon away and called for attention. "Henrik says there are two ships waiting for us further up the river. He's going to take us to the riverbank to see if we can lure them out. He wants us to stay in the cabin, or go below deck, and grab hold of anything we can use as weapons."

Nellie had expected a lot of complaints, but heard none. The women understood the threat and acted quickly, gathering up their things, children and friends, and filed into the sleeping cabins.

Nellie, Agatha in the kitchen, and Madame Sabine were the only ones left in the cabin.

Of course Madame Sabine wanted to take charge.

"Didn't you hear what Henrik told us to do?" Nellie asked.

"Hiding won't do any good," Madame Sabine said. "If these are my husband's men or bounty hunters, we need someone who knows how to talk to them."

And clearly Madame Sabine thought she was that person. "I don't think they'll be in the mood for talking." Heaven knew, they might even want to capture Madame Sabine and ransom her.

"Just in case they are. We arm ourselves in case they are not in the mood to talk. I don't presume this ship has weapons on board. Monks defend themselves with words and prayer, not swords."

She could be oddly practical.

"Failing that, as far as I know, the next best weapons are in the kitchen."

Madame Sabine walked past Nellie into the galley and came back a moment later with a few knives. She dropped them on a table and stuck the biggest one in her belt.

"Take one," she said, pushing the remaining knives in Nellie's direction.

Something about her movements said to Nellie that she was no stranger to this kind of action.

Such an odd woman.

Nellie weighed up which of the remaining knives would be the most suitable, and she settled on a small but sharp knife used to carve meat. The hilt felt warm in her hands, as if it had already been used.

Nellie slipped it in her pocket, hoping she wouldn't have to touch it.

Gisele came out of the passage to the sleeping cabins carrying her weapon of choice: a hammer. If Nellie remembered correctly, she also had a knife in the pocket of her habit.

She glanced at Madame Sabine, and some unspoken words went between them. They were both members of the Science Guild. Maybe some part of the group was about a lot more than science. Madame Sabine had called Nellie's father old-fashioned, as if she questioned his involvement and didn't agree with him. Had she even been in the Science Guild when her father had started the group? How did she know what he wanted? Why did she assume that she knew everything?

Nellie pushed her annoyance aside.

She did feel better knowing Henrik was not the only one who had any experience in fighting and talking their way out of difficult situations. She just wished that Madame Sabine didn't act like she was the natural leader of the group.

And where was Prince Bruno and his dragon box? Would the dragon have gained enough strength to scare off bandits or the Regent's soldiers?

The ship had almost come to a halt.

Nellie followed Madame Sabine and Gisele onto the deck. Henrik still stood there, peering at the horizon.

"Have you seen them yet?" Nellie asked.

"Three ships," he said.

"Mercenaries," Madame Sabine said.

Henrik gave her a sharp glance. "It's only a rumour that they're in this area."

"The rumour is true." Madame Sabine stuck her chin into the air.

"Who would hire them, though?"

"My dear husband."

"But he has no money."

"The church does."

"Why would the church be interested in hiring armed men when he's already got guards out here?"

"Those men are here to make sure no one enters the city and no one can leave it safely either. They patrol all the ways by which people leave or enter Saardam."

"Yes. They're groups of city guards looking for particular people or stolen items," Henrik said. "They have to do a posting here as part of their training and then again if they face punitive action."

Madame Sabine shook her head. "These are my husband's private men, placed under his name by the church."

Henrik frowned at her. The disturbed expression in his face made Nellie's heart jump.

A question came to her, which she was afraid to ask, and she was fearful of hearing the answer. What about all those people, like Jantien's husband, who had left the city and who had been unable to contact their families? Had they all been killed as soon as they ran into these men?

Henrik squinted at the riverbanks.

"If they're your husband's men, we should avoid engaging with them. They might not know he's dead."

"I'd say they wouldn't."

Henrik crossed the deck to the bar where all the sea cow reins were tied up. One by one, he began to loosen them.

"What are you doing?" Nellie asked.

"We're turning around."

"But you just said—"

"Yes, but that was before I knew about these men. We won't go back far. We passed the Rede River, and we can go up there."

"But my family lives along the Saar River."

"We won't go far, just until they've gone."

He pulled the reins off the bar, one by one. To the cows, it was a sign that they could graze. Because they were travelling against the current, the ship would start drifting backwards soon.

Nellie didn't want to go up the Rede River. That's where they'd gone last time with Mistress Johanna, only to find more death and destruction. Her memories were still full of ghosts and haunted castles and other terrible things she had seen.

"How do you know that the men will leave?" she asked.

"I don't. But I can't see what else we can do."

True. Having these mercenaries invade their ship was no solution either. They couldn't even pretend they were innocent river traders. For one, proper river traders would know how to get past these mercenaries, probably by paying bribes. But they would have no chance, not with this beautiful ship that everyone knew.

Soon enough, the ship started to drift back down the river. Henrik pulled the reins back in so that the sea cows pulled the ship straight. It felt wrong to go in this direction. The soft breeze came up, carrying wet mist over the river. It was cold up here.

Gisele called out from the back of the ship.

They all went to join her, to find she was pointing at the strip of land with the willow trees. And indeed, Henrik had been right. Three ships upstream had come into the middle of the river and were coming in their direction.

A chill went over Nellie's back.

She would have walked right into that trap. She wouldn't have seen them until it was too late.

"They're faster than us," Henrik said.

For a while, they drifted downriver. Nellie knew they shouldn't expect too much of the sea cows because it would be hard enough for them to turn back into the current later.

Then Madame Sabine yelled, "There. They were not alone."

Indeed, they were not. Two more ships were coming up the river. These had snuck up from behind and one of them was already so close that Nellie could see the men on the deck, and a glint of light on a weapon or a shield.

"It's a trap," Gisele said.

Nellie ran into the cabin.

As Henrik had ordered, the main cabin was empty, and everyone was below the deck in the sleeping cabins.

Nellie called at the top of stairs, "Bruno."

A muffled voice responded in the darkness.

Nellie told him, "Get your dragon."

He came up the stairs carrying the dragon box under his arm.

"Do you think he is strong enough to help us?" she asked.

He looked at her blankly.

She explained to him, "There are soldiers out there. We need the dragon to defend this ship."

He opened the box a crack. A couple of sparks glowed within.

"Come on." Nellie grabbed him by the arm and dragged him onto the deck. He didn't exactly protest, but he didn't seem keen either.

Henrik had collected his bow and arrows, but by himself he would be no match for the men on the other ship. They were in full armour, at least ten of them.

Madame Sabine and Gisele had collected an array of projectiles: bottles, jars, pots, tools. Gisele had lit two torches and filled the bottles with oil. She and Madame Sabine were speaking to each other in Lurezian, and it was as if they were old friends who had worked together before in similar situations.

By the Triune, what was Madame Sabine's history?

The ship was not within reach yet, but fast approaching.

"If you have any magic, now would be a good time to use it," she said to Prince Bruno.

He didn't respond, his face pale and terrified. Of course, if he'd had any powerful magic or known how to use it, he would have escaped captivity long ago.

"Come on, let the dragon go free." It would take the dragon a while to assume his solid form.

Prince Bruno set down the box and backed away, his gaze on the armoured men on the other ship.

Nellie picked it up and opened it. A shower of sparks came out and leapt into the air, whirling around. It was bright, even in daylight.

The men on the other ship saw it, too. They shouted, but the sound of their voices faded over the water and Nellie couldn't hear what they were saying. But the other boat came ever closer, and a few more men in dark clothing with big swords came to the deck. Nellie wondered who these men worked for. They didn't wear uniforms and she couldn't imagine that the church hired men like this. Look at the disgusting long hair and beards on them. These were savages.

How were the women supposed to survive this? They had no weapons. If they were boarded that would be the end of this adventure.

Gisele pulled on the sea cow reins to make the animals swim faster. Maybe they could escape between the river-bank and the other ship. A reed bed might stop the cows and the water might be too shallow, but they had to try.

On the deck, the sparks coalesced into a luminous shape. That dragon had better hurry, or there would be nothing left for him to fight.

All of a sudden, it sprang into the air. Its wings flapped, blowing air over Nellie's face.

The men on the deck of the other ship shouted.

One man put an arrow to his bow and pulled back, but didn't release it. They were still too far, arrows were scarce, and they couldn't harm the dragon.

Prince Bruno had taken shelter inside the door of the cabin. The dragon landed in front of him, stretching out his neck.

Prince Bruno patted the scaled skin. His eyes were still wide and his face pale. He looked so frail.

Nellie called, "Come on, make it scare them off!"

She had directed her comment at Prince Bruno, but the dragon lifted his head, gave her an alert look and took off, swooping low over the water.

He made straight for the other ship.

The mercenaries dived for shelter behind anything they could find. The dragon hissed fire over the ship. A section of the railing and a nearby coil of rope burst into flames.

One man ran onto the deck with a bucket to put it out.

"Come on!" Gisele shouted.

She held her burning torch to one of the bottles until the oil caught fire and threw the bottle, burning and all, to the other ship. It hit the top deck, the glass shattered and burning oil spread across the wood.

Meanwhile, the dragon flew across to the next ship.

"Quick," Gisele said. She was pulling on the sea cow reins, and the animals strained against the harness. They might have noticed the dragon and, being friendly to him, have been whispered into action. They might simply be scared of fire.

Whatever the case, they were tired and would not go far, but they would try.

The sun broke through the clouds ahead, turning the river into a wide expanse of silvery water. To the left was the entrance of a canal. Willow trees stood on both sides of the banks.

Gisele steered the boat in this direction, and the sea cows swam at full speed.

"What are you doing?" Nellie asked. "We can't turn around in that narrow canal. We'll be trapped."

"At the end of this canal is an estate where we can find safety."

It was too late anyway, because three ships were now in the canal behind them. Two were on fire. Men ran around on the decks, trying to put the fire out.

The canal was narrow, and with the sea cows going at full speed, the banks whizzed past. Nellie kept checking over her shoulders, seeing the flames spread over the first ship. It slowed and receded ever further as the crew became more occupied with saving themselves and less with continuing the pursuit.

The dragon swooped down and landed on the deck. Gone were the sparks that would leap from his body, gone was the rich red colour of the skin. The creature was ethereal and almost translucent. Prince Bruno opened the dragon box, and the dragon went inside without protesting.

He shut the lid.

Nellie hoped that they wouldn't get a hostile reception at the estate, because there would be no dragon to help them. He would need to gather strength first.

She met Bruno's eyes. That was the main thing he had been able to get the dragon to do so far—get him back into the box—but even that skill had eluded Nellie.

How much control did he have over the dragon? She was sure the dragon only pretended to listen to her out of habit. She had looked after him, and the creature understood loyalty.

Ahead, the estate's house was coming up. The silhouette of a windmill stuck above the low-hanging mist. A row of trees surrounded the main house, a sprawling building surrounded by a moat with a drawbridge.

The canal opened out into a square pond where two boats lay moored alongside a wooden jetty.

A couple of men in dark green livery waited there.

Nellie recognised the colour. This was Lord Verdonck's estate. And so they had ended up exactly where Nellie didn't want to go. It was almost as if Madame Sabine had ordered it that way.

Not only that, but a man in the company of two guards now walked across the drawbridge.

"It looks like we have visitors," Gisele said.

CHAPTER 3

THE MEN ON THE JETTY didn't move to either help or deny the ship access to the mooring posts and, since they didn't seem hostile, the women busied themselves with the practicalities of getting the ship to the jetty.

"There is no current here, so use the light ropes only," Gisele said.

Koby went to do as Gisele asked.

Nellie pulled the individual cow leads to release the animals from the harness so that they could graze.

Gisele and Henrik had tied up the ship by the time the Verdonck estate party reached them.

Nellie recognised neither the man on the horse nor the two guards with him. The man wore a cloak with the coat of arms of the Verdonck estate. She guessed he was the master of the estate in the lord's absence. Adalbert Verdonck had been at the palace when she left and was probably still there.

The man surveyed the ship full of ragtag women with suspicious eyes and then looked at the pursuing ship which burned back in the canal. The smoke hung close to the ground, but the silhouettes of men running from the wreck to another ship were visible.

"What is this, then?" the estate master asked. His voice sounded as haughty as that of Adalbert Verdonck himself. He turned to Henrik because apparently one could not possibly talk to a woman.

"I'm sorry to disturb you," Henrik said. "We're a group of women, children and a few men who have fled from Saardam, and we are looking for a safe place. We won't stay long."

"Yes, you will be staying long. We will have to clear the canal first."

"We can help with that."

The man sniffed. "What help are women going to be? Where did you come from anyway? How did you get that ship?"

A clear female voice said, "I will explain everything." Madame Sabine.

The man stiffened. His face twisted into a snarl. "I doubt my lord will consider you a welcome guest here."

"Did you hear me ask to be your guest?"

He gave her a hard stare, and she stared back.

"Is your master home?" Her voice was ice cold.

"Not yet. I expect him home later today. He will send all of you on your way with your stolen ship, I have no doubt."

"Man, have a bit of common decency," Henrik said. "We're refugees, mostly women and children. Allow us to stay here while we help you clear the canal."

"My master will have the final word about that."

"Let's wait for that, then." Under his breath, Henrik said, "No matter how stuck up Adalbert is, he's twice the human being you are."

Nellie stifled a chuckle.

The man said nothing further, and Gisele and Koby

put out the gangplank, ignoring him while he looked on from the shore.

The flames of the ship in the canal were dying because the wreckage sank further and further into the water. It was clear that the pursuers had fled in another vessel.

So they didn't like getting close to the Verdonck estate, huh?

Because the women had planned for a longer journey, there was plenty of food aboard the ship. Agatha and Mina suggested that they cook a meal, and Nellie walked along the deck to collect firewood.

The men on the jetty left.

"That won't be the last we've seen of them," Henrik said. "The old Verdonck had a habit of employing obstinate, distrusting characters. They travelled with him, but whenever he was at the palace, they would never come inside."

"As it turned out, they had good reasons," Madame Sabine said, referring to her lover's poisoning.

Maybe, but Nellie wasn't comfortable discussing it any further with Madame Sabine present. It became ever clearer that she had been working for someone else or in some other capacity. Was she her husband's victim, or evil in disguise? It was hard to tell.

FOR THE NEXT WHILE, they busied themselves with cooking the midday meal and looking after the weakest and the ill. Jantien's children were well behaved and carried bowls of Agatha's thick soup to everyone and then back to the kitchen for cleaning. Standing at the door to the galley, Nellie did a quick headcount. Not including Yolande the shopkeeper, who had not reacted well to imprisonment and being dunked in the harbour and was coughing, they numbered thirty-four. Wim was also not well, but at least he was out of bed, if looking old and frail.

Brother Martinus, the monk who had accidentally come on the journey, had ensconced himself in the study room.

Nellie met with Gisele and Henrik on the top deck after they finished eating. Gisele had found a map of this section of the river in the wheelhouse. She spread it out over the bench.

She pointed. "This is where we are."

They weren't far from the corner called the Bend, where the water flowed faster, where the river was a little narrower than other places and where, when the water was low, one could cross on a horse that was a strong swimmer.

Lord Verdonck's estate was marked on the map with all its orchards, two driveways and several sheds and staff houses. Apparently, a road from the other side of the estate led to the main road to the city. It went through an area of forest and more buildings on the other side.

"What are these?" Nellie asked.

"A nunnery," Gisele said. "They have extensive farms and they sell their produce to the traders who come past on the road. They're not far from the road, as you can see."

Nellie knew little about the villages that were on the road, other than that some of them had tolls for people to pass through and maintained the roads in return. She knew that people complained about the tolls a lot, and that Lord Verdonck's estate had something to do with it.

She had never heard of the nunnery, but that wasn't surprising. The church was run by men, and if the monks were poor, the nuns were even worse off. The most important function they had was to look after fallen girls who had illegitimate children or other problems that caused the parents to put them in the nunnery, or no parents at all.

"The estate is quite big," Gisele said.

Yes, Lord Verdonck was considered one of the rich citizens of the country. "So, what are we going to do? I don't think we can stay here."

"That will depend on the lord's mood, I guess," Gisele said.

"I don't think we should stay here," Henrik said. "Adalbert will not rest until he has found out who poisoned his father. If he doesn't get any answers that satisfy him, he will demand that his loans to the Regent be repaid, or he'll withhold his produce. He could starve the city if he wanted to. This estate is going to be the focus of a lot of attention and violence. I don't think we want to be in the middle of all that. As far as I've seen, we're nowhere near strong enough to undertake any kind of plan, and we need to be safe for the winter so we can gather strength."

Nellie said, "But if guards are on the river, then we can't keep going, and I don't want to go up the Rede River because no one there can help us."

"I was thinking we might offer to work as farmhands."

"But we know nothing about farming."

"We have a good number of healthy workers."

"Who wants women to work on their farms? If there is even any work, because it's winter."

Gisele said, "The nuns won't mind that we're mostly women."

Nellie looked at Gisele. She hadn't considered that, and it made perfect sense.

She was about to say something, when she heard the clop-clop of a horse's hooves and a man said, "Hello."

While they had been talking, the man had come down the path from the house. This time, Nellie recognised the young Lord Verdonck.

"Well met, my Lord," she said.

He narrowed his eyes and squinted up at her on the

deck of the ship. "Aren't you the same maid who came into our room at the palace?"

"I am."

He gave a dry chuckle. "The one accused of killing my father."

Nellie shuddered. "I thought they were blaming the dragon."

"Yes, but failing a dragon, a maid will do. You made the most daring escape from the city. With the monks' boat, too." Did he sound bemused?

"We have all the refugees here, my Lord, but we ran into some problems, and we came in here."

He snorted. "Call the problems by their names. Pirates. Filthy, uncivilised, murdering, raping pirates. Never travel upriver from here alone."

His eyes went to another part of the ship, and his face turned dark. "What is she doing here?"

Madame Sabine had come to the deck. She stood with her chin in the air.

"Her husband was going to drown her."

"Good riddance. The cheating harlot."

"Adalbert, my dear, always so welcoming," Madame Sabine said.

"If there is anyone I hold responsible for the death of my father, it's you and that husband of yours. Cheating two-timers. These people are welcome to stay here." He made a gesture at the boat. "But you are not. In fact, I want you to remove all your rubbish from my sheds, or I will burn it."

"You wouldn't dare. You know how much your father invested in it. He'd be rolling in his grave."

"My father was a good man, but his delusion about you knew no boundaries."

Nellie said, "Please, all we ask is to be allowed to be

moored here for a short time until we can clear the canal, and then we will leave."

"Hmph. Where will you go?"

"I have family in Stellem."

"That's around The Bend. I can't allow you to go there. There are rogues all along that stretch of the river. I couldn't live with myself knowing I'd sent you into trouble." Madame Sabine was obviously another matter. "I don't want to leave any of this group behind. We're few enough as it is. We risked our lives to rescue these people from certain death and it wouldn't be right to abandon them." That included Madame Sabine.

He snorted. "Hmph." And then he said nothing for a while and snorted again. "Very well. You can use the barn."

"Thank you very much," Nellie said.

She expected a protest from Madame Sabine, but none came.

He continued, "But I still want her gone as soon as possible. I will look for other options, and I also want to see both of you at the house for dinner."

"Me?" Nellie met Henrik's eyes. "Us?"

"You heard me. I'll send my housekeeper. Be ready."

He turned around and made his way back to the house with one of the guards, while he left the other to show Nellie to the barn.

Nellie watched him with a feeling of astonishment. "Why would he want to see me? I'm not a noble lady."

"Why do you always talk yourself down?"

"It's true. I'm just a kitchen maid. Why would he want to see me?"

"You have a lot of experience and what you've done is astonishing. He would be stupid not to want to talk with you. In the city, with all the other nobles, people have their own groups of influence. In the country, anyone can be a friend or an enemy, and you have to make sure you know where everyone stands."

True, but it still disturbed her. She didn't like to be put in a position where she had to speak for other people.

Nellie and Henrik went with the guard to the barn, a building visible from the deck of the ship. They walked along a tree-lined lane with fallow fields on both sides. The guard said that, in summer, the estate would grow wheat and barley here.

Barn was too humble a word for the solid stone building at the end of the lane. It didn't look like any animals had ever slept there, but instead it was a building for storing hay and other produce. Bales of raw wool lay stacked in the main room, and one of the smaller rooms in the building held a weaving loom and two spinning wheels.

The guard told them that the estate kept sheep and goats for shearing, and a few of the workers' wives would spin wool and weave fabrics.

Nellie was reminded that this was possibly the richest family outside the city, and from the way the man spoke, it was clear that people were proud to be part of it.

The space where they could sleep was dry and comfortable. It held a small stove used by the weavers, hay to sleep in and a rainwater barrel outside.

Nellie said they could cook aboard the ship, but the guard showed them into another room which had a complete kitchen with rows of tables. A stack of wood lay next to the fireplace, pots and pans stood on the shelves, spoons hung on a rack above the stove and shelves contained jars and pots with stoppers of the type Dora used in the kitchen for sugar and salt.

"The fruit-pickers use this room in autumn," the man said. "You should still find some of their supplies on the shelves. They haven't been gone long."

"Thank you so much," Nellie said again, and she meant it.

He left, and Nellie and Henrik walked back along the lane to the ship.

"Do you know what his disagreement is with Madame Sabine?" Nellie asked.

"They don't like each other," Henrik said. "That's all I know."

"I'd like to know if there is a reason other than that they don't get along. What's this 'stuff' he was talking about that he was going to burn?"

Henrik shrugged. "At the palace, she spent a lot of time in her room and going out after dark. The guards told each other lots of rumours about what she did, but none of them were ever proven true."

Ever since she had gone into Madame Sabine's room, Nellie had wondered where Madame Sabine stood and what her motivation was for stealing the dragon. She had never asked, because it was not her place and because she wouldn't have trusted the answer. But the time was coming when she would need to know. She didn't look forward to the discussion.

CHAPTER 4

BACK AT THE SHIP, Nellie and Henrik told the women to collect everything they needed and come with them to the barn.

Nellie kept a close eye on Madame Sabine. She didn't know what to think anymore. From any other noblewoman, she would have expected a protest, but again it didn't come.

Madame Sabine simply collected what meagre possessions she still had and then went to the kitchen to ask Agatha whether she needed to carry anything. Agatha gave her a stack of bowls, with the words, "I don't know if there is enough kitchenware."

Agatha then raised her eyebrows at Nellie while Madame Sabine left the kitchen. She mouthed, *What's up with her?*

Strangely, Nellie had the feeling that Agatha was happier if Madame Sabine made silly demands and argued with her.

They walked from the ship along the lane in a long file. Some children had been asleep and were cranky at having been woken up to brave the cold air.

The day had turned overcast and dreary. Everyone was tired. It could just be that no one had energy to argue because they realised they'd gone from one difficult situation to the next. Nellie wanted to speak to Madame Sabine, but people kept asking her questions.

First, Gisele wanted to know what the guard had said. "Did he want us to work for accommodation?" she asked.

"He didn't say. I said we would stay for a few days. It seems he doesn't want us to stay at the estate while his father's former lover is in our group. And I'm not sure if she is worth our protection."

"Madame Sabine has been quite good at hiding her real identity. She is not your average noblewoman."

"I figured as much. Have you known her long?"

"Known of her, yes, but I don't know much about her. She keeps her history private. I will tell you the few things I do know."

"You've known her for a while through the Science Guild, haven't you?"

"Yes, but even there she rarely talks about her history or anything that might let us know about her family or other activities. She says she comes to the meetings because she wants to foster business, but it's a particular type of business she's after."

"That would be magical business?"

"No, but something fairly close to it. Let me start at the beginning. This is what I know to be true: Madame Sabine is a cousin of the Lurezian king. Her mother was cast out from the royal family when she left her husband. This is very much frowned upon in the Belaman Church, but he was a cheater. Even after she had confronted him with evidence several times, he did not mend his ways. In that particular marriage, her mother was also the most powerful one. Her husband had come from a minor noble family who had sought to marry up. But in marrying

Madame Sabine's mother, the man had not bargained for her strong personality and her interests."

"I am guessing it is these interests that all this is about?"

"That is correct. Her mother was interested in the sciences. Madame Sabine is interested in ways to make people fly."

Nellie laughed. "People can't fly. They are not birds." Unless they're sitting on top of a dragon.

"I know, but the time of people trying to fly by jumping off mountains with wings strapped to their arms is over. Many people now make a giant structure called a balloon out of fabric, fill it with hot air or gas and tie a basket to the bottom. Those will fly short distances. They will fly further once all the problems with keeping the hot air inside the bladder have been solved."

"I've never heard of that. Have you seen this?"

"I have, once. I was with the monks at the wedding of Prince Pascal of Lurezia. He's the king's youngest son, a lout and miscreant."

"Like Casper?" Nellie said. She had never heard of Prince Pascal.

"Much worse, because he's older. Anyway, he likes extravagant things, so the king had invited a group of balloonists to show their flight. They took off and almost landed in the palace pond. Everyone was so drunk that they all tried to get into the basket, and a big brawl started because one of the guests said that the flying balloon was trickery. The problem is that this type of thing is not yet very reliable, and one of the reasons that Madame Sabine comes to the Science Guild is to find ways to make these balloons fly in the direction we want them to go. She's interested in everything the men report, and often asks them to come and work for her later."

Nellie now realised something else. Madame Sabine

had been interested in the dragon not because he was magic, but because he could fly. "But whatever is the use of flying? It's a frivolous thing for the rich people to spend their money on, but why spend so much effort on it?"

Gisele shook her head. "Not so frivolous. A part of the Lurezian army is looking at building these balloons. That way they can fly over an enemy city or a camp and drop things on them from the air where arrows can't reach them."

By the Triune.

Nellie felt cold. Part of why she had been so disturbed by Madame Sabine's actions was that she had never looked like a noblewoman with refined ways. Madame Sabine had always reminded her of a soldier.

She *was* a soldier. She was a Lurezian spy.

And Nellie had expected a story about wanting to trade magic and sell it to the church, which had already proven itself irrelevant because the Shepherd was a magician. Or that Madame Sabine wanted magic, that she disliked the church and had been trying to increase Lord Verdonck's influence over the Regent, and things like that. What Gisele told her changed everything.

She would have allowed Madame Sabine to stay as long as she found out enough about why the young Lord Verdonck hated her so much, but this moved her opinion towards banishing her from the group altogether.

Still, Nellie didn't want to do that.

Koby came to talk to Gisele, and Nellie continued walking by herself, deep in thought.

They arrived at the barn and installed themselves inside. Mina was delighted with the kitchen. "We will make sure we use our own food and clean everything as much as possible," she said. "I don't want to give any of these people the opportunity to say bad things about us. We may be poor, but we are not savages."

So much needed to be organised. Some of the women rolled out mats and blankets for sleeping in the hay, and they needed to close the door to the weaving room so the children wouldn't play there and damage the loom.

"I guess she told you all about me," Madame Sabine's voice said behind Nellie.

She turned around. If Madame Sabine was a cousin of the Lurezian king, she didn't look it. She looked just as worn out as everyone else. "Come, I need to talk to you."

Nellie preceded her outside. She didn't want any of the other women listening to this conversation.

The open area outside the barn was for carts to stop and turn around after having delivered or picked up produce. A horizontal wooden beam for tying horses rested on two posts. There was also a water trough—now empty. To the side of the barn stood a small shed, open on three sides, that contained neatly stacked firewood and a chopping block.

Even though it was only mid-afternoon, it was already getting dark.

Nellie began, "The young Lord has said we are welcome here, but you are not. You've been with us for a few days, and I need to know your position. I don't mind arguing with him on your behalf, but I need to know that you're not going to betray us."

Madame Sabine snorted. "I can argue for myself."

"Henrik and I have been invited to the house. Are you coming as well?"

She knew that Madame Sabine had not been invited, of course.

Madame Sabine laughed. "You have been *invited?*"

"Yes, he wants us to come to dinner."

"Well, well, fancy that."

"There is no need to talk down to me. I used to live in the room that's now taken by your youngest son. I spent all my days upstairs with the king and queen. You may not like me or trust me or think much of me, but don't tell me I don't know how to behave in noble company."

Madame Sabine gave her a suspicious look. "You're a strange one for a maid."

"You're a strange one for a noble lady."

Madame Sabine lifted her chin.

In fact, the more Nellie got to know her, the less she looked like a noble lady. Everything about her was scandalous and designed to be that way. Madame Sabine made a point of annoying people. "So, then, why doesn't Adalbert Verdonck like you?"

"That's none of your business."

"It is. We saved you. Adalbert Verdonck wants us to abandon you—"

"Then why don't you?"

"Because I'm not the type of person who abandons people, no matter how unfriendly or prickly they are to me."

"And you think I am, huh?"

"I don't know what you are. That's why we're here. I need to know if I should worry about protecting you. Why does Adalbert Verdonck want to see you leave?"

Madame Sabine shrugged. "Because he doesn't like Lurezians? Because I take the place of his mother? Who knows?"

"Or could it be because of the things you know?"

"Whatever do you mean?"

"Why, for example, do you have dragon scars on your back? Why did Lord Verdonck have dragon scars on the back of his leg? Why indeed did you have the dragon box?"

"Would you want the church to sit on this treasure? It's been very useful to us already, hasn't it?"

"That was not my question. The reason I took the box

from the chest was that my father wrote about it in his diary, which I received, and he warned about its powers."

"Oh yes, your father was always so good at knowing what to tell people to do."

Much as she wanted to defend her father, Nellie had to admit that this was right. And she was very good at telling people what to do, herself. So father, so daughter.

What little confidence she had in herself or her ability to lead fled her now. She was just becoming another preacher. People would hate her like they had hated her father. "I removed the box, because my father told me about people trying to abuse it. It had been owned by the church and I considered that the safest place for it to be."

"But you were wrong."

"Yes, but that is beyond the point. I took it because I was going to return it to the church. I need to know what you were going to do with it. If you intended to give it back to someone who legally owned it, like Prince Bruno, you wouldn't have opened it. And since you did open it, why did the dragon attack you? I opened the box, by accident, and the dragon did not attack me at all. Which makes me wonder what were you trying to do with him?"

"You would really like to know that, wouldn't you?"

"I would. And I will go even further. If you don't tell me, I will tell the Lord Verdonck that we have no further interest in protecting you and that he is free to send his guards to remove you from our group."

"You wouldn't do that. You would regret it."

"Maybe I would, but I will take utmost satisfaction from doing it anyway. Or you can just be nice and tell me. We are a group of very different people, but we have escaped from a great injustice that was being carried out by your husband and the church. We might as well try to survive together because we will have a better chance. If we have the dragon and the ship and all these people, we may see the next summer, and then we can consider our options."

Madame Sabine was silent for a while. They had stopped walking, and she was looking over the fence into the paddock where a couple of dopey horses grazed.

Nellie continued, "All right, since you are not very forthcoming, I'll tell you what I think. I think you're a spy for the Lurezian king or the Belaman Church."

"Lies. All lies. I don't spy for anyone. Those men accept your help and then when you have helped make them richer, they turn around and betray you."

"Then tell me what the story is."

"You're not going to give up, are you?"

Nellie shook her head. "We have all risked our lives getting here. I won't risk my life any further by supporting someone who may betray me."

Madame Sabine let out a breath. "I'm sure Gisele has told you all the sordid gossip about my family, about my cheating father and my brave mother."

"Some of it, yes."

"Soon after she left her husband, she fell ill and died. I was alone, sixteen, and my mother's family didn't know what to do with me, so they married me off to an old man. He owned the house where the Science Guild first met. He also forbade me from ever talking to anyone who visited, or ever going into the room where he kept all his experiments. He was not bad to me—he wasn't interested in me in any kind of way—he simply needed a wife to look after him. I secretly went into his room and looked at all the things he was doing. He was working on balloons. Unfortunately, he was old and died soon after. Some people in his family didn't like me. They said I was too outspoken for a woman, and they blamed me for his death. I had nowhere left to go, so I dressed myself as a man and went to the army because they were recruiting.

It took them about a year to figure out that I was a woman."

Nellie looked at her full figure and found it a bit hard to believe.

"I was a lot skinnier back then. That is one of the problems when you're not allowed to do anything. You end up eating too much."

Not that that had any ever been a problem in Nellie's life.

"But instead of casting me into the street, the commander had plans for me. He wanted me to infiltrate the Science Guild to see if there were useful developments in technology the army could use. So I visited all the meetings because they were not as difficult for a woman to get into as they were for a soldier. This is how I found out that the army wanted to use balloons, and began to consider the study of them as more than a frivolous pursuit. I studied everything there was to know about them, I made diagrams and sewed sheets together into huge gasbags. I helped make the baskets and I helped with the first very short flights. But once the project was starting to look like it might be successful, people didn't want me to get any credit for it. I had an argument with the commander and that was the end of my involvement with the army.

"But I didn't want to give up working with these new balloons. Especially not once the Eastern traders came with the iron ships and dragons. We can't sit and do nothing while people in other parts of the world develop new things. But I had no money and no one to support me. That was when I met Bernard, who offered to help me out if I married him. It seemed the lesser of two bad options. Whore myself honourably or dishonourably. The only thing he ever wanted from me was an heir, so when that was done, we lived separately."

Nellie wanted to ask whether she cared for the boys at

all, but she was almost afraid to hear the answer. It was clear to her that Madame Sabine did not.

Madame Sabine continued, "I later discovered that Bernard was a great deceiver. He pretended to have lots of money, and I only found out that he didn't after I had married him. He thought I had money because of my family. But my mother and I had not been nobles for years. That is my story."

"But what about the things you have in the young Lord Verdonck's shed that he said he was going to burn?"

"His father and I collected many items that would be helpful in our study of flight. We started to construct balloons. It would be a tragedy if they were burned."

"Can I see them?"

Madame Sabine gave her a suspicious look and shook her head. Nellie had expected her to say no, but then Madame Sabine said, "Why not? It's not far from here."

She looked around the countryside. "I don't think anyone will be watching. The fields are empty, and no one will see us."

Nellie wasn't so sure, but she wanted to know whether these things in the shed were worth her loyalty. She still wasn't quite sure whether to trust Madame Sabine, and history had proven that she probably should not, but she didn't want to make any decisions without knowing what all of this was about.

They set off along another lane. For a while they said nothing, and they walked next to each other with breath steaming in the misty air. The horses in the paddock barely moved. If Nellie had the dragon with her, they would be more interested.

"It's a tragedy that Ronald's son is so much against my work," Madame Sabine said eventually.

"Has he said why?"

"Don't ask me to explain the thoughts of men."

"Are you sure it's your work he has a problem with?"

A sharp look. "Well, he himself is not exactly a paragon of loyalty to his wife."

"Is he married?"

"He was, but his wife couldn't give him children, so he's looking for a new one."

Sometimes Nellie was glad she was not part of the noble class. These people were so horrible to each other. You would think they would look out for each other, instead of always stabbing each other in the back.

After walking for a while, they arrived at a second barn. From here, you could see a couple of houses in the valley.

"That is where the farm workers live," Madame Sabine said. "They'll probably notice us here and tell Adalbert that we have been here. He might think I'm going to remove all this from his shed." She opened the door to the shed, and they went inside.

At first Nellie didn't know what she was looking at. The floor of the barn was full of strange pieces of equipment. Wooden frames, metal struts, structures made from baskets.

On a big wooden beam that crossed the room and supported the roof hung a big piece of fabric. Next to it was leather harness much too big for a sea cow.

And now Nellie understood. "You wanted to get the dragon to pull you."

"It was a good idea, but it didn't work. The problem with these balloons is that they get carried by the wind. Another problem is that they are either too heavy or too light, and it is very hard to control how high they fly. You need to carry weight, and once you have dropped the weights the only way to get down is by letting air out of the bladder. That means you can't go back up again, and if there is a wall in your way when you're flying over a city, you don't want to be in that situation. So we heard of these magical flying creatures and wanted to try it for ourselves."

"How did you know where the dragon was?"

"Are you kidding? How did you know?"

Nellie knew through her father, obviously, but had Sabine ever met him? "How well did you know my father?"

"Not very well. When he died, I had just arrived at the palace. He was already old and bitter and had stopped working for the church. He didn't come to the meetings of the society that he started, and he said that we were all twisting his ideas."

"He was not a very easy man to get on with," Nellie said. It felt great to have finally admitted this. She was sick of defending her father. He might be dead, but he would not have liked her defending him. He would have been very capable of defending himself.

"He must have told some people about the dragon, because soon after I started going to the Science Guild meetings, two deacons broke into the church crypt and attempted to open the dragon box. We heard about it from a monk. The two deacons never said a word about what they had seen, but they almost burned down the crypt, so it was clear to us. Rumour went that when the dragon came out of the box, they had panicked and tried to kill it."

"Why did you think you wouldn't suffer the same fate?"

"We were different. We weren't going to harm the creature."

Then Nellie also noticed the scorch marks on the beams. "Let me guess. You paid someone who had access to the crypt to steal the box. You brought the dragon here, you opened the box, and then you tried to tie him into the harness as if he were a sea cow."

· · ·

"P RETTY MUCH."

"And the dragon decided that he didn't like to be treated that way and he attacked you."

"That was a wild night. We opened the box and the dragon came out in a ball of flames. We tried to tie it in the harness, but the creature ended up bucking and flying like crazy, dragging the gasbag behind it until the bag caught fire when it emptied and the dragon knocked over the oil lamp. All our work was ruined. I've had to make an entirely new balloon, but the good thing is that I could try a new design."

"How did you get the dragon back into the box?"

"Ronald managed to catch it with a magic net. We were lucky it didn't escape."

"I don't know how much the dragon can escape. I'm pretty sure he needs to stay close to the box. If you have the box, he will always come back to the area."

"And it will probably stay close to its owner. I don't think anyone else knew that the Prince was still alive, but the dragon did. It did not want to be in this barn without the prince."

And that, eventually made Nellie decide to trust Madame Sabine, at least for the time being. And even if she didn't trust Madame Sabine, she could see some uses for this contraption. She would do everything she could to prevent Adalbert Verdonck burning all this work.

And that meant they had to find another place to live.

CHAPTER 5

AS ADALBERT VERDONCK had promised, a guard came to the barn later in the afternoon.

Before that time, Nellie had scoured the ship to find something suitable to wear. She only had the clothes she had left the palace with, and they were very dirty. Not suitable at all for a visit to a lord's house. The cupboards below the deck held a few habits, and while Nellie hadn't expected to find any women's clothes there, she'd hoped for something to make herself a bit more respectable.

Not finding it, she tried to fix up her hair, but she had no comb, and she'd lost some of her hairpins.

Henrik still wore his smudged uniform. No amount of rubbing would remove a black stain from the lapel, and Nellie decided it was not that important. Running an agricultural estate, the young lord would be used to people coming into the house looking like peasants.

So when the guard turned up, Nellie and Henrik still looked very much like peasants, and dirty ones at that.

It was late in the afternoon, and the sun was already setting over the fields as they walked along the tree-lined lane through the fallow fields and leafless orchards. The estate lay in the middle of a well-tended garden with clipped bushes and a garden house where the lady of the house, if there was one, would entertain guests in summer —if they ever received guests this far out of the city.

A moat wide enough for a river ship surrounded the garden, and a drawbridge provided the only crossing to the safe island haven that surrounded the house.

This house was a sprawling affair, two storeys tall at most, with an attached stable, servant housing and storage sheds.

They went in through the main doors, where a servant took Henrik's coat. His shirt underneath had also once been cleaner. Nellie was a little embarrassed to see that there was a rip in the back of his shirt.

She herself probably looked no better.

They went across the hallway past a sweeping staircase into an audience room on the ground floor.

Through the tall windows, Nellie could see over the fields on the other side. They were full of sheep standing around feed troughs.

Adalbert Verdonck waited by the fire, seated in a broad armchair with a velvet covering.

"Well met and thank you for your hospitality," Nellie said.

"Sit down." He made a sweeping gesture at the couch opposite him. He wore a number of gold rings on his fingers. Nellie recognised the Verdonck family seal.

Nellie and Henrik sat, Nellie remaining on the edge of the couch because she was afraid to make it dirty.

He gestured at a tray with bread and tea that stood on a low table. "Help yourself."

Nellie was quite hungry, but felt too embarrassed to start attacking the food.

Henrik had no such inhibition, and he grabbed a hand

full of biscuits. He held one out to her. Nellie took it, feeling self-conscious.

"You may ask why I invited you here," Adalbert Verdonck began.

"Well . . . ," Nellie said.

"You did wonder, because if you were in the city you would never be asked to come to the house of the lord of an estate. It's different here. We need each other to survive. We need each other for news and must look out for each other. I treat my servants and workers well so they will be loyal to me."

Why was he saying this? Was there a reason he thought that his workers had not been loyal? Did this have to do with Madame Sabine? Was it a warning?

At any rate, it made Nellie uncomfortable, because he was drawing a clear line, telling them, *don't get too comfortable, because I will put you in your place at the first opportunity*.

"Now, tell me the reason you're here," he continued. "Tell me who you are, and who you are working for."

He was looking at Nellie while he said this, and Nellie had no idea what was safe to say. And didn't he already know who they were?

Henrik said, "We have already told you who we are. We are refugees."

The Lord's eyebrows flicked up. "That includes you? Last time I saw you, you were working at the palace as a guard, which is a coveted position no sane man would give up. How did you end up here with this stolen ship that, frankly, I'm going to get into a lot of trouble for sheltering?"

Henrik stiffened ever so slightly.

Nellie said, "Why worry about the ship? Your father was no friend of the church, and he would have been delighted to play games with the shepherd or the Regent over returning the ship. You can have it and play the games on his behalf. All we ask is a safe place to stay."

Henrik gave her a wide-eyed look.

Adalbert Verdonck looked merely amused.

Nellie continued, "We can work, we can clean, we can sew."

"My rules are simple: I am happy to have you, but that harlot is not staying on my land. She will be taking all her rubbish with her or I'll burn it."

"Do you know what it's for?" Nellie said.

"Witchery," he snorted. "I don't know why my father was taken with it. As if people could fly. Can you see us all flapping our hands and taking off into the air? We have enough chaos on land to deal with; we don't need people flying about the air. I don't need my neighbours attacking my sheds for it."

"The things she is doing are known to work. They don't strap wings onto people's arms anymore. They use bags filled with hot air."

"I've heard enough of it. It's all witchery. I want it gone. I want *her* gone. My father is dead because of her."

"All right, then lend us a wagon in exchange for the ship and we'll leave."

He looked taken aback. "What? All of you?"

"Yes. Either we all stay here or we all leave. We came here together, we all escaped death, and we're not leaving anyone behind in the middle of winter."

"You know who she is, do you?"

"We are not leaving her behind. Lend us a wagon and we will leave, *with* all her things."

"You won't find a wagon big enough."

"Then we will come back as many times as needed."

He looked at Henrik, then turned back to her, frowning, a perplexed look on his face. Oh, Adalbert Verdonck wasn't dumb. He would think if Nellie was so keen to hold onto Madame Sabine's balloon then he might be missing something.

"No," he said simply.

"What no?"

"I can't allow you to leave. It's very dangerous out there."

"Then Madame Sabine stays as well."

"I can arrange for her to travel back to her family, if that pleases you."

"She has no family that she cares about." In all the discussions with Madame Sabine, she had not mentioned going back to Lurezia even once.

Adalbert Verdonck's face twitched.

Henrik said, "Is there anything that could make you change your mind about her? Anything she can do?"

"As a guard, did you ever deliver mail or messages?"

What? Nellie frowned at Henrik.

"Sometimes. Why are you asking?"

Adalbert Verdonck got up from his seat. He walked across the room to his desk, picked up a letter and gave it to Henrik. "Does this strike you as real?"

Seated next to Henrik, Nellie looked over his shoulder.

The single-page letter was written in a neatly schooled hand. It bore the Regent's seal.

It said,

Most exalted of court advisors,

The news will have reached you that our father is dead. After his passing, things happened in the palace that are best left unsaid, except that all the paths laid out for the future of the Regentship were unpalatable to me, namely that all of them would result in the death of me and my brother or our banishing. I have chosen to prevent my own demise at the hands of the same cowards who killed my father and have declared myself Regent of Saardam. The first order of my tenure will be to establish good relationships with neighbouring estates. The custom of the city of Saardam has allowed you to live in a great deal of luxury. In order for this relationship to be mutually beneficial, I shall have an urgent need of a minimum of fifty men, supplied and fitted out for active guard duty, to serve the Regentship for a period of ten years. You will be well rewarded in our return custom of your produce.

Yours most kindly,

Casper

Henrik shook his head. "He even signs his first name only, like a reigning king. The hide of him."

"Is it real, though? Will his mother be able to tell the writing?"

"And if so, will she tell the truth?" Henrik asked.

"Those are all questions I'm wrestling with. In short, this is plea for help. Send soldiers."

"Only fifty."

"I suspect he thought asking for more would make me laugh. I don't have that many men to spare. If it's not a trap."

"You can ask Madame Sabine if she recognises her son's handwriting," Nellie said.

"And if he wrote it, how do we know whether he wrote it of his own volition or was forced?"

No one replied. It was impossible to know that.

Henrik spread his hands. "Why would anyone force him to write that?"

"To lure me into the city. I've asked for the repayment of loans. They try to make me sympathetic to this . . . boy who, when I last saw him, was behaving abominably and getting involved with families we would all rather not see increasing their influence."

Nellie shuddered and remembered walking in on Casper engaged in a certain activity with Baroness Hestia in the laundry room.

"Do you think he wrote this well-constructed and eloquent letter?" Adalbert asked Henrik.

"Two options. If he did, he has obviously sobered up and realised that if he doesn't start acting like an adult, he will be dead before the year is out. If he didn't write it, then who did and why? Do you have news that his claim that he's taken the Regentship is true?"

Henrik said, "My limited sources say that it is, yes."

"And where is Shepherd Wilfridus?" Nellie asked.

Adalbert Verdonck frowned. "Is the priest important?"

Now it was Nellie's turn to be surprised. "You do know what happened in Saardam, right?"

"Rest assured, I know. I know that the Regent was hit by an arrow in the chest and died instantly."

He eyed Henrik while saying this, and frowned.

"It's all right, I shot the arrow," Henrik said. "I don't want that to be a secret."

"I thought it was you. It's a . . . surprising action, to say the least."

"Is it? Would you be happy to stand by and watch while a man drowns his defenceless wife?"

"She is not defenceless, and she is not innocent. This is why I don't want her in this house. You're all taken by the fact that she is a woman, but she is a manipulating harlot."

"That's still no reason to drown her."

"He wouldn't have done that. He would have pardoned her at the last moment."

"Except he didn't. She went into the harbour with the others, while their sons were watching."

"What? Is the man mad?"

"That's what we asked ourselves, but the question is irrelevant. He won't do any more mad deeds."

Adalbert Verdonck eyed Henrik with an expression of renewed respect. Calculating. Nellie could see the thoughts whirl behind his eyes. Was Henrik mad? Did he speak for others? Did he have a lot of support? Did he have leadership ambitions?

Adalbert Verdonck was a very calculating man, much more so than his generous father. *That* was why Henrik and Nellie had been invited here: before he decided to remove this group from his land, he wanted to make sure removing them was in his best interests.

Although Nellie suspected that the interests of the group of women were somewhat aligned with Adalbert Verdonck's—they both wanted peace and openness to return to Saardam—she was developing an intense dislike for him. He viewed people as set pieces to be moved to his advantage.

Henrik asked, "You were not present at the punishment?"

"I don't lower myself to attend disgusting spectacles like that. I remained in my father's room at the palace. But after the Regent failed to return to the palace, there followed a period of expectant silence, as if one knew that something had happened but was unsure what. The guards returned with the body and the palace went into lockdown. The Guard commander ordered all his men into the hall and ordered them to crush down hard on any signs of unrest. The nobles at the palace argued over who should replace the Regent. They made a number of suggestions but that priest vetoed all of them. He had been attacked himself, he declared, and he wasn't going to appoint any noble until her knew which of them had ordered the attack on his life."

Nellie said, "Didn't anyone tell you what he did at the harbour?"

"What do you mean, what he did? The priest? The guards told me that the dragon made an appearance."

"It did, but that's not what I mean. Henrik shot two arrows, one of them destined for the Regent, the other for the shepherd. But before the arrow could hit the shepherd, he threw a ball of fire, which then turned into the same fire dog that has been terrorising the city at night. It fought with the dragon." Was it possible that the people on the quay hadn't seen this as clearly as she had?

He gave her a suspicious look. "No, I haven't heard that. Who told you that?"

"I didn't hear it, I saw it. Twice. People in the city have been worried about the fire dog and the magician who owns it. The magician is Shepherd Wilfridus. I have seen him conjuring it twice."

He frowned. "Are you saying that the shepherd is a magician?"

"He is the strongest magician in all the city. I think I understand why he has been chasing magicians, because magicians usually can feel other magicians, and since he is preaching against magic he didn't want anyone to know that he is a magician himself. He may believe that his magic is good and any other magic is bad, or that you need magic because the church is being attacked by magic, but whatever he says, he's a very strong magician."

While she spoke it was as if a light went on in Adalbert Verdonck's head. "That makes so much sense. Everything makes sense to me now. My father has always hated that priest. My father has always wanted him to back off from the Regent. Of course he appointed the Regent, but he should not have any influence over the Regent governing the country. But he meddles with everything. He tells the Regent exactly what to do."

"All of which is now irrelevant, because there is no more Regent," Nellie said.

As she said those words they all realised the horror of the situation.

Henrik said, "Who is in charge of the city now?"

"By all indications, it is that very shepherd," Adalbert

Verdonck said. "Who may pretend that this sixteen-year-old boy has taken the position of his father, and has written to me to lure me into this trap."

"That was his intention all along," Nellie said. "He chose Regent Bernard because he knew the man was weak and had few friends. Your father was one of the very few influential friends he had, and this was the reason the shepherd didn't like him. The shepherd was trying to hide his magic that he uses to make the people believe him and agree with him through the food he gives out from the stores. I have evidence that the shepherd killed your father."

The young Lord frowned at her. "A man of the cloth killed my father?"

"Not with his hand, but with poisoned gin. I know how he did it, because I have seen the evidence."

The young Lord put his fist on the table. "The sooner we're rid of this disease, this horrible church that poisons people's minds, the better. I never understood why my father pandered to them. Show me this evidence, and I'll make sure that the proper processes are put in place. My esteemed colleagues will see that it's a folly to continue to support this church. Most of them are heathens anyway."

Except he was talking about the nobles of Saardam who went to the banquets and had their minds poisoned by magic. And getting the evidence would mean going back to the city and unmasking Gisele's illegal gin business, and that would mean trouble to a lot more people.

But ultimately, she didn't want to tell him these things. Because who said that he would use them for the good of everyone? He'd said he looked after his servants, but he almost spoke as if he did this just to show what a good man he was, and expected praise for it, rather than because he believed it was the best thing to do.

He insisted that Nellie provide proof that the shepherd had killed his father, but he resisted all suggestions that he invite Madame Sabine to look at this letter to see if her son could have written it. He kept calling her "harlot" and wouldn't use her name.

"She never deserved to have two sons, for all the lack of care she has given them. Those two boys have never had a proper mother."

Nellie agreed with him on that front, but didn't understand why he said this to them. This was a very dangerous young man, angry with all the world. He continued to call magic "trickery" and called the members of the Science Guild "quacks" whose opinions his father had courted, but whom he would never have taken seriously.

Henrik asked what he thought the dragon was if not magic, and he declared that "there is likely a rational solution, if one looks properly." As to where he thought his father had obtained the scars on his leg, he said it was a hunting injury, inflicted by a bear.

He wanted to pay the women to visit the city on his behalf to check out what was happening, but Nellie managed to convince him that the women were much too scared to go back to the city. She was tempted to ask why these people should be asked to risk their lives in order to prove a crime that had no relationship to their lives, but that was not true. If it could be proven to the citizens that Shepherd Wilfridus was a magician and that he had killed Lord Verdonck, the citizens would . . . what, exactly? There was no higher authority in Saardam than the Church of the Triune. And the shepherd ruled the church.

The situation was bad. Too bad, perhaps, ever to return to the city.

She told Adalbert Verdonck that they wouldn't make use of his hospitality for long, that they would find another place, but that while the women were at the Verdonck estate, they would work. And that Madame Sabine wouldn't be going anywhere.

"She is not to come anywhere near the house."

Nellie had to agree with that condition.

With that, the meeting was over and Henrik and Nellie walked back to the barn. For the first part of the way, they were silent. Nellie felt uneasy saying less than flattering things about their host while they might still be within earshot.

Eventually, Henrik said, "What did you make of that?"

"He give the appearance of being strong and confident, but he's crazy. I wouldn't trust him at all."

"He is a noble. What do you expect?"

"I don't like how determined he is for us to get rid of Madame Sabine. Does he really hate her that much? I don't like it that he refuses to talk about magic. We've tried pretending magic didn't exist before, and it didn't work."

"What do you think he wants, then?"

"He might want the Regentship."

Henrik laughed. "When he has all this?" The land lay beyond the gesture of his hand in the dark, though they couldn't see it at the moment.

Nellie felt heat rush to her cheeks. "Well, if you know so well, why don't you tell me what you think he wants?"

Henrik laughed again. "I'm just teasing you."

"I'm not in the mood for teasing. This man disturbs me."

"I'm sorry. I honestly don't know what he wants," Henrik said. "I've been with these nobles long enough that I know they're propelled by money or power, but I can't see how he can get either out of this. He had few relations with the Saardam nobles, and I doubt they'd support him as Regent. Saarland is not big enough for him to risk his life. Certainly he appears to have been scornful of his father and his involvement with Madame Sabine. He doesn't like the Regent, he doesn't like the church, he doesn't like magic, he doesn't like the Science Guild. There is not much left for him to like."

"I don't want him in control of our group. We will find somewhere else as soon as we can." She knew it would not be easy, especially in winter. They might have to split up, stay quiet, and hope no one would ask questions about Prince Bruno or the dragon.

"What are these possessions of Madame Sabine's that he was talking about?" Henrik asked.

"Madame Sabine has an interesting history with the Lurezian army. They're balloons. Madame Sabine has the knowledge to make them. I think she was injured because she attempted to get the dragon to pull one with a harness, like the sea cows pull the boat."

"That's crazy."

Nellie nodded. Noble people did crazy things.

"Do you think the letter is real?" she asked.

"Oh, it's real. Casper wrote it. The seal is real. But I think someone made him write it, probably the shepherd. I think Adalbert Verdonck is right: the purpose of it is to lure him to the city so that someone can kill him, heirless. And then they can fight over all this land and his money, because the palace needs money. If they were already handing out food at the start of winter, the end of winter will be far worse. I repeat what I've said before: this estate will be the centre of a lot of trouble. We need to find another place to live."

CHAPTER 6

NELLIE AND HENRIK were almost at the barn when the hoofbeats of a galloping horse came from behind.

"That horse is going at great speed," Henrik said.

They stopped and turned around.

From out of the darkness came a pale shape. For a moment, Nellie thought it was a ghost horse, but it was making too much noise. It was a grey-white horse, one she had seen before: Madame Sabine's stallion.

As they watched, it took a giant leap over the fence of the sheep paddock. It made a sharp turn and ran down the road until it was swallowed by the darkness.

"Well, I never . . ." Henrik said.

"Do you think the horse has followed us all the way from Saardam?"

"Looks like it."

They waited for a bit, but the horse had vanished, so they went into the barn.

While they had been away, Lord Verdonck's men had delivered a wheelbarrow of winter vegetables: cabbages, parsnips, carrots, beets and dried peas, half a wheel of cheese and some ham. Agatha and Gertie were happily cooking.

The delivery included bread, even if it was a little bit dry, but they were provided with some real butter, and all the children were very happy about that.

Looking over the goings-on in the barn, Nellie felt uneasy. She didn't want to impose on the estate's hospitality for any longer than necessary. She knew that the young lord had invited them for a purpose, and she didn't like not knowing what that purpose was. But finding another place would be hard. If Stellem was as unreachable as Adalbert Verdonck had said, they might be stuck here for longer than planned.

But, for a while, all the talk was about food and the facilities.

Even Madame Sabine got into it, and now that Nellie knew she had served in some kind of special force, her impression of Madame Sabine had changed quite a bit.

She was not the pampered noblewoman that Nellie had thought her to be. From what she had heard, she didn't really belong at the court at all.

The children asked Nellie to tell her a story before bed, so Nellie sat on the floor and told them a story of a young boy who always wanted to travel, who went with his parents across the sea from the east and came to a country where everyone was very scared of them. The boy had magic, and magic was considered normal where he came from. His family had dragons and no one thought anything of that.

She was talking, of course, of Bruno's father Li Fai, who had come with his parents, even though he had been a little bit older than the story suggested.

Prince Bruno himself was sitting to the side, his knees drawn up to his chest and his arm slipped around his knees. His dark eyes roamed the inside of the barn, alternately looking to the women preparing dinner and the children listening to the story. The dragon box lay at his feet. Sometimes he smiled at Koby, who was helping the women.

Koby took a piece of bread to him and sat down next to him.

They started talking, but because Nellie was still telling the story, she couldn't give it any attention. At any rate, Prince Bruno appeared to be laughing and listening to Koby.

After dinner, Nellie went with Gisele to check on the sea cows. Gisele stopped at the jetty, peering out into the canal where moonlight softly glinted on the dark water. "We need to remove that wreck from the canal."

"Do you have the same urge as I to get out of here?" Nellie asked.

"I don't like this place," Gisele said. "Now, of course, the noble son doesn't like the church. I'm wearing a habit. It's quite likely that he has seen me at the palace. Of course he doesn't like me. But I have the feeling he knows something he's not sharing, or he wants something and knows we will be important in getting whatever he wants."

"Yes," Nellie said. "I have this feeling that he's trying to use us against the church. I don't like it. I don't want to be used as a weapon against anything. And the church is not bad."

They were silent for a while. In the distance an owl hooted in the woods.

"You were talking about a nunnery? Would it be possible that we could offer our services there?" Nellie asked.

"They have a farm," Gisele said. "It's a farm I like very much. I've spent some time there in the past years. The soil is rich and the land produces plenty. It's a place of solace."

"But?" Nellie suspected there was a but.

"The abbess died last year. She was very old. I would have trusted her with my life, but I don't know much about the new one."

"Could we visit, perhaps, to see if they could offer us a barn in return for our work?"

"I've been thinking this. A few of us could go. If they can't accommodate us, we might find work in a village on the other side of the nunnery. The only problem is that it's on the road from Saardam to the ferry to Burovia, so it's more likely that soldiers and rogues looking for us would be there."

"Let's try the nunnery first." It sounded like an ideal place to Nellie.

They walked back to the barn in silence.

From a distance the sound of children singing drifted on the cold night air.

When they went into the barn, they found the women seated by the fire, singing and clapping with some of the smaller children. Wim was getting carried away by the game. He still bore bruises and scabs from his time in the dungeons, but otherwise he appeared to be recovering well.

Mina had made a steaming pot of tea.

Henrik, and Jantien's son Ewout, carried wood to the fire, and Henrik showed him how to feed the flames. Nellie knew that Henrik had grandchildren and thought he must miss them.

Prince Bruno sat with Koby and a couple of the older children, including Anneke. He held the Dragon box on his lap, and let others touch the lid.

Nellie pretended to go to the sleeping area, so that she could walk behind them. "Can you feel it?" Anneke said.

The little girl who had her hand on the box shook her head. "He isn't really in there."

"He is so," Anneke said. "You can feel the magic in the lid. The same as when you touch Boots."

"He is only warm," the other girl said.

"No, it's magic," Anneke said.

Meanwhile, the adults were talking while seated around the fire.

Nellie listened with half an ear to how some of the women wanted to stay here because it was warm and dry, and how some others didn't like being guests of a noble family.

"Before we know it, we'll be drawn into servitude," Agatha said.

"What do you want then, to freeze to death out in the forest where there is nothing? I have no interest in being a martyr for some sort of noble cause."

"You don't understand what these rich people can do to you," Agatha said. "And what they can do to your children."

She glanced at her daughter and son, who were still with Bruno and Henrik. Anneke was still arguing with the other girl about whether you could or could not feel magic. Prince Bruno had moved to the other side of the group, glaring across the barn with his arms crossed over his chest.

Nellie left the group of adults, and went to him. "Did the children say anything to upset you?" she asked.

"They know nothing." His voice sounded angry.

"Nobody can know everything. They are only young children."

"This is my dragon."

"No one ever said he was anyone else's." She tried to make her voice soft and soothing, but he didn't even look at her.

"They said he was yours."

"He's not. I looked after him, but he's yours."

"He listens to you better than he listens to me."

"Maybe you need to give him time to get used to you."

"He has to listen to me. I want to use him to punish those who punished me."

"Punishing is not always the best thing to do."

"Not even when they hit me for no reason at all, and they made me sit in the chapel without clothes on in the middle of winter until I was so cold that I fainted? Not even if they made me cite the Book of Verses off by heart and lashed me each time I got something wrong? Not even if they killed my mother and stepfather and told my father to go away and never come back?" His voice was shrill. "And they killed my sister and said she was evil, and this stupid fat man sits on the throne where my stepfather should be, and he talks to the priests that hit me, and pretends they are good people. Shouldn't those people be killed?"

"Punishment is only good if it teaches people a lesson. If those people won't do it again—"

"They won't if they're dead."

"Or if other people can see it and they know the punishment was just and they know that whoever ordered the punishment is a just and not a vengeful person."

"I think it's fair. I suffered for many years. They will only suffer for a short time."

"But if they're dead, they can never apologise or tell other people how wrong they were."

He had to think about that for a while. "You said yourself that the priests should be punished. Why are we here in this barn listening to the stupid man in the big house up the lane when we should be in the city fighting the stupid monks? I want the dragon to kill all of them."

"The dragon is a gentle creature. He won't kill someone just because you say so."

"See? He listens to you, not to me."

"He listens to himself and decides what is right."

"That makes no sense. He has to listen to me."

His anger disturbed her. Sure, she would be angry if she had been locked up, but he had gone from an injured, timid boy to a really angry adolescent in a very short time.

"We will go back to the city and you will get your revenge, I promise."

He pressed his lips together, but said nothing.

"We need to get ourselves better organised, because there is no way we can escape the guards with just this small group. We need to wait until spring when we're all strong again."

He still said nothing, so she suggested that he go to sleep, although that wouldn't solve anything. But morning made everything so much better. She would know what to say to him in the morning. Tonight, the Triune would touch her in her sleep and tell her what to say.

Bruno sat down in the straw, and when the children asked him to play a game he played with them.

Nellie was somewhat reassured by this, but to be honest, he didn't really belong with the children anymore, if he ever had. He seemed to like Koby, so maybe she should talk to Koby about keeping an eye on him.

Nellie returned to the fire with the adults, where people discussed what they should do next.

Jantien wanted to travel to Florisheim to see if she could find her husband. "Now that the Regent is dead, he'll be coming back to Saardam and if he finds us gone, he'll be beside himself with worry."

"You could go back to Saardam," Agatha said. "A couple of us want to go."

"You can't ask Jantien to go back there," Floris said. "She almost got killed."

"I'll go back," Yolande said from where she lay in the straw. Her voice was rough and, after she had spoken, a hacking cough racked her body. "I'm dying anyway. I'll die on the bastard's doorstep and he can dispose of my body. Which is easy because I'll be in the church anyway." She chuckled and her voice faded in another coughing fit.

"I think Yolande is the reason we should stay here," Hilde said. "She is too ill to travel. I don't understand why you're all so keen to leave again. Lord Verdonck is friendly, he is happy to have us stay, the barn is comfortable, it's warm here and we have enough food. What more do you want?"

"He says that if we want to stay here, Madame Sabine can't stay here. Since we rescued her and she has come here with us, I think we should all either stay or go. I don't want to make any exceptions."

"If you wish, I can go with Sabine and take her to one of the order's monasteries," Brother Martinus said.

Everyone turned to him. He rarely said anything.

Hilde spread her hands. "See? The solution is easy."

But Nellie didn't want that at all. She was sure that if Brother Martinus reached any of the monasteries along the river, he would tell them where to find the missing ship and there would be all kinds of trouble. Besides, she didn't trust either him or Madame Sabine not to betray the group.

So she told the women what she and Gisele had already discussed, that a few people would go to the nearby nunnery to see if they could house a group of thirty-five people for the winter in return for work.

Gisele then explained what sort of place this nunnery was, that she had been there and that it was very comfortable and not very far.

And finally everyone agreed that it was at least worth investigating. Gisele said that she would ask the groundsman for a wagon tomorrow.

CHAPTER 7

"**I'VE BORROWED A HORSE** and cart," Gisele said at breakfast the next morning.

Nellie had just risen, her head still fuzzy from sleep, and she sat on one of the hard benches in the fruit picker's kitchen, eating porridge. As usual when she worried, she'd lain awake until well into the small hours, listening to Yolande's coughing; but, unlike Yolande, she couldn't sleep in.

Gisele looked far too awake, her cheeks rosy from the cold.

"It's not far to the nuns' farm," Gisele said. "There is a forest in between the Verdonck estate and the main road. The farm is just the other side of the forest."

They could easily visit in a day.

Next was the question of who should come. Nellie, obviously. Gisele, to introduce them and steer the cart. She wanted to take Henrik, but he said it would be best for him to stay in case there was trouble. That could be trouble from outside as well as within the group.

Bruno ate at the table by himself, with his dragon box,

still with an angry expression on his face. Apparently he wanted to come.

Henrik had to promise him to teach him to shoot with a bow and arrow.

"I can come," Brother Martinus said.

That was the second time now that he'd offered to do something that took him away from the group. No, he was definitely staying here.

Nellie chose Wim as their last companion. He had found a heavy cloak with a sheepskin lining on the ship. It was so big that he almost disappeared in it. Despite tasting all the Regent's food, Wim was a skinny man.

The cart stood outside the barn, a simple flatbed affair with a single bench and a tray. The horse was very big and looked dopey.

Nellie, Gisele, and Wim got in. Gisele took the reins, Nellie sat next to her and Wim climbed into the tray.

Just as they were about to leave, Koby came from the barn.

"Oh, Gisele, can I come, please?"

"Come on then, hop on."

Koby climbed into the tray with Wim, and they were off.

First they travelled through the estate's fields, now fallow because it was winter. A frosting of ice dusted the stubble on the ground. It would probably thaw out later, but for now the world was frozen in silence. The cows moped over a soggy pile of hay and the sheep nosed around in the dead grass. Not a single bird gave a peep.

They crested the low ridge. Ahead lay a grazing field—the grass now brown—interspersed with corpses of willow trees. The road wound through this field, occasionally avoiding wet marshy areas. They came to the edge of the forest.

For Nellie, having travelled through the forests of the

east, this was not a real forest. The willow trees were not very tall, and the leafless branches let through plenty of light.

In the middle, they passed another marshy area surrounding a pond, where a number of deer took flight. It was quite soothing and pretty.

Only some of the willows were harvested, to make baskets from their supple branches. Most of the trees had their natural shape. Being winter, the branches bore no leaves, and the grass between the trees was dead.

It was because of this sparse vegetation that Nellie spotted what looked like a hut in the middle of the forest. And then another one. She also thought she could see a wagon, and a grazing horse.

She pointed. "What's that?"

Gisele squinted. "I don't know. The map said nothing about a village."

She unrolled the map on her knees just to be sure. "Oh, I see. It's a water mill. I guess the miller keeps some horses."

They could now see the house as well. A plume of smoke rose from the chimney.

"All this land belongs to the church," Gisele said. "Adalbert Verdonck is not happy about it, because his mother gave it to the nuns when she found out that his father was cheating on her."

"With Madame Sabine?"

"Long before that time. Lady Verdonck has been dead many years. She was a very generous and devout woman. Ronald Verdonck was a habitual cheater."

Nellie wondered how well "devout" would have gone down in a household where the men openly declared hatred of the church.

"At the end of her life, Lady Verdonck lived at the farm. You can still see her rooms if you ask the nuns. They maintain the flower garden as well. The rumour goes that Adalbert wants to repossess the land and is offering the nuns good payment. Unfortunately for him, the nuns care little about payment. They grow everything they need and sell the rest to people who take it to the markets."

Gisele knew such a lot about people's lives. It was sad that she didn't appear to have had much of a life of her own.

The cart trundled through another field and up another low hill, and when they got to the top they could see a couple of buildings along the creek. The buildings were surrounded by small plots of land, with empty bean stakes and cabbages still growing, an orchard of leafless trees, barns and fields with horses and cows.

No people were in sight, but trails of smoke drifted from several chimneys in the sprawling complex of buildings. When they came closer, Nellie could see the chapel tower and the entrance of the building with columns around the front.

They were coming to the farm from the back entrance. A lane lined with trees led from the buildings to the main road between Saardam and Burovia, which was visible in the distance, as well as the church tower of a village.

The cart turned into the long driveway through empty paddocks. A bit further along, a horse clopped to the fence, looking curious. When they entered the grounds, someone came onto the porch, a middle-aged woman dressed in a light-brown habit.

Nellie had heard of the nuns but, unlike the monks, they did not usually come into the city.

"That's Sister Anna," Gisele said.

She came down the steps and met the cart in the middle of the forecourt.

"Brother Gerard, Fancy seeing you here."

"Well met, Sister Anna. May the holy Triune be with you."

"You are welcome at our humble abode. Who are these guests you have brought?"

"These are people from the city. There has been unrest, and as we all know, the poor people are living a very hard life in the city. I've come with a number of women and children to Lord Verdonck's estate, but he doesn't want to house all of us. We're looking for a safe place to stay the winter. The women are all good people, no thieves or charlatans."

The nun looked at Nellie.

Nellie self-consciously flattened her hair.

Sister Anna snorted. "And the Lord Verdonck would rather have all his food spoil before he gives it to the poor people."

Clearly, there was no love lost between the neighbours.

"Come in. You must warm yourselves by the fire. Our monastery is not as luxurious as a castle, but you will have everything you need."

Nellie, Koby, Gisele and Wim followed her inside.

It was very dark inside the building. A long corridor stretched into the darkness, lit only by the light from the single torch. The walls and floors were made of plain stone, the floors without any covering. A number of doors opened into the passage. Most of them were open, giving Nellie little glimpses into rooms for cheesemaking, processing wool, preserving jams, and smoking sausages.

The smell made Nellie's mouth water.

By the broad hips underneath the sister's habit, Nellie judged that hunger, at least, was not one of the problems in this place. They seemed well provisioned and well organised.

The passage opened into a room where a number of

nuns sat at tables, drinking tea. When Sister Anna came in, they all turned to the door.

"We have visitors," Sister Anna said.

The women got up and came to meet the newcomers. They were young and old, most local but one or two with dark skin. A middle-aged woman greeted them.

"Welcome to our humble place," she said. "My name is Sister Louisa. I am the abbess of this monastery."

"Thank you for receiving us," Nellie said.

Sister Anna explained, "Brother Gerard here told me about a group of women and children who have fled from the city. They're looking for a place to stay for the winter."

"We are most all strong and healthy," Nellie said. "We can work in the fields and many of us have experience in cooking and cleaning and craft."

The sister looked her up and down. "Are they all your age?"

"No. Most of the women are younger, but some are older. Some have children. Most of us are healthy and everyone is willing to work."

Another look. "What about you? Where did you come from?"

"I was born in Saardam. I have worked as a servant for many different families."

Nellie chose not to mention the palace or the Regent or the queen, because she didn't know what that would make these women think of her.

"Do you have any men with you?"

"Only four. And there is one boy who is fourteen."

Nellie expected her to say that men weren't welcome, but she gave Nellie another look. "We do a lot of hard work here. We work in the fields in summer and in winter we produce craft. We have a tannery and we make shoes and leather belts and jerkins. We bring wood to the sawmill and do carpentry. We weave carpets. We dye and spin wool. We make lotions and teas and ointments from plants we grow in the garden."

"Some of us have experience with that."

"We can always use hands to help us, if the people are honest."

"We are."

"We also require prayer twice a day. Would you come and pray with us?"

"That would be good. My father used to work for the church, and I could recite entire services."

Sister Louisa gave a small nod. Whether that signified approval or not Nellie didn't know. "Very well. I will show you to the chapel."

She preceded Nellie through a maze of corridors that went through high-ceilinged halls, workshops where women in light-brown habits were weaving, past a smoking room where sausages hung on the ceiling, and a quiet room where nuns could study the verses and a library.

"This is amazing," Nellie said.

"I told you this place is nice," Gisele said in a low voice.

Sister Louisa turned to Nellie. "Life is hard in the city these days, is it?"

"Have you heard that the Regent is dead?"

"No, I haven't. The Triune's judgement is final. I'm sure he will be replaced. We choose to live away from the madness of the city. The rich men jostle for power and corrupt each other's thoughts with greed and gluttony. It's of no importance to us."

"But you sell your produce to the city?"

"A few merchants come to collect food and bring it to the city. With the money, we pay the sawmill and buy items for the farm. We have built a church in town. We support poor families who have met with misfortune. We don't care for games of power. Money is of no importance to us. We can survive very well without it. It is nice to be able to buy new tablecloths of the finest fabric, but we can survive without them as we have for hundreds of years. We can weave our own fabric, we can make our own sausages, we grow our own food. We have nothing that we want from the city. It is a place of sinners and wasteful excess."

She pushed open an intricately carved door, letting them into the chapel.

The circular space beyond was full of light and warm colours, from the wood of the pews that stood in a circle around a basin with a statue in the middle of the chapel to the bright colours of the paintings on the walls. Wooden beams with intricately carved panels supported the roof.

The walls were painted red, golden-yellow drapes graced the sides of the windows, and each pew contained a neat row of embroidered cushions.

Nellie said, "Wow." This room was the product of years and years of loving craftsmanship.

"We built this room for the Triune all by ourselves."

"But certainly you had people from the city come in to make all of these things, like the furniture and the buildings?"

Sister Louisa lifted her chin. "Nobody from the city ever touched this building. We made it all with our hands and our tools."

Nellie was amazed. She felt like she had stepped into a dream. This was where she wanted to spend the rest of her days. She wanted to learn to make all these things with her hands. What a way to live away from the city and all its crazy nobles.

"There is no altar," she said.

"No, we believe that all are equal. We will sometimes hold readings, but we take turns delivering them. No priests tell us what to do or how to interpret the verses. Now, let us pray."

She led the small group into one of the pews and

kneeled. Nellie kneeled next to her, then Gisele and Wim, and Koby at the end. It was clear that Koby didn't know what she was supposed to be doing. She looked around nervously. Good grief, had that girl never been inside a church?

Nellie prayed to the Triune that all the refugees would be safe, that they would not be punished for taking the ship, and that no one would find them here until the end of winter.

Sister Louisa sprinkled some water from the basin into Nellie's face.

She gasped with the icy cold.

"You're lucky it isn't frozen."

Then the sister showed them the guest dormitory rooms where they could stay.

"Normally we would have girls here from the city whose parents send them to us to make them into obedient girls, but we don't get many girls these days."

"I know a monastery where they do that with noble boys," Nellie said.

"It's not always an easy task, but we do it to give back to the community."

It seemed generally that the community didn't really appreciate this beautiful place.

Sister Louisa agreed that the group could come, and walked with Nellie and the others back through the maze of hallways and workshops to the main entrance. It was windy and cold outside, and Nellie rugged up in the cart as it went through the fields back to the forest.

First, they came through the garden of little plots. Having seen the rooms where lotions and ointments were made, Nellie now recognised the herb garden. "They're growing a lot of different types of plants."

"Yes, this garden is full of wild plants in summer. It's very pretty and smells really nice. Most of the herbs that you will see in the city are grown here. The most famous product from the herb garden is a healing tea."

"Did you sense any magic being used in the preparation rooms?" Nellie asked Gisele.

"No. Why? They're nuns. They wouldn't use magic."

"A lot of herb sellers use it."

But as the cart trundled in the direction of the forest, another cart turned from the main road into the lane that led to the farm. A donkey, not a horse, pulled the cart. Nellie knew only one person who had a donkey: Zelda.

CHAPTER 8

"**DID YOU SEE?** That was Zelda," Nellie said to Gisele as the cart made its way through the fields.

"Who is Zelda?" Gisele asked.

Nellie explained to her how, when the dragon had taken her from the palace, she had found a group of old friends and other outcasts living in a warehouse in the artisan quarter, and how Zelda was using the women to help her sell her magic tea to merchant wives with more money than sense.

"It's plain quackery," Nellie said. "There is nothing special in the tea, and the fact that she says she gets it from Mr Oliver doesn't make it any more special. It's just chamomile and a number of herbs from the meadows around here. I've seen what she puts in it. I've seen how she makes ointments and then charges ridiculous prices for them. I've seen how she sets the children to beg. I don't want her to know that we are anywhere in this area. She'll betray us like she betrayed us before. She will sell the knowledge of where we are to the guards, because she's only interested in money."

"Yes, you can't trust that one," Wim said.

"Do you know her?" Nellie asked.

"I caught her trying to sneak into the palace stores once. When I asked her what she was doing, she gave me a story about her poor children and having no money."

"She has no children," Nellie said.

"A few days later she was trying to butter up the guards by giving them biscuits. They seemed happy about it, too. Just an old woman, they said."

"Did they eat the biscuits?"

"What else would you do with biscuits?"

"You didn't test them first?"

"No. I would only test what the Regent ate." He frowned at her. "Do you think there was a problem? None of the guards complained about the biscuits. They were only biscuits."

"They may have been part of a larger plan. I know why the nobles of the city have been so placid about the Regent's excesses and have allowed themselves to be insulted by him. Shepherd Wilfridus is a magician. For many years, since the Regent came to power, the shepherd has controlled the citizens through the food they ate, using the Regent as a front. At first he only needed to control the nobles, because the nobles own the businesses and they have the influence. But because of the winter and because not much produce is coming into the city, the citizens are becoming unhappy, so he told the Regent to open up the stores; and he's been distributing food laced with magic to all the citizens of the city so that they would do whatever the Regent told them."

Both Gisele and Wim frowned at her.

Wim said, "I never got sick from any of the food. I tested all of it." He looked distinctly uncomfortable.

"This wasn't magic to make you sick, but magic that made people numb and more likely to believe what the shepherd and the Regent said. Haven't you noticed that you've asked a lot more questions since leaving the palace?"

"Being convicted of a crime I didn't commit has that effect."

"Not just you, everyone who has left the palace. I don't know how and where the magic entered the palace and what he used to spread it. I do know that Zelda sells magical concoctions to merchants. I know they all think she's wonderful. I know she is an informant for the palace."

Wim's eyes met hers. "But I never saw any foul play in the kitchens."

"That's why I think the magic went into the food before it reached the kitchen, and that Zelda may have had something to do with the spreading of it. And Zelda comes to the nunnery to buy her supplies. I'm not sure I want to come here anymore."

Gisele gave her sideways look. "I don't understand. There are remedies against magic. They will involve dandelion, anise or blackberry. I don't know the recipe, but I'm sure someone will know how to use these ingredients, especially if the magic isn't strong."

"The problem is, you have to believe it enough to realise that a potion will help you. If you don't see the problem, you won't see the need for taking a remedy."

So much magic had been used on everyone, and none of the other nobles saw the problem either. Except Adalbert Verdonck, who would never eat in the palace. But his father had. He must have been taking a potion against magic.

The weather had turned windy. Gisele sat at the reins hidden in the cowl of her habit. Wim and Koby were huddled up inside Wim's cloak. Nellie had pulled a shawl over her head to protect herself from the biting wind that howled through the barren branches.

Probably because of the bad weather, they didn't hear the thunder of the approaching horse's hooves until the horse ran past. It galloped past them through the forest, followed by a number of other horses all in different colours, manes and tails flying. At the front was Madame Sabine's white stallion; it was followed by a black horse, a brown horse and a dappled horse, as well, as a bit later, a cow, a couple of goats and a most peculiar squat pony that was white- and black-striped.

"Whatever by the Triune is that?" Wim called out.

All of a sudden everyone was alert. Gisele sat up and ordered the cart horse to stop.

The troupe of animals disappeared into the forest. The thundering of hooves and cracking of branches faded in the distance.

"They're going to the old water mill over there," Koby said.

It was true. And now Nellie heard the loud whistle like a shepherd calling his flock.

From the barren trees came an ear-splitting screech, a sound that brought Nellie back to her youth.

She'd been fourteen or fifteen when the man named Mustafa opened his animal park in the artisan quarter of the city. He owned a couple of squat black- and white-striped ponies called zebra horses. They were cranky things and you couldn't ride them. He also owned two red-and-blue birds with enormous curved beaks. They would screech so loudly that you could hear them even in the street outside the park.

She had wondered where Mustafa and his animals had gone. They had just discovered the place, but what was he doing all the way out here? People wouldn't come all this way to look at his animals. "Let's go and have a look."

Gisele turned the cart into a narrow, bumpy track that went in the direction of the water mill.

It was a most idyllic place with a small lake upstream from the mill and weeping willows standing by the side. The house overlooked a meadow, now brown but which would be green and filled with flowers in summer.

When the cart came down the driveway, a man came out of the house. He was quite short and stocky, smoked a pipe and wore a beret.

He had aged a lot, and his face was not as dark as it had seemed back when he was the first dark-skinned person she had seen, but Nellie recognised the owner of the animals, Mustafa.

"Why, I seem to have visitors."

Nellie said, "I just noticed your zebra horse running through the forest. I hope it didn't escape."

"Naw, it's fine. I feed the animals here so they always come back."

"What are you doing here with this menagerie? Last time I saw you, you had a park in the city."

"Those were the good days, when all I had to worry about was the ladies getting upset about the parrot's language. I've been minding my own business lately," he said. "It's no longer safe in the city, so I've moved my troupe here where I can wait until there are better places to go. It's a nice place, isn't it?"

He had left the door to the house open, and another animal stalked out. It was shaped like a cat but as large as a giant dog. Its pelt was creamy yellow with hundreds of little black spots. It lifted its head and surveyed the newcomers with curious interest, swishing its long tail from side to side.

"Is that a leopard?" Koby asked.

"It is."

"Aren't they dangerous?"

"Not to me. Lila chases away wild boars and any people I don't want around here. She catches rabbits for me. It so happens I was just cooking one. You want a bite and some tea?"

Tea sounded good.

Gisele tied the horse to a tree, and they followed Mustafa inside. Koby made sure she kept a good distance away from the leopard, which kept looking over its shoulder.

It was very warm inside the barn. The air was humid, laced with the scent of animals. A fire roared in the hearth. A piece of meat hung on a spit on front of the fire. The smell was heavenly.

The room only had a few small windows and was quite dark. It took Nellie's eyes a little while to get used to the low light, but she sensed other animals inside. She could smell them. The straw rustled in the dark and something very big snorted.

A table with two benches stood in the glow of the fire.

"Sit down, sit down," Mustafa said.

Nellie, Gisele, Wim and Koby sat on the benches while Mustafa busied himself getting a stack of chipped and dirty cups and carrying the battered and blackened teapot over from the fire.

The tea was almost black.

"I have milk but no sugar, I'm afraid," he said. "It's not safe for me to go into town to buy things, and I have to make do with what I have and darn my gloves rather than get new ones." He held up his woollen gloves where the fingers had been darned with different colours of wool. "I just look after myself and wait until things get better. I can survive here with my animals."

He had sat on the bench. The spotted cat curled up at his feet.

"Why were they all running through the forest?" Koby asked.

"I don't know what's gotten into these creatures the last few days. I let them out of the barn because they were very restless. Normally a time spent outside calms them down, but this white horse turned up and some other horses that I'm sure belong to Lord Verdonck. I haven't touched them, because he is very precious about his horses. I have no idea how they got out. I don't know about the cows either. They're not mine. They must belong to the other neighbour from across the creek. There's something up with these animals. You can see they're nervous."

He got up from the bench and crossed to the dark side of the barn, where Nellie had noticed the snorts of a large animal.

A *very* large animal.

A massive shape moved in the dark, and a flexible, snake-like thing thicker than a man's arm sniffed at Mustafa's pockets. Trunk. Elephant. Nellie had seen these creatures travelling with the circus.

He pulled something out of his pocket, and the creature came out of the shadows. It was huge and grey, with wrinkled, dusty skin. It held out its nose to Mustafa.

"Ohhh!" Koby shuffled back on her bench, her eyes wide.

"This is Esme. She's very friendly. Here, give her a carrot." He tossed Koby a carrot from his pocket.

Koby got up from her seat, holding the carrot as if it were something dirty.

"Hold it out like this," Mustafa said.

He produced another carrot, which the elephant grabbed with its trunk, brought to its mouth and proceeded to crunch loudly.

"Carrots," Mustafa said. "I don't know where that bag came from. It suddenly appeared."

Nellie knew. The dragon. He stole bags of carrots.

Of course, *that* was why the horses had been so excited. The dragon attracted animals, like kittens, puppies, horses and sea cows. And elephants.

Koby held out her hand and shuffled closer. She squealed when the elephant reached out and grabbed the carrot from her hand. The carrot went *crunch* in the elephant's mouth and then the trunk came out again.

"Pat her," Mustafa said. He demonstrated, rubbing the trunk with his hand. Koby very gingerly copied him, giving little squeals when the elephant probed the sleeves of her coat.

Nellie said, "I think I might understand why the animals are nervous and running through the forest. If I'm right, it's my fault, and I'm sorry."

"Naw, that dopey old horse of yours is not going to stir any of my animals—excuse me."

He rose from the table and went to the door. When he opened it, the two colourful birds flew in, screeching.

He put one on his shoulder and the other flew across the barn and landed in the middle of the table, almost upsetting Koby's tea.

"My, they're big," Koby said. "Look at all those colours and the strange beak."

The bird made a few strange noises that sounded almost like a horse neighing, and then it said, "You're a dickhead."

"What?" Koby squealed. "It talks. It talks!"

"Omar is a parrot," Mustafa said. "Parrots talk."

"It's not very polite," Nellie said.

"He doesn't know what he's saying," Mustafa said. "They just make the sounds, not the words."

The other bird jumped from his shoulder onto the table. It yelled, "What the fuck?"

Koby almost fell from her seat laughing.

Wim said, "I imagine that when you were in the city, the noble visitors to your park would take offence to this bird."

"I had to keep it at the back of the park, because the rascal children from the area would sneak over the fence at night and teach the birds bad language. They used to belong to a sailor, and unfortunately I haven't been able to teach them manners."

"What other animals do you have?" Koby asked.

Apart from the parrots, the elephant, the leopard and the zebra horse, Mustafa had three sheep with big horns, two large horses, a spotted snake that lived in his shirt, a number of chickens and a cow.

People left him alone in the old water mill, which apparently used to belong to either the Verdonck estate or the nuns, depending on what year it was.

Apart from the occasional disagreement about the land, life was quiet here. Mustafa had lived in the farmhouse for the best part of the Regent's reign.

"I loved the park, but I had to go," he said. "The guards would come and accuse me of using magic to make the parrots talk. Then I got Esme. She was but a young thing about this high." He held his hand at shoulder height. "She was born in a circus and the owner couldn't keep her because business was bad. But the guards wouldn't let me take Esme to my park because they said it was impossible to control a large creature without magic, and magic was forbidden."

"I loved the park," Nellie said.

"Why, thank you. I loved it, too."

"It's still there, empty and overgrown with weeds."

He sighed.

"Would you come back if you could?"

"If I could, maybe, but I would need a bigger park, because Esme needs a nice piece of land. I would love to dress her up and give children rides through the streets."

Koby's eyes widened. "Really? That would be amazing."

"A lot would need to change for that to happen, though," he said.

"The Regent is dead," Wim said.

"Yes, but the shepherd is still in control."

"And you definitely don't have magic?" Nellie asked.

He shrugged. "It's changed so many times what they call magic. Animals feel attracted to me. Some of the circus troupes keep their animals in cages. That's cruel. I don't like cages. My animals can walk. The horses like walking, Esme likes walking."

"What about the dangerous animals?" Koby asked.

"Lila? She's not dangerous. I used to have a lioness, and had to put her in a cage when she was up to no good. But I would know when she was in a mood. I guess you could call that magic. I never had any magic like where you raise your hands and fire comes out. That's what I call magic."

Nellie looked around nervously and asked him where the lioness was.

"Unfortunately, she died of old age. She was very old. She'd been with me since I was a little mite and my father owned the menagerie."

She asked, "Do you know anything about dragons?"

He gave her a sharp look. "Real dragons or magical dragons?"

"Is there a difference?"

"Real dragons are much smaller. They normally live in or near the water. I've seen people who have owned them. They eat a lot of bugs and they're good to have around when you don't want ants around the house."

"I guess I mean a magical dragon."

Another sideways look, guarded, suspicious. Here was the proof that his magic was real. He could feel the presence of the dragon in the area

"Magical dragons are rare, and I wouldn't keep one, because they're not like normal creatures and you need to be a magician to rule them. But they do help normal people sometimes, bringing them things they need."

"Like bags of carrots."

Another sharp look. Yes, he knew what she was talking about.

They chatted for a while. Having learned of sea cows, Koby wanted to know what an elephant ate and how Mustafa obtained those things. He shared pieces of roast rabbit with the group—caught by Lila the leopard, who lay on a sheepskin by the fire.

Nellie had to force herself to drink all the tea, since it was much too strong for her liking.

When they went back outside, an amazing sight greeted them. Madame Sabine's white horse stood next to the cart, as well as the other horses they had seen earlier. With them were three cows, two goats and a whole flock of spotted deer. There were at least thirty of them, some with antlers and some without.

"Well, that's interesting," Mustafa said. "These animals are behaving ever stranger."

"It's because of the dragon," Nellie said. "The dragon likes animals and he pays his dues by leaving bags of carrots. The dragon came with us into this area."

Nellie, Gisele, Wim and Koby climbed back into the cart. Nellie assured Mustafa that they would visit again, and that they would try to bring him things he could use that he found hard to get. Like wool for fixing his gloves.

Then they went back to the main track from the nuns' farm to Lord Verdonck's house.

"Interesting fellow," Wim said.

"Don't you remember his animal park in town?"

"No, I don't."

"Really? We used to go there all the time as kids."

"I went into the army when I was sixteen. Spent most of my youth marching around Estland."

Right. And he was a year or two older than her. She didn't remember when Mustafa had come, but it couldn't have been long before her memories because it had been a time of discovering new lands. She wasn't sure where Mustafa had come from. He wasn't Phenician, but his home was somewhere in the south-east.

And so the cleansing continued. Foreigners had magic, and therefore they had to leave the city. Like Mustafa, like Madame Sabine.

"What are we going to tell the others?" Wim said.

"I don't know anymore," Nellie said. "I thought the nunnery looked good, but if they sell to Zelda, she will betray us."

"Maybe we should tell Madame Sabine to leave. Then we can stay on the estate."

"Where would she go by herself?"

"She's a noblewoman; she has money to figure that out."

Nellie shook her head. "She's not rich, and she doesn't have friends and relatives anywhere who will help her. She spoke to me yesterday and told me about an important part of her history."

"Witchcraft?" Wim asked.

"No, she's the Lurezian king's cousin once removed, from a really good family, but they fell on bad times. She has always needed to work for her survival. She's a member of the Science Guild, and when she lived in Lurezia, she was in the army and made balloons. She started making balloons in Lord Verdonck's sheds, but the son doesn't like it. She showed me her project. I also know that she arranged for the dragon to be stolen from the church crypts not because he is a magic creature, but because he can fly. Apparently the king of Lurezia has offered a large reward for a person who make humans fly reliably. They can do this with balloons, but the balloons are hard to steer, since they go wherever the wind blows. She tried to get the dragon to pull the balloon, in a way that sea cows pull the ship. But the dragon didn't agree with that, and he attacked her and her lover. I believe they wanted to try again. All the equipment to make balloons is still in the shed. Lord Verdonck wants her to get rid of it."

Gisele snorted. "Why ever would he do that? Think of being the first person to make people fly!"

"I guess he thinks it's frivolous."

"A lot of people think it's frivolous! But still . . ."

"The Lurezian army paid her to make the balloons. They wanted to use balloons in war, to drop stuff on enemy camps, or something like that. The unsolved problem was, she said, to make the balloon go where you wanted it to go. That's why she wanted the dragon."

Wim stared at her. "Do you think Lurezia wants to attack Saardam?"

Nellie was going to say she couldn't see why, but of course she could, because attacks had been common in the past. The sea was muddy and full of sand banks. Reliable safe harbours were rare, and Saardam had such a harbour. Wars had been fought over it before.

Gisele said, "Then we have a choice. We can stay in the barn where we are, or we can go somewhere else."

"I don't like Adalbert Verdonck at all, but I have more trust in him as an honest man who won't betray us than I have in Zelda. The fact that the nuns sell to Zelda means that either the nuns have no idea what they're doing, or they agree with Zelda's position. I don't think we can afford to be involved with that."

"Then that means we stay where we are," Wim said. "That suits me fine. I wasn't looking forward to having to move anyway. I don't think Yolande would survive that." And he had taken to looking after her, since they were the oldest two people in the group.

"No, it would probably be better for the people who are not well to stay where we are," Gisele said.

"But we have to remain careful," Nellie said, remembering Henrik's words about violence.

Gisele raised her eyebrows. "Isn't that always the case?"

"I don't trust Lord Verdonck. I don't want him to drive out Madame Sabine. I feel that we might need her."

CHAPTER 9

THE VISIT OF ZELDA to the nunnery put the group in a difficult position, because what were they going to do now? Stay at the Verdonck estate and be in the middle of arguments between Adalbert Verdonck and the palace about loans? Or go to the nunnery and risk discovery?

It could be that Zelda only came occasionally and only bought from the nuns if she needed something they sold.

Or it could be that the nuns worked with her and were part of Zelda's moneymaking scheme.

At any rate, it would only be a matter of time before these nuns discovered that Nellie and the others were wanted by the palace.

Nellie disliked feeling like a political pawn with Adalbert Verdonck, and the Lord did not want the ragtag group on his estate, anyway. While he might allow Madame Sabine to stay for now, Nellie had no illusion that he would make it easy or comfortable for them.

Staying with the nuns, who were happy to have them, would be less safe, even if many of the women would prefer that. What would she say to the women? There is a nice, comfortable place, but we can't go there because I don't trust one of their customers?

Would it be possible for the women to keep themselves hidden from Zelda? Would the Abbess allow it?

In the end, they were all in this together.

On the ride back to the Verdonck estate, they decided to put the matter to the group. But when they arrived back at the barn, it was to the sound of raised voices from within. She could hear Agatha, and Henrik as well.

Goodness, what was going on?

While Gisele went to take the cart back to wherever she had borrowed it, Nellie opened the door.

The dragon sat at the far end breathing smoke over the floor of the barn.

Several women called, "Nellie! You're back!" They sounded glad.

Nellie called out, "Someone tell that dragon to stop trying to set fire to the barn." She hated to think what the Lord Verdonck could charge them if the barn burnt down. They would be bound to eternal servitude.

Then she realised that Prince Bruno was standing in front of the dragon. Henrik and Agatha had been facing him, but they now turned around to the door.

The dragon had lifted his head, and smoke no longer came out of its nostrils. That was something at least.

"What by the Triune is going on?" Nellie asked.

"I told them I want to go and see my father," Prince Bruno said.

Henrik said, "But you can't. No one even knows where he is."

"I'm not going to find out if I stay in this stupid barn, am I?" Bruno's voice sounded shrill.

Nellie said, "We are here for your and everyone's safety."

Agatha said, "Don't waste your breath, Nellie. We have argued with him ever since you left."

"You want to hide me again!" Bruno called out. "Why did you even free me when I'm not allowed to go wherever I want? This is my country. You should listen to what I say."

Heavens, what had gotten into that boy? "Well, if you are going to behave like that, we will tell all these people that you are not Prince Bruno after all, and then no one will listen to you."

He stared her, opened mouth, and then closed it again.

Some form of adult intelligence was going on behind those eyes. Nellie could see that he was thinking. She could see that he knew he had gone too far. He lacked any form of education about how he to behave, but she sensed that he could grow into a strong-willed young man.

He sat down in the straw, and tightened his arms about his chest. "I still want to see my father."

"I understand, but that's not going to be easy. I would like to see your father, too. I thought he was a very respectable man." Nellie sat next to him.

He looked up, his dark and beautiful eyes meeting hers. "Did you know my father?"

"I was with him and your mother all the time, and you, too, even though you don't remember any of it."

He said nothing.

Nellie felt that he might want to apologise, but he was simply too proud to do so. "We will make sure you see your father."

"You will make sure that we go to the palace, too?"

Nellie cringed. "Eventually, maybe. But I think you are a bit too young to be fighting wars."

"I can fight."

Nellie looked at a scrawny arms and his thin legs. "I

believe it. But I think you may want to have a bit more training before you rush off to get yourself killed."

"Can I start the training now?"

"If you eat well, and if you stop behaving like a child and start listening to what we say."

He fell silent. Then he walked across the barn and picked up the broom that apparently he had been asked to use before the argument broke out. He started sweeping the floor.

Henrik looked at Nellie, his eyes wide. "However did you do that?"

"Years of practice dealing with King Roald."

With that settled, they started cooking dinner, and Nellie told the women of their trip to the nunnery.

The women's eyes lit up when she spoke of the nice building and the fields and quiet spaces, and specially the absence of men.

"But won't they have any problems with the men in our group?" Hilde asked.

"They said everyone was welcome."

Josie said, "Then we must go there. It sounds like the ideal place."

"I thought so, too, until we left and a visitor came into the place."

"Who was it?"

"Zelda."

Gasps. The women stared at her, their mouths open.

Josie said, "Zelda came to the nunnery?" Josie in particular had made her dislike of Zelda overly clear in the days since she had been rescued. It was because of Zelda that she, Jantien, and most others had almost died.

"We didn't stick around for long enough, but I think Zelda was buying produce from the nunnery. And then I became unsure of whether it was a safe place for us, seeing how Zelda betrayed us before."

"I can well see that," Mina said.

Agatha said, "So then, what can we do? We don't want to stay here because this lord whatever is a stuck-up you-know-what and he will sell us to whoever offers the most money, dragon included."

Nellie didn't believe that Adalbert Verdonck would do that. To him, knowledge and power was more important than money. "That's what we need to discuss. There are a number of options," Nellie said.

"What options?"

"We can stay here."

Mina shook her head. "No. This man worries me. He will sell us or we will be drawn into something evil."

"Or we can go to the nunnery."

"I don't like that," Jantien said. "Not after Zelda betrayed us."

Jantien was shy and didn't speak up often, but when she did, people tended to listen.

Hilde said, "We can go there but make sure that we stay hidden."

"Can we do that? There are so many of us, and we can't hide children for very long. We don't know what Zelda does there, or how long she stays. We don't know whether she just comes to the door, or if she goes into the building."

"Zelda does not strike me as a religious person," Mina said. "She may just come to the door to buy her things."

"No." Jantien was adamant. "I'm not going where Zelda is. She already betrayed us once."

Henrik asked, "Is there another option?"

Nellie said, "Maybe we can send only the people who can stay there safely. Only the ones who don't know Zelda or who Zelda won't recognise."

"And then what about the rest of us?" Agatha said. "I

propose something else. I propose that we talk to Zelda to see what she actually wants and who she works for."

Several women shouted her down. Jantien called out, "Didn't you listen to what I said? I don't want to have anything to do with that woman anymore."

And again, the issue of Zelda had divided them. Nellie wished she could just understand who worked for who.

"Jantien is right," said a cultured voice.

In all the commotion, Nellie hadn't even thought about Madame Sabine, but of course she had been in the barn all along, unable to go anywhere else.

She continued, "Zelda is not a person you should trust, ever. The wayfarer families have a very strong circle of associates in almost every city and town. They have become that way out of necessity. Wayfarers are poor people and they will do anything for money."

"Excuse me? I don't do 'anything' for money," Agatha said.

"You're not a wayfarer."

"No, but I'm poor. Being poor doesn't mean you do anything for money."

"Well, you have to survive, right?" Madame Sabine said.

"There are ways of surviving that you wouldn't have a clue about."

"And how do you know what I don't have a clue about? What do you know about me?"

"Enough to know that you don't have a clue."

"Please, please." Nellie held up her hands. "Sniping at each other doesn't achieve anything."

"Then she should stop acting like she knows and owns everything." Agatha crossed her arms over her chest.

"I know and own a lot more than you."

"Like, a husband who wants to kill you and two sons who don't even care enough about you to cry about you?"

"I'm not even going to honour that with a reply,"

Madame Sabine said, her voice ice cold.

"Good," Nellie said. "We're all in this together."

"I'm not," said Brother Martinus. "I want to return to one of the order's monasteries as soon as possible. I don't believe any of your stories about Shepherd Wilfridus being a magician. I believe you should let me and Madame Sabine go."

Agatha said, "So that you can report us to the nearest guard station?" at the same time as Madame Sabine said, "I'd rather be dead than seen travelling with a monk of that despicable church."

And so the impasse remained. No one knew what to do.

The soup was done, and Mina started handing out bowls. They sat around eating, but the atmosphere in the group was far from happy.

Splitting up the group—with all the risks that would bring—seemed the only option. For a moment Nellie even considered taking the boat back onto the water, but the rivers were not safe.

What were they to do?

After they finished eating, Nellie went to clean the bowls in the ice-cold water of the basin that they had set up outside for that purpose.

She tried to lead this group but she wasn't sure she was cut out for leadership. *You're too nice and forgiving,* Mistress Johanna would say. Well, if she had to be nasty in order to be a leader, she preferred not to be a leader. Let them split up, let each person go their own way. At least they had survived this far because of her. Now they could look after themselves.

But that wasn't how she wanted things to be. She'd dreamed of the time when she was with Mistress Johanna and Prince Roald and they had come back to the city to oust the Fire Wizard.

They had a group; they had a prince. They even had a dragon. So why was everything wrong?

The door to the barn opened, letting out a strip of golden light in the gathering dusk. Henrik came out.

"Are you all right?" he asked, his voice kind.

"I never knew how frustrating it is to get a group of people all to do the same thing."

He chuckled. "My family helped me get over that hurdle."

That hit home with her. "You must miss them very much."

"I miss Martha, but she is never coming back. I'm glad she doesn't have to see me like this. My daughters are grown up and married. They can look after themselves. I'm sure we'll get back to the city and I can visit them."

But as the man who had shot the Regent, that might not be so simple. Nellie still didn't understand quite why he had done it, because it had destroyed his comfortable life. He had said that it was because the Regent was going to kill his own wife in front of his son's eyes, but there had to be more to it.

"What do you think we should do?" she asked.

"I'm going to make this about Bruno. I'm worried about him, and we need to make sure he doesn't do anything stupid. He's the best chance we have of getting rid of these power-grabbing tyrants."

"I'm worried about him, too," Nellie said. "He's very impatient and asks disturbing questions."

"He does. I need to be stronger with him."

"It's not your fault. He's lived locked up for ten years, and spent the most important years of his life in a dark prison. Of course he's angry."

"We have to make sure he uses that anger in a good way, though. He seems to think that everyone is trying to hold him back. He wants the dragon to take him to see his father, and he thinks we know where Li Fai is. He also thinks that you have turned the dragon against him, because it won't listen to him the same way it listens to you."

Nellie snorted. "The dragon listens to me? That's news."

"It listens to you better than it listens to anyone."

"No. He follows animals better than he follows people. He attracts animals, too."

"Anyone human I mean. Like this afternoon, you told it to stop trying to set fire to the barn, and it did."

He was right, she realised with a shock. "I don't mean to take that away from Bruno."

"I know, but the dragon seems to have an opinion of who to follow and what's right and wrong."

A phrase bubbled up in Nellie's memories. "The Great Just Dragon."

"What?"

"I'm not sure. It came into my mind—wait, it was a story that Mistress Johanna told the children. I think it was an eastern story. It was about how a dragon saves a village. The dragon refused to obey its master because the master was the village mayor and made unreasonable demands of his villagers."

"Maybe there is some truth in it somewhere that dragons will follow sensibility over orders."

"And I am the pinnacle of sensibility," Nellie said in a mocking voice.

"You are. You always have been. I'm not joking."

The idea that the dragon should choose to listen to her over Bruno disturbed her. The boy seemed so fragile, and it wasn't right to take what he considered his. If it continued, he would only get more disturbed and angry.

"How can I make sure the dragon knows he belongs to Bruno?"

"I suspect Bruno will have to earn the right to command the dragon."

"Could you possibly start training him in fighting and swordcraft?"

"He's still really young and not very strong."

"I know, but it will give him something to do and stop his brooding over all the things he can't do. He'll feel involved and active, even if he may still be too weak to be any good at it."

Henrik let a small silence lapse. "I don't have any equipment."

"I'm sure we can make a fake sword out of stuff we find in the barn. I've seen lengths of wood lying around. I'll show you."

She picked up the stack of bowls and walked to the door of the barn. It would be cold tonight, because the air already bit into the skin of her face.

But Henrik remained at the bench.

"Is anything wrong?"

"Nellie, you always so perfectly manage to steer the conversation away from yourself."

"What do you mean? This isn't about me."

"I know, but I asked if *you* were all right."

"You didn't. You asked about Bruno."

"No, I came out here because I wanted to know if you are all right. It was the first question I asked."

"I don't like talking about myself." As Nellie spoke, she realised just how true it was. "This expedition isn't about me. I could have stayed in the palace just fine."

"Then why didn't you?"

"Why did you shoot the Regent?"

"See? You're doing it again. We do the things we do, because we believe they are right. How *are* you doing?"

"I'm fine."

But she didn't think he believed that.

CHAPTER 10

WHILE NELLIE LAY IN the straw trying to sleep that night, the conversation played in her mind many times.

Henrik made her uncomfortable. Whenever she spoke to him, it was as if he held up a mirror to her face and forced her to look into it. And she didn't like what she saw: that she was self-righteous, that she didn't know anything about other people's lives, even if she thought she did, and that she was hopeless at leading groups of people, always having been in the shadow of much more powerful leaders. She simply couldn't be like Mistress Johanna. She could only be herself.

If the group couldn't agree about what to do, they would split up; and Nellie would never be able to break the stranglehold over the city held by the shepherd, a man who, curse his soul, used the cover of the church to propel himself into the leadership over Saarland, because "there is no clear heir to the throne." Yes, there was, and he'd lived in the church dungeons for ten years.

The shepherd, a man who forbade magic because "it is evil", and then made sure that no one in the church found out he had magic. He punished citizens who had small amounts of magic "for the safety of the citizens" while in truth he did it to drive his rivals away.

That was the only thing he'd done: make sure that no one who would ask pointy questions or challenge him came near.

And she would make sure that this evil man didn't destroy the city and the church she loved, so all these women and their husbands could go back. So all the foreign merchants who had left came back to the city, so the ocean ships returned with their trade. So magic would be taught to children. And so Shepherd Adrianus could return.

Her mind went around and around in circles, and while she lay there she wasn't sleeping. Everyone else had been exhausted, including the dragon, who was snoring loudly.

She was exhausted, but the worry consumed her mind.

The next morning, as he had promised, Henrik started Bruno's sword training. He got up early, and then had some trouble waking Bruno.

"Can we go bit later? It is still so cold."

"If you want to learn, you have to do the work. Soldiers get up early and don't complain."

Bruno sprang up, and got dressed, even if in low morning light, Nellie could see that he was shivering. She hoped that Henrik would not be too hard on him.

They both went outside. Not much later Nellie got up as well, and started the preparations for

breakfast. She wondered where Koby was, because usually she helped.

But then she discovered Koby outside, watching while Henrik and Bruno were lifting pieces of firewood in the first pink light of the

dawn. Henrik's piece of wood was much bigger than Bruno's, but Bruno scrunched up his face and lifted his piece above his head and then let it drop again and lifted it again and let it drop again.

"What are they doing?" Nellie asked.

Koby said, "Bruno wanted to be trained to be a fighter."

"Yes, I understand, but I would think they might do something useful, like practice fighting moves."

As she said this, Henrik took off running up the road. Bruno took a little while to figure out that his mentor had gone, and then dropped his wood and followed him. At the end of the laneway, Henrik turned around and came running back again. His face was red from the cold and exertion. Nellie thought it was amazing that he was still this strong and healthy at his age.

When they were back at the barn, Bruno seemed much more exhausted then Henrik was.

"Are you coming to have breakfast?" Nellie asked them.

"Is it ready?" Henrik said.

"Almost."

Henrik held up his hand when Bruno joined him to stop his pupil running down the lane again. They were both breathing heavily, but Henrik seemed the one who was actually enjoying himself.

"How is he doing?" Nellie asked Henrik when he came inside.

"He could use a lot more training, but he seems quite keen. Although he's very impatient. He asked me several times whether he could use a weapon. He will have to learn a bit of patience to be a good fighter."

"Good luck with that. I think you'll have to watch him closely."

"Well, we can't train with a weapon, because I don't have a training weapon, and we don't have any money to buy one either."

"Thank goodness for that."

They all sat around the fire eating breakfast and drinking tea. Bruno's face was red, and his eyes were bright.

"You enjoyed that, didn't you?" Nellie asked him when she handed a bowl of porridge to him.

"Of course I enjoyed it. Anything that teaches me how to kill that evil man."

A chill went over Nellie's back. Even if she thought the shepherd was evil, she didn't think about killing in such a glorified way.

"You're not very strong yet."

"But I will be, soon, and then we can go to the city, and we will get rid of all these evil men."

"They will always be more evil men."

"But then we can go to the palace, and the palace is mine, and I will bring peace. And then my father can come back, and everything can be good again."

Nellie didn't think it was going to be quite as simple as that. For one, not everyone in town would be happy to see the eastern traders in a position of power. Li Fai was in Anglia, and a return would bring Anglian people they might not be happy to see.

"Tell me how many rooms the palace has," Bruno said.

What a strange question. "I've never counted them."

"What did my mother do with all those rooms?"

"They are all different, and only a few of them are for the family to live in. Most of them are public rooms, for holding audiences and dinners and meetings and music performances."

"Audiences, that's where people come to bow to the king and ask him favours, isn't it?"

The way he said that made Nellie feel cold. This boy needed to be taught a lot of manners, preferably before he came anywhere near the palace.

"An audience is where people from the general citizenship can come to have their problems heard. They will discuss it with the ruler, the king or queen or regent, and the ruler will then make sure that something is done about it, especially if a lot of people ask for the same thing, and if it is at all within their power to give."

"But it *is* where people come to ask for things, isn't it?"

"It is where common people come to discuss their problems," Nellie repeated, more forcefully. "The king or queen who doesn't listen to the voice of the people will not last very long."

He gave her a blank look. "And how many of these citizens are there?" As if citizens were sheep or horses.

"I haven't counted them. Thousands, tens of thousands? I don't know. A lot. A lot more than any king or queen wants to make angry."

"But if they are angry, the king has guards?"

"Yes, he does. But, like Henrik, they are people who will sometimes also have problems, and they have families who will have problems, so the guards might actually agree with what the common people coming for an audience are saying."

His frown deepened. "But aren't guards supposed to listen to the King?"

"They are, and they will, for as long as the king looks after the guards, by listening to their problems and attempting to fix them."

"Oh, but I would feed them well and make sure that they are never cold."

"And the guards have families who live in city."

"I would look after the families as well."

"And the families have neighbours, who might be jealous when they see how much the guards' families are getting."

"I would bring all the families in the palace."

"I don't think the palace is that big."

"But you said it was very big."

"Well, it is very big, but the palace is still not on an island, and if the citizens of the city don't like it, they can rise up and burn down the palace, because there are many more citizens than any number of people who will fit in the palace."

He had to think about that for a while, and the chill that Nellie felt grew into a blizzard.

Whatever was going on inside the head of this boy, he was assuming that everything was his far too soon. What had these priests and monks done to him?

She mentioned this to Henrik after breakfast, when he had sent Bruno with Wim to collect firewood.

"I wouldn't worry too much about it. He's a young boy, and so he's very impatient," Henrik said. "Believe me, I was once that young boy. I was going to protect the king all by myself. I was going to slay the fire demons, even if I had no idea how to do that or even what a fire demon looked like. I was going to protect my king from the evil Red Baron, and when I finally saw the Red Baron, even though he was much taller than me and twice the width I thought I could fight him. It is a very common thing for young boys to think like this. He wants to prove himself. He's angry, and I can't blame him. To me, it's a wonder that his ordeal hasn't turned him completely crazy."

And Nellie wasn't so sure it hadn't. The mad King Roald was not the boy's father, but there were some disturbing similarities.

But she had to trust Henrik's judgement. She kept an eye on the two of them as they continued their training during the day.

The day was sunny but cold and frosty, and by the time the light turned golden and Henrik and Bruno came back inside, even Henrik looked tired.

"I hope you look after yourself," Nellie said.

"Don't worry about me."

During dinner, Nellie noticed that when Bruno had finished eating, he could barely keep his eyes open. His cheeks were bright red, and he sat with his arms looped around his knees, trying to be brave and stay awake. He didn't even listen to Koby's chatter, and his eyes kept falling shut.

Everyone was tired, and they went to bed early. For a change, Nellie slept well because it was quite warm in the barn, and she didn't have to worry about people invading.

Throughout the day, groups of people had still been talking about what they would do, but whichever way she thought about it, Nellie thought it would be better to stay here rather than go to the nuns and risk the mercenaries from the city finding them again.

She couldn't imagine that Casper had anything intelligent to say about what needed to be done with the undesirable people the mercenaries found outside the city. From what Henrik had said, the Regent probably had little influence on these men anyway. And Casper would be far too busy making sure he didn't get killed.

If the women were betrayed, the guards would find everyone in this group, throw them in jail and burn them at the stake. Once, there would have been citizens in the city who would rise up and protest, but by now they were all kept quiet with the shepherd's magic.

Over the next few days, it became clear that it was not just Bruno who was impatient. Madame Sabine sent Jantien's daughter Jette—who was enamoured with Madame Sabine's curls—to the house to ask for pens and parchment. She demanded the right to correspond with acquaintances who could "help her escape this dreadful situation". No word of thanks to Nellie for rescuing her. No word, either, about her sons.

Nellie hoped this didn't mean that she didn't care

about the boys, just that she didn't want to ask the group to help rescue them.

She remained a strange and very closed woman.

As for Nellie herself, it was hard to imagine that she could feel any worse about the situation. They may have saved the lives of the prisoners, but no one seemed to know what to do next, and they lived as virtual exiles, without the ability to organise themselves or to do anything about the dreadful situation in the city. With winter coming, it would be a long time before the weather was good enough to travel back, and then there didn't seem to be any reason to do so.

Nellie mostly kept these thoughts to herself as she watched Henrik and Bruno do their regular training, and as she watched groups of animals congregate outside the barn.

The dragon was growing stronger, and had once been let out of the box so that he would keep the children warm at night.

Adalbert Verdonck didn't care much about them, although Nellie spotted him going into the shed where Madame Sabine's balloons were stored. As it turned out, he arranged for all the experiments to be packed up into crates.

Madame Sabine was not happy about this, and Nellie remembered the threat he had made to burn all her things.

She also heard that Madame Sabine had an argument with one of Lord Verdonck's house staff about sending a letter. He would not pay for it, and she had no money. She argued that if he wanted everything out of his shed, he should give her the opportunity to arrange it, to which he said that she could take her horse, since it was roaming around the field stirring up *his* horses.

The attempt by Madame Sabine to capture the horse would've been amusing if she hadn't been so angry.

"I don't know what's gotten into that animal," she said. "It was trained extremely well. Someone has gone and spoiled it."

Apparently, this someone was supposed to have been Henrik, because he often went and gave the horse carrots when he and Bruno were training outside.

Of course, Nellie felt sure it was the magical influence of the dragon. The horse didn't understand what was going on but, like Mustafa's animals, it felt the excitement of the presence of the dragon, and no longer wanted to listen to human commands.

But trying to command the dragon was another thing altogether.

Increasingly, he wandered freely around the fields. If the women shut the barn door and didn't want him to come in or go out, he would revert to his ethereal form and slip underneath the door in the form of a cloud of sparks.

Bruno would sometimes try to make him come and, when he did, he would try to climb on his back, but so far the only person who had ridden the dragon was Nellie, and that had been a total accident.

Nellie could, however, ask the dragon to come inside at night, and usually he would do so for a short period. In a way, the dragon was like cat. He would come when there was food or he wanted to sit by the fire, but he got bored quickly and asked for the owner to open the door. The dragon didn't need to do this. He would simply dissolve into sparks. Nellie usually got the dragon to come when the children went to sleep. She suspected that the dragon simply liked sleeping with the children, because the children were innocent, their intentions were clear, and they didn't try to take advantage of the dragon.

But every time she called the dragon, Bruno was watching.

"I want to do that. He is my dragon," he would say.

And several times she showed him what she did and told him to hold out his hand and what words to say so that the dragon knew it was bedtime. Which he probably knew anyway.

Bruno tried a few times, but she didn't think he was genuine or polite enough. The dragon didn't like commands, and didn't like when people shouted at him. He also tended to protect animals more than people.

The stray horses that had been with Madame Sabine's horse had all been recaptured by their owners, mostly people who lived on the estate, but a flock of sheep persistently hung around, and no one was clear where they'd come from. When the groundsman tried to chase them out of the vegetable garden, the dragon flew across and chased the man off. Bruno ran after them whistling and yelling at the dragon to kill the man, but Nellie had to explain that this was not something the dragon liked.

"How can he not like spitting fire? That's what a dragon does. He's a dangerous creature."

"Yes, but when dangerous creatures are good and just, they only use violence as a threat. They try at all times to use their abilities to terrify people."

And it seemed that finally Bruno was starting to understand. He had to be friends with the dragon before the dragon would do what he said. The dragon had to trust him. In the evening, he went into the paddock and called out to the dragon. He scratched the heads and ears of the sheep that always hung around with the dragon. Today, there were two goats as well, and Madame Sabine's horse was never far.

He picked up the little kitten that was still following them around and was now a slightly bigger kitten. Only when he had shown his affection to all these animals would the dragon come in and take his position with the children. Bruno told them a story as well, even if he was a little upset that none of the children knew what a pulpit was, and then he was upset that some of them fell asleep.

That wasn't really because the story was boring—even if it was—but because the children were tired.

All the while this was happening, Nellie was looking on, happy that at least something was going right. If they had to wait in this barn until spring came before they could do anything, they might as well use it to be as prepared as possible.

CHAPTER 11

IT WAS ONLY JUST LIGHT when Nellie woke to someone touching her shoulder.

She opened her eyes to see that Henrik had kneeled next to her. He held his finger to his lips and said, "The boy is gone."

Nellie pushed herself up. "What do you mean?"

Next to her, Hilde was still asleep.

Henrik whispered, "The boy. Bruno. He's gone."

"Are you sure?"

"I can't see him anywhere. We were supposed to start training."

"Maybe he got really keen." Bruno had not complained as much about getting up early recently.

"I don't think so. Come, have a look."

Nellie jumped to her feet and went to the place where Bruno had been sleeping with the other children. The children were all still there, fast asleep with rosy cheeks. During the last few nights, the dragon had slipped out of the barn during the night, and it no longer lay in the straw.

Henrik had been right. Not just the prince was gone, but all of the possessions he had collected were gone as well, including the habit Gisele had given him to disguise himself as a monk. And including the dragon box.

"Maybe he's gone training," Nellie said. She wasn't hopeful that this would actually be the case. If he had taken those things, he was gone, and he was up to something.

"Let's check outside." Henrik set off past the dying fire to the barn doors. He lifted the latch and opened the door. The sun hadn't yet risen, and a soft mist hung over the pale fields. The hoar frost had turned the world into a white wonderland.

It was completely silent, with not a sign of the prince or dragon.

Nellie shivered, pulling her coat around her.

Henrik crossed to the fence of the horse paddock. He pointed. "Look here."

Nellie went to see.

In the frosted dead grass in the paddock were tracks of a very large animal. They went a number of paces into the white grass and then disappeared. The tracks were too broad to belong to any of the horses, and those stood very quietly down at the other end of the paddock.

She met Henrik's eyes. They both knew what it meant. These were paw prints of the dragon. Where they disappeared, the dragon had taken off.

Henrik scratched his head. "I thought he was struggling to talk to the dragon, never mind climb onto its back."

"He managed to call it yesterday," Nellie said.

But either yesterday's interaction had been more significant than she had realised, or he had been tricking them about how he couldn't control the dragon all along.

Either way Bruno was gone. "By the Triune, where do you think he is?"

Henrik shrugged. "To kill the shepherd? To go to the

palace? To find his father? Whatever, none of those things are good."

No, they weren't. Not only that, but if they had any hope of defeating the shepherd and reinstating the royal family, they needed the dragon and Bruno.

And what was more, she felt betrayed. Recently, she had assumed that people were right and that the dragon did listen to her. It was still a magical creature and did its own thing, but she thought she understood it better than anyone else. That it liked animals, that it attracted animals and would defend them, and that the way to get it to defend you was to treat it well and be an honest person. But if Prince Bruno had lied about being able to interact with the dragon, then her understanding was a lie, too.

She couldn't imagine it.

When Celine and Bruno were little, Li Fai would tell them stories of legendary dragons of the past, and Nellie had also heard versions of those stories from the sailors who used to work for Mistress Johanna's father. Stories of the Great Just Dragon were too common for them to be based on a fallacy.

Dragons stood up for people who did the right thing. That was a fact.

Nellie and Henrik went back into the barn, where Agatha and Mina had woken up and started on breakfast.

"Did anyone see Bruno leave?" Nellie asked them.

Mina shook her head. "No. Did he leave?"

"He took his possessions and the dragon."

Mina frowned. "Did he take any food?"

That was a good question. "I don't think so."

"Then he can't have gone far."

Good old Mina always remained level-headed and practical.

After a quick breakfast, Nellie and Henrik went out to

see if they could find out more about where Bruno might have gone.

First they went to the estate's horse stables, where the stable master had noticed that the horses were very nervous early in the morning.

"They've quietened down a lot now, mind, so whatever spooked them has gone."

Nellie and Henrik didn't say anything about the dragon to these people. Lord Verdonck might suspect that they had it, but he hadn't mentioned it since they arrived at the estate.

They checked in the village where the estate's workers lived, but everything was quiet there.

They also checked in the shed that contained Madame Sabine's balloons.

The crates containing the fabric and other material still stood in the corner ready to be taken away.

"It would be a pity if all this is lost," Nellie said.

Henrik scoffed. "I'm sure some rich noble in Lurezia will continue to make balloons. It's of no concern to us."

"I think it is."

"How so?"

She explained how an army could drop things on an enemy from the air.

Henrik gave her a disturbed look.

"When you're in the air, no one can reach you, and no one can hear what you say." And she knew this from the terrifying experience flying on the dragon's back.

"But that would be all the more reason to destroy this."

"Except that Lurezian nobles will continue with these balloons. And if they come to us with armies that have balloons, we want to have our own balloons."

He raised his eyebrows. "We?"

"Well, Saardam in general. Because if invaders have balloons and use them to drop things on us, then we'll be as defenceless as we are now against magic. And pretending this doesn't exist isn't going to stop other people using it."

"Isn't one of the problems with the balloons that they go where the wind blows and you can't control their path?"

"It is. That's why Madame Sabine and the old Lord Verdonck stole the dragon box: so that the dragon could pull the balloons like sea cows pull a boat. Except the dragon didn't like it." Because one had to earn the trust of a dragon before you could get it to do anything.

"You could use something else to keep a balloon under control. You could use a boat. You could attach a long rope and let the balloon fly over the city while the boat stays at a safe distance."

Nellie nodded. One could also use another animal, like . . . an elephant. That might work for a circus troupe for the novelty of attracting a crowd.

She sighed. "Anyway, first we need to find Bruno. If he's gone in search of his father, then I don't know that he'll survive the journey. It's a long way over the ocean to Anglia and it's very, very cold up there."

She still shivered when she thought about her short adventure on the dragon's back.

Henrik shook his head. "I'm not sure he's gone that far. In the past few days, he never stopped talking about how he was going to avenge his father and pay the church back for the time he spent locked up in the crypts. I think he's gone to Saardam."

"Where he's likely to get killed. Without him, there's not much point trying to show the citizens of Saardam what Shepherd Wilfridus is doing to them. We might as well move to Lurezia."

"It's not a nice place for foreigners, I hear."

"No, and I don't want to move there, but Bruno is the

only reason we can get the citizens behind us: if we have the rightful heir to the throne, they'll support us."

"We'll have to find him, before he gets himself into trouble. And don't worry, Nellie, I'm not about to give up."

But nobody they met on the estate had seen anything out of the ordinary. They didn't even find Madame Sabine's horse any more.

That was the clearest sign Nellie had seen that the dragon had left the area.

There was only one thing left to be done. That was to inform Adalbert Verdonck himself and ask if he could offer any assistance.

They walked down the tree-lined lane to the house, talking about what they would and would not say. Henrik agreed that it was best not to trust Adalbert Verdonck too much, because *rich men are never your friends*.

But when they arrived at the house, it was to find that another visitor was already there, judging by the horse tied to a pole for that purpose outside. This animal was not a dopey farm horse, but a sleek brown horse that looked fast.

Henrik eyed it suspiciously.

"Do you know that horse?" Nellie asked. There was always a danger that someone from the city would be here and would recognise them.

"No. But it looks like a military horse to me. It's been a while since I was in the Army, but they used to have that type of saddlebag."

"Do you still want to go in?"

"I'm not entirely sure. Maybe we should wait until the visitor departs."

But as he said that, the front door open and a man came out.

Henrik pulled Nellie behind a big tree.

The visitor was not a military man; at least, his long

black coat didn't look like a uniform, although his tall black boots might once have belonged to a soldier.

He walked in quick strides, went down the steps to the gravel, untied the horse and climbed in the saddle. The horse took off at a trot.

Henrik didn't speak until he was halfway down the lane to the main road. "I know that man. It's Sigfrid Emmel. He used to be a lieutenant when I was in the army. Retired with an injury and started his own mercenary army."

"Is his visit here a good thing or a bad thing?"

"Adalbert Verdonck has served in the army, too. They could be friends. Or it could be a business meeting. I'm not sure."

"You're not sure about many things today."

He sighed. "I guess it's not my day, then."

She had noticed that he looked very tired and worried. "Apart from the fact that Bruno is gone, is anything else wrong?"

"I have sworn to protect the boy," he said. His face was haunted. "I've failed."

"You've sworn? Who did you promise that to?" This was the first Nellie heard of it.

"His father. He also asked me not to tell anyone, but there's not much point keeping it secret now."

"You were in contact with Li Fai in Anglia?"

"Not me, but someone I know well was. A number of years ago, the boy's father asked us to keep an eye on him after his mother had been killed. He knew what had happened, and although he was travelling, he was never able to come back to find his son, because his magic wouldn't allow him to come into the country. We were aware that the boy's body had never been found and became aware not much later that there was a good chance that the boy was still alive. To quell the rumours, the church ordered graves for both Bruno and Celine, but everyone knew there were no bodies in those graves. We even had both graves opened to prove it. So when Li Fai contacted us, we swore to protect him."

"Who is we?"

"Myself and a group of friends. You may meet them at some point. They're all guards."

"City guards or palace guards?"

"Both. And some are ex-soldiers also."

"And did this group know that Prince Bruno was in the church crypts?"

"We suspected he might spend some time there, but we know he also spent time in other places like some of the church's monasteries that are closed to visitors. Once it became clear that you had freed him, it was my duty to protect him from his captors."

A light went on in Nellie's mind. "That was why you came. I wondered why you made that bold move to jump onto the ship and shoot the Regent, but now I know."

"Not the only reason, but an important reason, yes."

"And here I was thinking that you came with us because of me."

"I'm sorry to disappoint you."

"So when you shot those arrows, you meant to kill the shepherd more desperately than the Regent?"

"That's true. But my main aim was to create enough chaos for us to be able to get away. I aimed for the Regent because he is a despicable man who allowed all this to take place, but I really wanted to kill the shepherd. Because I knew how much he would want to come after you and how much his death would solve. I swore to protect the prince, and did everything to ensure that people believed I only protected the regent."

So much of Henrik's behaviour now made sense.

When he was at the palace, he had been unable to

agree with her because he was playing the role of the faithful guard.

"So what are we going to do now?"

"Knowing what we know about how the shepherd controls people with magic, we cannot allow Adalbert Verdonck to hire mercenaries to take the town by force. It would be a bloodbath. So I'm going to talk to him."

"I don't really trust Adalbert Verdonck. Are we going to tell him the truth?"

"I can't see another option. We'll tell him as much as he needs to know."

CHAPTER 12

NELLIE FOLLOWED HENRIK across the forecourt up the steps to the front door. When he knocked, the sound reverberated in the hollow space beyond.

A moment later Lord Verdonck's housekeeper opened the door.

Henrik said, "We would like to speak with your master, please."

"May I ask what this is about?"

"It's a confidential matter of extreme importance."

Henrik clearly had experience in sounding very authoritative and convincing.

The housekeeper showed them to a small room and told them to wait while he went to inform the master.

The sound of male voices drifted across the hall from the library. Having been inside the room before, Nellie could imagine Adalbert sitting by the fire.

Not much later the housekeeper came back. "The master will see you now." He led Henrik and Nellie into the library.

Adalbert Verdonck sat behind the big desk, and when

Nellie and Henrik came into the room, he pushed away the paper that he had been writing on.

An agreement he didn't want them to see? A budget for sending out an army? A letter to someone else to join him?

"This is an unusual visit," he said.

"It's an unusual situation," Henrik said. "I spotted Master Emmel outside."

"Dear man, do you wish to criticise who I receive as guests?"

"I know him well and I know what he does, so I cannot help but question his presence here."

"What would you say to 'That's none of your business?'"

"I accept that, yet it *is* my business. Knowing the things I know, I would strongly advise you against sending mercenaries into Saardam."

Adalbert Verdonck snorted and lifted his eyebrows. "What makes you think I'm going to do that?"

"Master Emmel's presence, for one. And the things you've said while in the palace."

Another snort. "The place is in chaos, and someone needs to bring order. Apparently, the Regent's son has truly taken his father's position, and the church supports him."

Nellie couldn't stop herself exclaiming, "Casper?"

"Yes. That utter ill-mannered brat. He's taken to ordering the guards about on ridiculous tasks. He's sent me another letter asking for my assistance, *financial* assistance, of course."

Nellie thought of the previous letter he had shown her. "What did you respond to the first letter?"

He spread his hands. "And now *you* want to know my business as well? Yes, I responded. I told the young brat that if he really wanted to be a ruler, he'd start by taking a mentor and marrying a princess." He laughed.

Nellie pushed down annoyance.

"Ruling a country is a serious business, not to be placed in the hands of a sixteen-year-old boy. Someone has to teach him a lesson."

"I agree, but sending in troops is not how to do it," Henrik said.

Adalbert Verdonck raised his eyebrows. "He's a *boy*. What can go wrong?"

"As long as the church supports him, everything."

Adalbert wrinkled his nose. "Priests. I will hear no more of them."

"Dangerous magical priests. You think a boy of sixteen can control them? You think mercenaries are the answer to a strong magician?"

Adalbert Verdonck hesitated. A small frown crossed his face. He might have dismissed their stories about magic during their last visit, but he was not stupid. He'd learn what there was to learn about a situation, and then he would use as much as he could.

He gestured at the couch.

Henrik took the hint and sat down. Nellie sat down next to him.

Lord Verdonck took a piece of parchment from the top of the stack of books next to his desk. He handed it to Henrik, presuming Nellie couldn't read.

But Nellie looked over his shoulder.

"I received this from a friend," Lord Verdonck said. "I know you believe otherwise, but it was one of the reasons Master Emmel was here: to deliver that letter. He and I go back a long way. We used to live on the same street."

"So did we," Nellie said. "Henrik went into the guards, and I ended up working in the palace for the queen. I also went with her to Florisheim."

Nellie was quite sick of this young noble acting like he thought less of her.

"Is that so?"

He looked at her with renewed curiosity as if he couldn't believe that a maid could have any use.

Meanwhile, Henrik was reading. The letter was written in a very neat handwriting, and Nellie recognised a seal at the top as being from one of the council families. She even thought she knew which family. The father was a grumpy old man who refused to come to any of the Regent's banquets. Normally she would question what he knew, but in this case it was a good sign.

"Things have really started to go bad," Henrik said.

Adalbert Verdonck nodded, as if he expected Henrik to agree with his proposition to send an army.

"Did he really do that?"

"Yes, Master Emmel was talking to me about it because he had to confirm what they said was true. The young upstart got the other young boys who taunted him in his youth to come to the palace, take off their pants, and run laps around the forecourt."

"It might just be a little teasing," Henrik said.

"I wouldn't think so. There is that trollop Baroness Hestia egging him on. And the church should know better and should stop it. Already some of the noble families are angry, but apparently some of their young sons have given the lout money."

"They should be livid."

"Take it from me, I'm sure they are, and I'm sure that some action won't be far away, especially if we show up at the palace gates with an army."

"What would you do if it were your son?" Nellie asked. She didn't know if he had a son; she guessed probably not, because of what Gisele had told her.

"If I had a son, I would be there demanding my loans

back immediately, except I have already done that and I am not exactly known for my patience. Most of these lazy people have a lot more patience than I do."

"But this is such a dangerous situation, with a young boy playing these games at the expense of the country."

He gave her a suspicious look, as if wondering where she was going with this.

"My point is, I don't think anyone who is sensible, like you, would put up with this any longer than it takes for your son to walk home without his pants and be laughed at by all the citizens."

He pressed his lips together.

"Now I guess a lot of these men are your friends. Would you suggest that they wouldn't do exactly the same if a member of their family was insulted? In fact, I observed Casper ridiculing the mayor's daughter and making crude comments about her. The mayor was very angry indeed, so it is not as if it is the first time that Casper has been insulting people. Shouldn't they be much angrier than they are?"

She could see in his eyes that he finally saw that she might be right. "Why are they not acting in a way that suggests that they're angry?"

He gave a small shrug. "Because it takes time to get protest organised. Oh, it's easy enough to storm into the palace and make your displeasure known, but it's another thing altogether to do it in such a way that it has an effect."

"Your friends in Saardam have been doing this?"

"Not as fast as I would have liked. But I can't see into their affairs. There may have been issues that necessitated a delay in their actions. It's difficult to judge from here."

Nellie asked, "All the while doing this, have there been any more dinners?"

"I suspect they are more lavish than ever," Henrik said.

Adalbert Verdonck scoffed. "The letter says that despicable priest even takes part in most of them. He fills the young gentlemen's heads with rubbish, from what I hear, and they behave like animals without their parents around."

"Just to be clear, you haven't offered him any support?"

He gave her a *What do you take me for?* look. "I thought my father's support of the Regent was already too much, even if I accepted his arguments for it. I think this young lout well crosses the boundaries of acceptability."

"But that same letter he sent you, he would have written to others, and some have obviously given him their support."

He snorted. "It seems so, although I have no idea why."

"Magic in the food," Nellie said. "I told you this last time we were here."

And obviously, he had discounted her words.

She continued, her voice low. "I have noticed it myself, after leaving the palace. My thoughts have become much clearer, and I've felt more able to ask questions."

His frown deepened. It was now a few days ago that he had last visited the palace. The effect of anything he'd eaten there would have worn off.

He spoke slowly. "You mean they support him because there is some sort of magic poison in the food that is served at the banquets?"

"I don't think it comes from the kitchen," Nellie said. "I worked in the kitchens, and I can tell you that nothing suspicious happened there. The food arrives at the palace already infused with magic. I have seen how they do it with gin. I told you this last time, too. I think at the time you had just come back from the palace and you didn't believe me."

"I don't even remember that you said it." Adalbert Verdonck was looking decidedly disturbed now. His face was haunted and his expression dark. After a long silence, he said, "I feel a like an idiot, and believe me, I do not like admitting that. My father talked about this magic a lot. But he was always taking all those pills for his health, and he was fine whenever he visited the palace. Even when he got sick in the palace I thought it was just his way of complaining that he didn't want to go to the banquet. He was always everywhere, but he got sick of people very quickly and he always left early."

That was true.

"I laughed about his pill taking, but I never really questioned what was in all these things. He was very particular about what he ate and told me not to trust any food served by anyone whom you didn't consider a friend, but said nothing more about the food that was served at the palace. I didn't go to the banquets. I brought my own food, because I disliked the company. He may have been trying to protect me."

"Do you have any of those pills he was taking?" Nellie asked.

"Maybe. I will have to search for them. Why?"

"I have heard of some herbal remedies that work against magic. I suspect they only work against low forms of magic and that a direct attack by magic will still require a magician to be defeated. But if people in the city—important people at least—could be convinced to take these pills, then you would get a lot more support if you came to drive Casper out of the palace."

Now he was looking at her with renewed interest. "So, if I found these pills, could you tell what's in them?"

"I can't, but some of the women would probably know."

"And you could make more of these pills?"

"Probably. We have with us a woman who used to run a shop selling sweets. I'm sure she knows how to make pills."

"But how would we get them out there and how would we let people know that they should take these pills?"

"I don't know. I'm just making this up as I go." Then, thinking of Zelda, she added, "We could pretend to be medicine women, although you'll find it hard to get many in my group to go back to Saardam. Most of them are terrified of being recaptured. Maybe your soldiers could enter the city and hand out food like the shepherd does."

"We don't want the *poor* people to eat it. We want to reach the nobles. We have to put it in the food that's served at the banquet."

"In that case, I don't know. I'm not at the palace anymore and it's too dangerous for me to go there."

"I agree it would be dangerous to go into town. You've made me think, though."

Hopefully he'd think for long enough to see that taking an army into the city was a bad idea. Maybe he'd heard the fire dog rumours from his friends. Who knew what sort of contacts these rich men had?

Meanwhile, Henrik continued, "We actually came here today because a boy from our group has gone missing. In the past few days, he appeared homesick and we think he's either hiding somewhere or he has gone to Saardam. We would like your assistance in trying to find him. Anything you can think of, but most of all, we would like you to tell your men to look out for a skinny young boy, fourteen years of age, with dark hair and dark eyes."

"This boy came with you on the ship?"

"Yes."

He gave both Henrik and Nellie a sharp look. Did he suspect this was Bruno? And then a horrible thought: Adalbert Verdonck considered himself eligible for the throne. What if he had recognised Bruno and made him disappear?

But it was clear from the tracks in the frozen grass that

Bruno had left on the dragon's back. And certainly the dragon wouldn't allow Bruno to be captured.

While Nellie struggled with her suspicion, Henrik said that they wanted only to borrow two horses and a cart. He explained it was for himself and Nellie, because the two of them were the people the boy knew best and trusted most.

"All right," Adalbert Verdonck said. "If you want I can lend you some men to search for him. I have a house in the city that is currently empty. You can use it if you want. There are three permanent staff in the house."

Henrik bowed. "Thank you very much, but the latter is not necessary. I have family in Saardam."

Nellie and Henrik left the room, walked across the hall and out the front door. It was not until they were halfway down the lane that Henrik spoke.

"That sneaky bastard. I think he intended to storm into the city, depose Casper and take the throne for himself."

"Do you think we shouldn't have told him about the magic?"

"No, because it offends me to send fellow soldiers to their deaths, and I think he may hesitate sending his men now that he knows about the magic."

"I think he might know about Bruno," Nellie said.

"Probably, although Bruno definitely left of his own will, or that dragon would have made such a ruckus that all of us would have been awake."

That confirmed Nellie's thoughts on the matter. "But what if he promised Bruno something?"

"That would have required him having spoken to Bruno, and no one came near the barn, not even when you were away."

"Do you think he would do Bruno any harm?" Nellie's heart was thudding. She did and didn't want to hear the reply to this question, but she had to know whether

Adalbert could be as bad as her fears made him out to be.

But Henrik shook his head. "I don't think so. He doesn't seem that type of man. Although he may stand by the side while we look for him and probably won't mind if we don't find him. I suspect there are a great number of people who will object if Adalbert makes a grab for the throne, and it's probably why the church has never made haste determining who the rightful heir is, anyway. They can't reject him too publicly, because of his loans to the city, so they're doing this careful dance instead."

"Does he have any claim to the throne?"

"The joke goes that there isn't a noble in all of the lowlands who doesn't have a claim to the throne, no matter how distant. If there was a line for the throne, however, he would be somewhere at the back."

"You think that's what the mercenaries were for?"

"It's possible that he only had a friend visit him, but in my experience, these men don't have friends. They have associates and business partners. If Master Emmel was here, he was here for a reason. Either to protect Lord Verdonck on a trip, or to get rid of bandits, or protect the estate. But there is no danger that requires an army of men."

"He could just be nervous."

"Not him, I don't think. He's the bold and loud type. He dislikes spying and scheming."

Nellie said, "I don't think he's a bad man, just very impatient."

"No, he isn't, but he's a very brusque person and will have everyone in Saardam fighting before he even gets there to assume power that isn't his to take. We won't be using his house, and we won't be using any of his people. We will use his horses, because at least horses can't talk.

We are going straight to the city now before he can warn anybody. We'll find Bruno without his help and meddling."

"I don't like leaving the others here, though," Nellie said.

"They should be safe. He's not interested in paupers. They're better off here than at that nunnery. It's only when we find Bruno that he will become more dangerous. There is only one thing you can do with men like him."

"And that is?"

"Use them. Be smart and get them to do what you need done while letting them believe it was their idea and they're doing it to benefit themselves. I bet that, right now, he's going through his father's bedroom to find those pills. What's the bet he's going to come to the barn to ask for the women's assistance in figuring out what's in these pills? That was quite smart, the way you mentioned how magic affects the nobles."

"It was an accident. It was just a thought. I probably shouldn't have mentioned it at all. That man frightens me."

"He frightens me, too. That's why we need to use him."

CHAPTER 13

NELLIE HAD BEEN prepared to go back to the city to find Bruno accompanied only by Henrik, but she was unprepared for the reaction they got at the barn. It was time for the evening meal, and Agatha and Mina were putting out plates. The smell of hearty cooking was heavenly. Nellie had sent Ewout and Bas to get some rabbits from Mustafa. It was a long time since they had eaten meat.

"Of course, we won't let you go alone," Mina said. "We've come with you all this way, and done all those crazy things with you. Do you think we would give up so easily?"

"I think you should all stay here, especially people with children," Nellie protested.

"And let you go by yourself?" Wim said.

"I'm in much less danger than you."

Gertie said, "You escape the palace with a dragon, and people call you the Dragonspeaker, and you're in less danger than any of us?"

"I was never in jail and wasn't going to be drowned."

"It's dangerous for all of us," Henrik said. "But it's more dangerous not to know where Bruno is."

"But I'm not missing any of the action," Agatha said. "I can come. I've done nothing wrong. They can't prove anything against me. I'm just a poor woman. They don't care about poor women."

Nellie did *not* want Agatha on this trip. "Please. It's going to be a very quick trip, just to find Bruno. We'll all go back to Saardam later, when we have a plan."

Whatever that plan would be, and if Adalbert Verdonck wasn't going to take the throne by force with a hired army first, in which case any plan would be irrelevant.

"You saved all of us," Wim said. "You risked your life, and you didn't need to do that. You risked your life for Bruno. And as many of us as possible will go to help you now."

"Yes, I haven't come all this way to let this boy turn me into an exile," Gisele said.

Jantien said nothing, but when Nellie met her eyes she said, "I have to think of the children. They are far too young to do anything, but believe me if I didn't have them I would come with you."

"I believe you," Nellie said she was close to tears with all the support she was getting. She had not expected this at all.

In fact, the only one who said nothing was the only person Nellie thought would have a very good reason to visit Saardam: Madame Sabine.

She sat in the corner of the fruit-picker's kitchen in the barn, cradling a cup of tea. She didn't look up or show any sign that she heard what was discussed.

Nellie didn't understand her. She had to know about the situation her sons were in without their father. Did she really care nothing for two vulnerable boys, no matter how poorly they behaved?

Henrik assured the women that they'd be careful, and

told them that on this trip, more people wouldn't be a help. The two of them would be safer on their own, but there would be plenty of time for the others to help Nellie later.

But first she and Henrik needed to find Bruno and bring him back or make sure that he was otherwise in a safe place in Saardam.

The idea of the dragon being with the prince clamped a cold hand around Nellie's heart. What would he order it to do? She knew the dragon couldn't defeat the fire dog by itself. It might need Bruno's magic to help it, and as far as Nellie knew, magic was worth little when untrained.

Nellie ate while Henrik told the group that they would leave in the morning the next day and would be back as soon as possible.

One by one, the women finished eating and left the kitchen. Mina had insisted that they work for their keep, so Lord Verdonck's housekeeper had brought a large basket with items that needed mending, mostly men's clothes that needed to be made smaller. Nellie suspected they were the father's clothes needing to fit the son.

Only a few people were left in the room when Madame Sabine slipped into the seat opposite Nellie. In the low light, her face looked haunted.

"Did he say anything about the boys?"

So she *did* care. "Nothing more than I've already told you. Casper has assumed the position of Regent. He seems to be supported by the church."

"That filthy priest." Her face twisted into a snarl. "He had my husband around his little finger. I don't suspect my sons have anything to say against him. They're just as weak as their father."

"Wouldn't you want to help them?"

She laughed. "As if they would listen to me. Nobody listens to me. I can't even arrange a ride out of this place.

Their father has spoiled those boys rotten. What can I tell them? Study science. Work hard. They're not interested in any of that. They want easy lives sucking on the teat of the church."

Unfortunately, Nellie had to agree with her, but she didn't want to say anything bad about the boys in front of their mother. If even a mother couldn't find it in her heart to love her children, then things were very bad indeed.

She had finished her meal and made to get up from the table when Madame Sabine said, "Sweets."

Nellie stopped. "Excuse me?"

"Sweet. They love sweets."

"Sure." Which person didn't love sweets?

"If you need to get into their rooms, offer them sweets. I used to do it all the time, until they figured out that when I gave them sweets, I wanted something in return and it stopped working."

All right. "Thank you for letting me know."

Nellie had no intention of trying to see Casper or Frederick.

"I used to worry about their teeth," Madame Sabine continued.

Nellie thought, *Used to?*

Madame Sabine didn't follow it up with more information, so Nellie picked up her plate again. When she turned away, she noticed the glitter in Madame Sabine's eyes.

Madame Sabine noticed that Nellie had seen it and turned away.

Nellie gave her plate to Koby who was helping Agatha with the washing up and went to the main part of the barn. It was much colder here and the women who had gone to work on Lord Verdonck's clothes sat around the fire with blankets over their legs.

Nellie would have joined them, but since she and Henrik were leaving early in the morning, she needed to pack her meagre possessions for the journey. Henrik had said they could stay at the house of one of his daughters and Nellie wanted those people to have a good impression of her. She might *be* a pauper right now, but that didn't mean she had to look like one.

Walking past the door to the kitchen, she heard voices.

Was Agatha really talking to Madame Sabine?

TRUE TO HIS WORD, Lord Verdonck sent a stablehand to the barn with two horses and a cart the next morning. Nellie and Henrik had packed up—not that there was much to pack.

Most of her clothes, she wore, and the rest could fit into a small bag. She debated whether to leave her father's book behind, but she didn't know if she would be back here, and they might need it. She even packed her copy of the Book of Verses, although she had debated giving it to one of the children who needed it more than she did.

Nellie and Henrik sat on the driver's bench and the tray remained conspicuously empty except for the blanket that Bruno had used when he slept in the barn.

Nellie and Henrik travelled through the countryside, following the road that Zelda must also take to the city. It was the only road, and it led past the front of Lord Verdonck's estate. They went down the long lane and then turned right to go to the city. This early in the morning, a few people travelled along the road on their way to market with their produce or crafts. They sat on their carts huddled in their coats and barely acknowledged Henrik and Nellie whose cart—being empty—was much faster.

The cart trundled along the cobblestones. Henrik asked her if she wanted to ride for a while, but it was a very long time since Nellie had ridden and she remembered how sore her backside had been back then.

The sun was up and provided only a tiny bit of warmth to their cold bones. The frost was just starting to melt and the low hanging fog did little to increase the temperature.

Gradually they encountered more houses and more people with carts and horses coming the other way, and people mending fences and doing other farm work.

The Verdonck estate was not very far from the city, and on the same side of the river, and gradually, little settlements dotted the countryside.

People greeted Nellie and Henrik along the way, and occasionally a bored guard waved them through a checkpoint. They looked like peasants going to the market. But Henrik said that they weren't bothered because Adalbert Verdonck controlled this land and the Verdonck seal adorned the horses' headgear.

"We're so close to Saardam," Nellie said. Already, she could see the spire of the church tower poking above the horizon.

So pretty.

"I hope we will find it as peaceful as it looks," Henrik said.

"I hope nothing bad has happened to Bruno. If he's been caught and locked up, I'm not sure I could get him out again."

"That boy is a danger to himself."

"I hope he isn't a danger to others."

And with that they had arrived back at the subject that Nellie dreaded. Having seen how King Roald was unsuited to govern, she wondered if it took a particular type of person to become a good ruler. You couldn't assume that just because someone was born into a family, he or she was a good match for the job. And if Bruno wasn't a good match to be king, who would take the position?

So many people were waiting in line to take over. They could appoint another Regent—they would have to because Bruno was only fourteen—but would the people of the city accept the new Regent knowing what a disaster the previous Regent had been?

The closer they got to the city the less certain she was that this would all work out. They were rushed into doing things, they would be discovered, they would all be thrown in jail and that would be the end of the royal family.

"I don't know what we'll do any more," Nellie said. "It seems that, wherever we turn, people try to take advantage of each other and of us. When we came to that nunnery I thought we had found where I would be happy to spend the rest of my days. Then Zelda came in, and it turns out that they're in with the same plot."

"You've seen all the things that different families do when they're in power and when they want to have power. Nothing should surprise you any more."

"It doesn't. But that doesn't mean it doesn't disappoint me."

And then they talked of all their memories of old king Nicholaos and of the time that they had to flee the city. It turned out that Henrik had been commandeered to work for the Fire Wizard, and had managed to get away with being placed with the city guards.

"That was a crazy time," he said. "Of course, I was much younger then, but part of me wonders whether, if the time ever came back, I would be swayed as easily as I was then to do as I did. I was no hero. But Martha and the girls needed me, and I had seen what happened to people who went against the Fire Wizard's word."

"We were all much younger," Nellie said. "I was very naive back then. I truly thought that only if everyone went to church they would know what was good and bad. It never occurred to me to think that people in the church could be bad. Misguided, yes; but evil, no. Because otherwise the Triune would never accept them, let alone allow them to rise to important positions in the church."

"The Triune doesn't allow people to do things. The church is made up out of people who allow other people to do things, and people are fallible."

That was true, too. Her father's experience had made that clear.

Henrik snorted. "Here I was, thinking about retirement."

"I've been wondering about that too."

"The winters get colder every year, and it becomes harder to get out of bed. Especially when I'm on duty very early."

"I have nowhere else to go." But that had been her fear when she lived at the palace. She had nowhere else to go when she worked in the palace. Now that she didn't work there anymore, she was already at the nowhere that she didn't have to go to. It was strangely liberating. She had nothing left to lose.

Henrik said, "I'm still thinking I might join another army, but I may be too old. Otherwise, one of my daughters may have to put up with me."

And then they both laughed, because being sad about not having anywhere to go in old age was just a strange thing.

He continued, "I have some savings. I was thinking I might be able to work for a landowner family or something like that."

Nellie said, "I would really like a small house somewhere where I can grow my own food and have some chickens and then maybe sell some eggs and some vegetables or pickles or embroidery."

By now, they had come to the outskirts of the city. Saardam was not a fortress city, and while a past king had built a wall with a gate, it had since become obsolete because people had built outside the old city walls, and no one patrolled the gate any more. In short, people were leaving the city and no one cared very much about who came into the city. The Regent had never had enough guards to patrol the gates very closely.

They took the cart and the horses to a stable where they paid for some hay. Then they went into the city.

Nellie was surprised how perfectly normal the streets were. There was no sign of any disturbance. She listened for gossip on the street, but the talk was all about normal daily things. In fact, it was disturbing how normal everything looked. When she had come back while the Fire Wizard was ruling the city, the signs of fear and destruction had been everywhere. She had expected the city to be somewhat like that, but nothing could be further from the truth.

In the marketplace, there were even more sellers than there had been when Nellie was still in the city. It seemed as if some people had deemed it safe to come out. Maybe they were desperate for money. "They probably just come because of the better weather," Henrik said.

That could be true, too. The weather had been dry, even if sometimes misty, but the snow was gone.

In winter, people did pick the best times to make the journey to the city.

They walked across the market square, looked at the produce and listened to the gossip, but what they heard was all about trivial things: annoyances, weddings, deaths, that sort of thing.

Then Nellie came across a cheese seller who was talking to someone at a neighbouring stand.

"And then, according to my friend, he said bring all the staff into the audience room. And when they came, he made them all kneel on the floor and bow their heads to him as he walked between them telling them how useless they were."

"I have heard that he does this all the time."

"It's a disgrace and an embarrassment. They should send in some adults to sort them out."

A customer came to the stand and the conversation turned to cheese.

Nellie and Henrik continued, and Henrik said to Nellie. "Casper is making himself very popular, I hear."

But there was no word of where Bruno might be.

In between the market stalls they could see the palace gates, and although it was the middle of the day, the gates were closed. A few guards stood there, and Henrik knew them, so he didn't want to go too close.

A man went up to the guards and proceeded to argue with them, with much waving of hands. Nellie went closer to listen, but Henrik didn't like it.

"Those men are trained to know everyone who walks through the palace gates. They will know and recognise you."

So Nellie had to stay in between the market stalls, and caught only shards of the conversation, which appeared to be about some prearranged business the man had in the palace that he was now prevented from entering.

"Why?" He wanted to know. "I've known the young lord since he was a little mite and have made trousers for him since he was a little boy. What is happening behind those gates that can't see the light of day?"

To which the reply was that the guards had detected the activity of traitors, and that the housekeeper had ordered the gates closed so that they could conduct a search of the palace.

That was nonsense. Nellie knew that the housekeeper was just a servant and had nowhere near that level of authority.

So. Casper had ordered the gates closed? No, because the guards would have said so.

The shepherd had ordered the gates closed?

Regardless of the influence of magic, Nellie liked to think that the citizens of Saardam would have a problem with the shepherd ordering anything.

The question remained: what had happened that had made someone—possibly the shepherd—order the gates closed and all visits cancelled?

No mention of Bruno anywhere, of course. And they weren't here to investigate the palace's problems.

"If you had to make a guess, where would you expect him to go?" Henrik asked.

"The shepherd's house, the church, maybe the houses at the back where the monks are staying."

"Well then, why don't we go to the church?"

CHAPTER 14

NELLIE HAD FEARED they would end up having to go to the church.

By now, little was left of the institution she had loved. She feared meeting the shepherd, and she had never considered the main church to be welcoming in the first place. With the things in the crypts, with the scenes she had witnessed under its vaulted ceiling, the church had become a daunting place to visit. It felt wrong.

A steady trickle of people were going in and out through the open church doors. Mothers with children, a group of young men, two older women.

To be honest, Nellie had never seen many people visit the church during daytime. Yes, the doors were always open, but the only people who came in regularly were older women coming to light a candle for sick relatives.

Especially unusual were the young men who now walked down the steps and turned into the street that ran past the side of the church.

Nellie felt the wrongness the moment she and Henrik stepped into the dark vestibule. First was the smell of burnt wood. Then, so many people were here who normally would never come. They all either walked down the centre aisle to or from the altar, or they stood in front of a line of wooden chairs with a rope strung between them that closed off an area around the altar. They were looking at something. They knelt to pray.

"What's going on?" Nellie whispered to Henrik.

But Henrik, being only a casual church visitor by virtue of his job, had no idea.

Walking down the aisle, the first thing Nellie noticed in addition to the scent of burned wood was that little was left of the wood panelling of the pulpit. The pretty dark wood had burnt to ashes, and the flames had made sooty black marks on the pillar behind the pulpit all the way up to the ceiling.

The cupboards and shelves against the back wall—where the Shepherd would put items to be used in the service, carried to the altar by young boys—were also burnt, as well as the carpet, part of the table where the candles and the goblet with wine would stand and indeed part of the altar itself.

The contents of some of those cupboards lay on the ground: thick, leather-bound books with half-burned pages.

In big sooty letters was scrawled across the back wall, *The King Will Come.*

A young woman with a little girl came to stand next to Nellie. She didn't know the woman.

"Look," the mother said. "That's where the evil creature tried to take the shepherd."

"Is the evil creature going to come back?" the girl asked.

"No. The shepherd defeated it."

Nellie turned to the mother. "Excuse me, I've been out of town. What happened here?"

"Well, the day before yesterday, we were woken up with

this terrible screeching and, when we went to have look, we met a man who said he saw the good shepherd fighting off a flying fire demon. He said the fire demon attacked the shepherd when he came into the church for the morning service and the shepherd fought it off by writing on the wall."

"What does it say?" the little girl asked.

"It says, 'The King Will Come'. The king is the Holy Father."

"And the demon was so afraid that it fled?"

"Yes."

Nellie nodded her thanks to the woman and walked along the rope barrier.

A big group of people came in, and Nellie jerked her head at Henrik. The two of them made their way back to the vestibule.

"What do you think happened?" Henrik asked her.

"I don't know, but that woman's story is rubbish. The shepherd would never scrawl on the walls of his own church. He's spent all his life trying to be completely normal."

Henrik agreed. "Scrawling on walls is the sign of a madman. He's too smart to do that."

"So what did happen? Any ideas?"

"I think there was a fight," Henrik said.

"With Bruno?"

He sighed. "I don't see who else would be involved. I know he never stopped talking about punishing the shepherd for locking him up."

"The question is: did he win or lose the fight?"

Henrik shook his head. "It's not looking good. I heard someone say that the flying demon, presumably the dragon, dragged itself out of the church."

"And where is he now? No mention of a boy?"

He shook his head again.

They had left the church and were standing on top of the church steps. From here, you could see over the market stalls. The palace, with its closed gates, was directly opposite the church entrance.

Nellie had seen the dragon when it had spent all its magical energy, leaking sparks. It could not have gone far.

The King Will Come.

"I wouldn't be surprised if Bruno wrote on the church wall," she said. "I think he considers himself the king, and a king belongs in the palace. What if he went across from the church to the palace? And the shepherd locked the gates pretending nothing was wrong, because the dragon can't defeat the fire dog, but the dog can't win the fight, either."

Henrik nodded, slowly. "I'd love to know what's going on behind those gates."

"I can probably find out. I could pay a visit to the kitchens. If anyone knows any gossip, it's Dora."

At first, Henrik would hear none of it. He protested. "I don't want you to endanger yourself."

"Then we should have stayed where we were. Of the two of us, you have already admitted that it's too dangerous for you to go into the palace—"

"But I've sworn to protect the boy."

"What do you think about me, then? I looked after that boy for the first years of his life. He may not remember or appreciate me, but I owe it to his mother's memory to make sure he is safe."

Henrik glared at her and she glared back at him and said, "I can get into the palace through the back gate. They still need to eat and people will still work in the kitchens. I have brought my apron."

"But the people will recognise you."

"That's the point. They're my friends."

And then she realised that Henrik's former friends

with the guards were no longer his friends, since they were still sworn to protect the palace, even if there was no longer a ruler to protect.

Henrik still didn't like it, but he saw no other option.

So they went to the palace's back gate, and found it attended by a young guard Henrik knew, but Nellie didn't.

"He's a good kid. I don't think he'd let me through, but if you put on the apron and tell him you're coming to work in the kitchens, he'll let you through. Just don't stay away too long."

Nellie took off her coat and shawl and replaced them with the apron and a scarf. It was good that she didn't have to walk far, because it was cold in this outfit.

Henrik took her coat and shawl and promised to wait for her in a street opposite the palace's back entrance, out of view of the guard.

Nellie went up to the guard, told him she'd been asked to come and work in the kitchen and he let her through. She proceeded into the back yard, past the noisy pigs. Her heart was hammering and her hands were sweaty.

She climbed up the back steps and opened the door.

"Nellie!"

Dora had been standing at the stove, and when Nellie came in, abandoned her pot and ran to the door. She swept Nellie up in a strong hug that smelled of hearty cooking.

"Where have you been? We heard all kinds of stories about you escaping the city and saving people who were about to be drowned. I could barely believe those stories, but apparently they were true. I said, is this really the quiet Nellie I know?"

"I know it sounds crazy, and I'm not the only one in the group. We have thirty-five people."

"Anyone I know?"

"Wim is with us," Nellie said.

"So it's true? And I heard that you even saved Madame Sabine."

"Yes, that's true, although she doesn't seem to be very happy about it."

"She doesn't like living at a farm, right?" Dora laughed.

"I think she would prefer to live in luxury." It was a very odd conversation, strangely distant. Dora's world was so different from hers these days.

"Oh no, she wouldn't dare come back. The guards would have her killed."

"So who has replaced the Regent?" Nellie hated playing innocent with Dora, but there were many other people in the kitchen who could overhear what she said, so it was best not to put anyone else in danger.

"It's the most ridiculous thing. We get to serve a boy."

"His son? But he is only sixteen."

"Tell me about it. He is the most insolent brat I know. Of course, he makes us do ridiculous things, and he holds the stupid meetings where he screams at the nobles and demands that they do all kinds of things for him and give him whatever he wants, including their daughters."

"And do they actually do this?"

"They have to. Because he has a lot of guards and they put anyone who doesn't listen to him in prison."

"And the guards have no problems with this?"

"The guards are terrified. I don't quite understand why, but they don't seem to want to stop him at all."

Nellie understood well enough.

"Is that what's going on at the moment? I noticed the gates were closed."

"Oh, no. I'm not exactly sure what happened, but there was a fire in the church one night and I've been told the shepherd blames Casper or his ill-behaved friends. Apparently they wrote all over the church walls. The shepherd was livid, and Casper told him to get out, and that's where we're up to now. The youngsters are all in the ballroom, where apparently Casper holds a court, and the other kids are his councillors. We don't get to go in. We just have to put the food outside the door and they take it inside."

"Do they sleep in there?"

"Yes. They're all together and won't talk to any of us."

"Can't the guards go in?"

"The shepherd says for them to wait."

"And the shepherd? Is he doing anything else about this? He would be the person people look up to. He should talk to them." More lies. Nellie hated it.

"The shepherd has been told he's no longer a court advisor. He comes to the palace sometimes, but he only speaks to the guards. He certainly doesn't come to dinners like he used to. In fact, most of the banquets have finished. We haven't had one since you left."

"That also explains why it's so quiet here."

"That, and a lot of people are just too afraid to come here any more. The only ones you'll see in the kitchen are those who have nowhere else to go."

"Does Casper get any advice from an adult?"

"Some nobles have tried. But all of them have been insulted and sent away by the brat, like the mayor and church deacons."

"Did he give reasons?"

"None that he would mention to us. But this is all so depressing that it makes me want to tear my hair out. What about you. How are you coping?"

"We're fine."

"Are you coming back to live here at all?"

"It's too dangerous at the moment."

"I understand. But life must be hard out there in the country. Do tell me where you are, because I would love to send you a package with goodies, like sweets and dried fruit."

"We're fine, truly."

"And I would like to visit you when I can." What was it with this insistence that she tell Dora where they were staying?

And all of a sudden Nellie grew cold. When she came here after having fled from the palace with the dragon, she had told Dora where they were, and then the guards had shown up. And Dora did the main part of the cooking for the banquet.

Had *Dora* told the city guards where they could find the dragon? Was *Dora* now trying to find out where the women were staying? Had *Dora* helped the Shepherd spread magic-infused food. Why hadn't she though of this before?

It grew too hot in the kitchen. She had to get out of here as quickly as possible but without raising any suspicion.

Corrie joined them at the table. Her ankle had healed, but between the cheerful replies, Nellie saw that her face was lined and she looked tired and worried. The other people in the kitchen were not working as hard as before. It was quiet and cold in here.

"What about the two sisters Els and Maartje?" Nellie asked.

Dora said, "I haven't seen them any more either. Not that it really matters, because we have no more work for them."

Nellie had what she wanted. She bade Dora goodbye, and left the kitchen again as quickly as she could.

While she was in the kitchen, it had started to get dark outside.

She crossed the muddy yard, where the pigs shuffled in their pen, and went through the lane out the gate. She pulled her scarf as far forward as it would go so that her face was in shadow and scooted past the guard. He wasn't concerned with people leaving the palace.

She met Henrik in the street opposite the gate. He stood waiting on the corner with his hands in his pocket and his collar drawn up around his neck. His breath steamed in the light of a lantern a bit further down.

He looked up when he heard her footsteps, and his face split into a grin when he recognised her.

"I wasn't gone that long," she said.

"No, but things are afoot in the city. I don't like the thought of you being out there by yourself."

"I know where I'm going. But yes, I agree, things are not good." And she told him that Casper and his friends had locked themselves in the ballroom and no one was sure what was going on inside.

"Bruno could still be there," Henrik said.

"He could be, but I expect Dora would know about it if a strange boy who damaged the church had sheltered in the palace." Or was Dora lying? It hurt her to think like this. She'd considered Dora a friend.

"It sounds a terrible situation, and the boys must be desperate."

"Or they could be smart."

"What do you mean?"

"You know how Adalbert Verdonck showed us the letter Casper had written to him asking for support? Casper obviously watched his father really well. He must have gotten some support, and it could well be that he figured out the shepherd was trying to use him, and now he's barricaded himself into the ballroom with his friends."

And then she told him about Dora. "I always thought that Zelda betrayed us, and she always insisted she didn't. She might be right."

That didn't mean Nellie was now going to trust Zelda,

because Zelda was not the kind of person she wanted to trust, but maybe Zelda's herb trade was less dangerous than Nellie had assumed, except to the pockets of the rich.

The thought made her sick, as if everyone used the situation to benefit themselves. "So. We still don't know for sure where Bruno is. If only we could figure out how to get into the palace while remaining undetected, when the guards are controlled by magic and the shepherd prowls with his fire dog, and the only thing that could possibly defeat the fire dog—the dragon—is either inside, injured or weak."

"Pretty much," Henrik said. "But there will be plenty of talk about this. It's dark now, and we won't find anything else tonight. Let's go and find something to eat."

CHAPTER 15

THEY WALKED ON for a little while in silence. Their footsteps echoed in the empty streets.

Nellie expected to be followed, or for someone to spring from the shadows at every corner or porch they passed, but the streets remained quiet.

"Where are we going?" she asked.

"I said we were getting something to eat."

"But isn't your daughter's house over on the other side of town?"

"We're not going to her house yet. I'm taking you to a favourite place of mine."

"Here? In the harbour?" She didn't think Henrik would visit sailor's taverns and whorehouses, but she didn't know of any reputable guesthouses in this area of town.

"Trust me. It's very respectable."

A moment later he turned into a narrow alley that went past the back of the houses. It was very dark here, and they had to be careful not to trip over uneven paving.

At the end of the alley, they came to a small courtyard with a couple of doors. Nellie guessed these were the backs doors of shops, through which the people who lived above the shops entered.

Henrik knocked on one of the doors. It opened, revealing a dimly lit room, and a man whom Nellie could see only in silhouette.

"Who is there?" the man said, his voice pleasant.

"I'm an old friend," Henrik said. "We are weary and cold in the night."

The man open the door further without another word.

Henrik stepped into the room beyond, and Nellie followed him.

The hall was only lit by a single oil lamp standing on a tall table against the wall.

By its light, she saw that the man who had opened the door wore a uniform in the colours of the city guard.

He said, "We thought you would never return. Some people even said that you were dead, drowned in the harbour."

"They can't get rid of me as easy as that," Henrik said.

"How did you get back? Where are you staying? Somewhere safe, I hope?"

"We're fine for the night. I was hoping you would be able to help us with a meal."

"Of course, my dear friend. Are you hungry?"

"Always."

And then Henrik stepped back and the man looked at Nellie. "Why, it's our Dragonspeaker."

Nellie smiled uneasily. The dragon had escaped with Bruno. "I don't deserve any heroic names. I'm Nellie." She held out her hand, and he shook it.

"You are welcome Nellie, to the humble abode of the Guard Guild. My name is August, and I work for the city guards."

"I didn't know that a Guard Guild existed."

"Officially, it doesn't," August said. "The members who

meet here do so at great risk to themselves and their families, and even most guards don't know about this place. If they did, we'd all be jailed, if not worse."

"Why?" Guilds were a good idea, because they helped tradespeople. Her father had been a member of several, including the semi-legal Science Guild, and had dealings with several more. They were respected organisations, and some even had their own premises.

"WHERE WOULD BE AN EASIER place to arrange an armed uprising than where armed men get together?"

Nellie frowned at him. "So who made it illegal? Or was it always so?"

He chuckled. "It's too cold in this hall to get into a detailed history of our organisation. Let's go somewhere warm."

He preceded them down a dark corridor, where the floor creaked and their footsteps sounded muffled on greasy carpet underfoot. He opened a door.

In this room it was warm and a number of people, both men and women, sat on easy chairs while a lusty fire burned in the hearth.

The first thing Nellie noticed was a big portrait of King Roald above the hearth. If she was right, this portrait used to hang in the king's small audience room, which had been divided into two guest rooms since Regent Bernard moved into the palace.

It seemed Nellie had not been the only one to rescue things from the palace stores.

Several of the men rose when Henrik came in and greeted him with cheers and claps on the shoulder. Some of them wore palace guard uniforms, and others were city guards. Nellie wasn't sure what the few women in the room where doing there. They didn't look like servants, and they were not noblewomen—at least, she didn't think so.

Meanwhile, August yelled to someone in the next room, "Bring us two plates and some good food."

He gestured to some empty tables and seats. "Sit down."

Nellie and Henrik sat.

A number of the men came to join them, and one of the women, too. They wanted to know what had happened, and Henrik told them his version of events.

They looked at Nellie with admiration. Henrik said several times that the prisoner escape plan had been her idea, and that he had only watched from the shadows. "But I knew that once they were out in the open, they needed a big distraction to let them get away."

August nodded. "It was a big distraction all right."

"The Regent's death has caused quite a lot of trouble, even if I can't fault your action," another man said. "I've been itching to shoot that man. How can he betray his own wife like that? And then to drown her in front of his sons. No wonder the boys misbehave."

August said, "Yes, but one way or another this has probably hastened the process of finding a permanent solution. The boy regent won't last."

Everyone around the table nodded.

"Now we only have to make sure that it's a permanent solution that's to the benefit of the citizens." The man who said this sounded cynical.

Another man said, "At this point, anything except the brat will do. Someone needs to take him down."

An older man said, "He's a brat, but he doesn't deserve to die. It's our task to protect him and we will, until such time as he commits crimes, or sins against his family or advisors."

Several people laughed. One said, "What advisors? A

bunch of adolescents who hold drunken meetings on how best to screw each other, with live demonstrations? There are women in this room, but I could tell you things—"

"I assure you, Cees, there is nothing you can say that I don't already know," one of the women said from near the hearth. Her voice was quite dark.

Nellie knew the man. He was also a guard at the palace.

"That still doesn't make it right or appropriate to discuss the details. Believe me, people don't need to know anything except that the young boy has become utterly corrupted by his obsession with pleasures of the flesh."

"As do most adolescent boys," the woman said.

The man gave a snort. Nellie realised she also knew the woman. She had been one of the long string of women the Regent had burned through while finding a governess for his sons.

The woman continued, "I just hope that it can be resolved without too many deaths or people losing their homes."

"Is there anyone left in the palace who has influence on Casper?" Henrik asked.

The guard Cees said, "The Shepherd could control him, if he wanted, but instead, he appears to be egging him on, bringing books about obscene subjects, and the boy is just lapping it up."

By the Triune, he was talking about the books from the secret library in the crypt. Nellie felt sick.

Not only that, it didn't fit with the picture she had formed from Casper's polite and well-written letters to Adalbert Verdonck asking for help.

What if Casper was much smarter than he let himself appear? He had spent the past ten years watching his father and the nobles of the city do a delicate dance with the shepherd, and losing the fight at each step. He might even, because of Lord Verdonck, be suspicious of the shepherd. Coming from Burovia, where magic was much more common, he might suspect that magic was involved.

He had watched the spectacle in the harbour from an upstairs window. He might have seen the fire dog and recognised it for what it was.

But Nellie didn't say anything about this to these people.

August was saying, "The brat is not the issue. His days are probably numbered, with the way he behaves. It's all by design that he is allowed to behave like this. Several people have tried to steer him into more adult behaviour, but the shepherd won't let anyone near him. He lets the boy free reign. He can misbehave however he wants. He has proven throughout his short life that he's well capable of upsetting a great number of people. He is ill mannered and rude to everyone, from the servants to the nobles to the rulers of the neighbouring countries. He doesn't know or doesn't understand how to behave. The shepherd is allowing this to take place, because he knows that Casper will make himself so hated that someone will kill him soon enough. And then, when the country descends into chaos, when all the nobles are fighting each other over who is going to sit on the throne, the shepherd will step up as the saviour of the town. I know that a lot of us have experience with who the shepherd really is, and what he does, but he is still enormously popular with a lot of the people who go to the church and are happy to follow his teachings. The church is full whenever he preaches. The people lap up his sermons about the evil of magic, because they like to blame someone for their situation. They don't know any of the things that we know."

Several people gave solemn nods.

A young man came out of the other door, carrying two

plates with fresh bread, fried eggs and ham and pieces of roast vegetables. It smelled heavenly.

"Your own produce?" Nellie asked.

"The family of one of our members has a farm. This food is as fresh as you can get it."

That wasn't the reason Nellie asked. The food was also untouched by magic.

While they ate, the men talked about Casper's recent tricks, which included teaching the noble son who the boss was by letting him run naked in the palace forecourt.

"If it wasn't so sad, it would be funny," August said.

The door opened and a man came in. He was very tall, wore dark clothing including a long cloak, and had his grey hair in a ponytail.

Several people rose and offered him their seats.

"Henrik." The man crossed the room and clapped Henrik on the shoulder.

Henrik made the introductions. "Nellie, this is Master Thiele, secret guild master. This is Nellie Dreessen, the Dragonspeaker."

"Please, you're embarrassing me," Nellie said.

"Not at all. You have brought us many steps forward. We waited and observed for years, wondering how we were going to get into the crypt to rescue the boy."

"Surely, you could have just cut through the metal?"

"We could, but without reasonable cause to do so, we would be committing a crime and incur the anger of the church which, in turn, would anger the citizens; and it might have led to ugly situations, both for ourselves, for the boy, and for the city. We always do what is in the best interests of the greatest number of people, which isn't always the same as what seems right."

"Well, we have a problem now," Henrik said. "Because our prince has gone missing."

"Yes. And when you're finished eating, you must come to my office and we can talk."

Nellie and Henrik quickly finished eating, and then the two of them followed Master Thiele out of the room back into the dark corridor and up the stairs into another corridor where it was very cold.

He opened a door and let them into a firelit office. The room was quite large and well appointed with a big desk, a couple of easy chairs around the fire, and many bookcases full of big, heavy leather-bound tomes.

"Sit down," he said, gesturing at the chairs.

There were only two, and Nellie felt a little embarrassed to take the last one, but he pulled the chair from behind his desk and sat on that one.

"Now tell us what has happened," he said.

Henrik told in a few sentences how they had fled with Bruno, but how he had been impatient and angry and Henrik had been unable to control him.

"I am sorry. I have failed. The boy is strong willed and it's not easy to subdue his impatience. I fear I may have endangered all of us."

Master Thiele folded his hands. "This is what we know so far, but the picture is incomplete. Two days ago, in the early morning, the boy must have arrived in the city. Nobody has come forward to tell us how he arrived. It happened in the very early morning when citizens were asleep. The first records we have that anything was amiss were reports from merchants arriving at the markets that there was a black sooty trail across the pavement leading from the open church doors. It became weaker the further away from the church it got, but appeared to lead to the palace. Not a single person has come forward who knows how this trail was made."

"What about what happened in the church?" Henrik asked.

"We know little. The church has always preferred to keep church matters to itself. None of the city guards ever got to investigate the cause of the fire in the crypts, for example. They don't like officers pouring over their affairs."

"But you've gone inside and looked at the damage, I'm sure?"

"Oh, we have, but although I have ideas about what may have happened, we have no witness accounts, and it's not in our interest to speculate."

"So how did you know Bruno was in the city?"

"One of our members spotted him in the palace with young Casper and the other young nobles before the guards were no longer allowed inside and the doors were locked. He said . . ." Master Thiele reached out to his desk and grabbed a piece of paper. "He said that he saw *a boy, fourteen or fifteen years of age, thin and pale, with night black hair and dark eyes. He sat at the table next to Casper, holding a wooden box of some sort on his lap. His cheek was bruised and the skin on his right hand bore blisters.*"

Nellie nodded. "We suspected Bruno might have fled into the palace."

"What do you think happened?" Master Thiele asked. "You know him better than any of us."

Henrik sighed. "I was training the boy because I felt it was a good idea, because he needed to do something. He was still quite weak and by no means ready for any kind of fight. Frequently when we were training, he would ask me questions about the palace and the church and when we were going back there. He told me a few times that the first thing he wanted to do was to was to punish the church for locking him up. So we assume that he went to the church and there was a confrontation between him and Shepherd Wilfridus, which he lost, after which he fled to the next place he wanted to go: the palace."

"Has anyone seen the shepherd since that day?" Nellie asked.

Master Thiele shook his head. "From what I understand, the services in the church have been suspended until they can clean it up."

Nellie asked, "How many people understood what they saw in the harbour that day? We were at the water, and the fight between the dragon and the fire dog happened quite close to us, but I understand that many people on the shore couldn't see what was happening. They blame us for the magic."

"They do, and to be sure, I have heard no reliable reports on what happened from people on the shore."

"I thought it was clear to all who witnessed it that the shepherd is a very strong magician."

Master Thiele shook his head. "Not clear at all. We strongly suspected it, and we have been very careful, but we haven't seen irrefutable proof that will stand up to the scrutiny of a full session of the court of nobles."

"I saw it," Henrik said. "I hope that is enough proof for you."

Master Thiele nodded. "You don't have to convince me, Henrik, you know that."

"As directed, I shot at him. I thought I would create confusion to make it look like it was meant to be an assassination of the Regent, but instead I seem to have made things worse rather than better."

"You were directed to kill the shepherd?" Nellie asked.

"We have a very short list of people that are better off dead than alive."

Master Thiele gestured at a board on the wall where a couple of names were written in chalk. The list included four names. One of them was Dirk Gouwens, which was the proper name of Shepherd Wilfridus. Nellie didn't know the other men. They were likely to be common criminals.

"Did you have that much evidence against him?"

"The man has a long string of common crimes, involving theft from bereaved widows and organising a network of peddlers and magicians to defraud ordinary citizens."

A memory came to Nellie's mind. "Zelda, the wayfarer."

"She is part of it. She gives him a lot of money for the sales of her wares that at best don't work. We are still dealing with complaints from her dragon ointment. You should see the injuries that some people got all over their skin. But those potions and pills are full of magic. We've been in contact with the Science Guild to establish that."

And then Nellie realised something else. "You used to be part of the King's Guard. Whenever people had a complaint about misconduct by guards or military, they requested an audience with the King's Guard. You would investigate to see if there was a reason to take them to task."

"That's right. Only, when the Regent came in, he wanted none of our meddling, as he said, so he disbanded us. As it turned out, the Regent had nothing to say about this but the shepherd didn't want any of it either, for obvious reasons. That man has a list of crimes longer than my arm. I could list all of them, but I would be here all night. We have no way of sending him to jail, because the citizens adore him."

"So you have him up on that board because he is a common criminal or because he's a magician?"

"For his criminal pursuits. We strongly suspected there was something else going on, but he is smart and he doesn't make it obvious to anyone who doesn't have to know."

"But that's why people adore him: because he uses magic to make people support him."

Nellie then told him about what she and Gisele had learned about the gin poisoned through magic.

Master Thiele gave her a wide-eyed look. "I strongly suspected that the Shepherd had something to do with Lord Verdonck's death. It's not a secret that he hated the man, and he was too obviously offering for us to test the monastery's wine, as if he wanted us to find something there."

"A man was sentenced to death because supposedly the wine was poisoned," Nellie said.

Master Thiele nodded. "I'm beginning to see what's been going on. I spoke to Commander Patrick of the palace guards, and he gave me no reason I could believe to convict the Regent's former taster. I didn't understand how he had come to the conclusion that the taster was guilty, even when it was clear the wine was not poisoned. He was also unable to explain it to me. I should have taken that as a strong sign that something important was amiss."

"You make and eat your own food here," Nellie said. "That has saved you from being afflicted with magic. The others have all eaten at the palace."

Master Thiele let out a heavy breath. "Every time when I think things are bad, they keep getting worse. So what can we do to get the boy out of the palace? Time is of essence. Not only do I have no idea how he is going to survive this, but when his father contacts us, we want to avoid a severe embarrassment."

"You're still in contact with his father?" Nellie said.

"He writes to us, once or twice a year. We write back to him, saying that everything is still as it was before, which is that the Prince is held somewhere in the church and that we haven't been able to free him."

"Well, now he's free."

"He is, but he may be in more danger than being mistreated. The church clearly had a reason to keep him alive, otherwise they would have killed him or let him starve to death long ago. The boy clearly has a strong constitution, because otherwise he would have succumbed to disease. The church had plans for him, and we have disrupted those plans, so they are likely to do something dramatic. I dread the day that we have to tell his father that he's gone. I would dread to tell the country that their best heir to the throne is dead."

"What are you going to do?" Henrik asked.

"I don't think we have any option but to get into the palace by force and free the boys to make sure nothing bad happens to them."

Henrik gave him a sharp look. "Would you stand against other guards?"

"If necessary, but only if we absolutely can't avoid it and if we have enough support to guarantee everyone's survival. We're not into suicide missions."

"You do know that all of them are likely to be influenced by magic?" Nellie said.

"We know, but that can't be helped at the moment. To reverse those effects, we would need a magician. We don't have one, and we don't have the time to look for one, at least not before we can break this situation with the youngsters locked in the palace ballroom."

"Can I help?" Henrik asked.

"Thank you. We will start in the morning. First we need to get our men together to see if we have the numbers to overwhelm the palace guards. We'll send out our men in the morning. No use sending out anyone now."

"This is essentially a mutiny." Henrik's face was grave.

"Hopefully, one that people can see is for the good of their city, but make no mistake, it will be dangerous. We've tried to avoid stepping out of the shadows like this. One mistake, and plenty of people can kill you, even my own men. Be here in the morning, and sleep well. I presume you have somewhere to stay?"

"My eldest daughter's house," Henrik said.

"All right then. Have a good rest."

On the way down the stairs, Nellie wondered if this was what being a spy was like.

CHAPTER 16

NELLIE AND HENRIK walked through the harbour and then into a street along the canals.

Henrik's family was not terribly rich, but they were not poor either. They lived in a house one block back from the canal, in a respectable street, where the neighbours worked in the trades or were employees for the larger companies. Warm light radiated from the windows, and the scent of wood fires hung in the air.

Nellie hid in the collar of her coat. She longed to be warm again.

Henrik had not sent a message to his daughter because he didn't want to risk people who shouldn't know finding out he was back in the city. He knocked on the front door.

Surprised voices came from inside the house. Nellie imagined that not many people visited after dark.

The door opened, and a young woman with blonde hair and freckled face looked out. Her eyes widened when she saw Henrik. "Papa!"

"Clara!" Henrik swept her up in his arms.

She called into the house, "Oh Jan, Annie, come have a look who it is."

Two young children came into the hallway, a boy and girl. "Grandpa!" They ran to Henrik, and they all piled together in hug.

Finally, Henrik's daughter's husband came into the hall. "Henrik. It's good to see you," he said. "We were all afraid we'd never see you again."

And then they looked at Nellie in an uneasy silence.

"This is Nellie," Henrik said. "She's an old childhood friend who used to live a few houses down the street where I grew up. Nellie, this is my eldest daughter Clara and my son-in-law Gus."

"My papa's friends are my friends," the woman said. "Come into the kitchen. Have you had anything to eat?"

"We have," Henrik said. "But some tea would be nice."

They followed her to a warm, well-lit kitchen. A table with a red-and-white checkered tablecloth stood in the middle, with cabinets of the family's tableware around the sides. A door opposite probably led to the dining room, but this room was where the family spent their evenings. It was warm, and the table held a slate for children to learn to write, and a ball of wool and a pair of knitting needles.

Clara set a pot to boil for making tea.

They all sat around the table, including the children. The boy Jan was the older, about five or six. He still had soft curls and rounded cheeks.

The girl was not much more than a year younger. With her red cheeks and flaxen hair, she reminded Nellie of Anneke.

Clara said, "Now be nice, children. I know it's past your bedtime, but if you behave you can have a glass of milk and talk to grandpa."

"Are you coming back to live with us, Grandpa?" Jan asked.

"Maybe for a little while," Henrik said.

"Surely you're kidding?" Gus said. "The guards are

combing the streets in search of you." His eyes met Nellie's. "Both of you."

"We have ways of avoiding them," Henrik said.

"Do be careful, papa," Clara said. "We don't want anything to happen to you. The guards have already been to the house once to ask where you were. I wouldn't know what to do if they came while you were here."

She brought the teapot to the table and poured some hot milk out of the pan for the children who sat very quietly in their seats, looking on with wide eyes.

"What else did they want?" Henrik asked. "Magic trinkets?"

"No, they asked specifically for you. They had a long list of accusations to do with the Regent's death. I told them that I didn't know about any of it, but that you're one of the most respected guards in the city, and you never do anything without a very good and just reason."

Henrik put his hand over his daughter's. "Thank you."

Her eyes widened. She realised what that meant.

Henrik told them of the things that had happened since they fled the harbour. He left out the details about Prince Bruno, because it was better that not too many people knew.

"So are you coming back here to live?" Annie asked.

"I would like to, but I don't know if that would be safe for you."

"Don't be silly, papa, you're always welcome here. Your friend is welcome, too. I mean what I said. If you did anything, I'm sure you had a very good reason."

While they drank tea, talk was about general things, for the sake of the children. Clara then went to take them to bed.

Left in the kitchen with Nellie and Henrik, Gus asked, "Did you do it?"

"Yes," Henrik said. "There were reasons that I can't talk about."

Gus nodded, and everyone was silent until Clara came back into the kitchen. Gus was a bookkeeper, and as far removed from violence as possible. He was clearly uncomfortable with the idea that his father-in-law had killed someone in view of the public.

"I'll show you upstairs." Clara smiled at her father. "No, we haven't rented out your room yet."

"I was worried there for a moment."

She preceded Nellie and Henrik up a narrow flight of stairs. Several rooms opened up into the hallway. From one door came the giggling voices of children.

"Be quiet now. It's bedtime," Clara said as they walked past.

The room at the back of the house contained a double bed, a couple of chairs and a wardrobe with a palace guard uniform on a hanger on the outside of the door. Up an even narrower flight of stairs was the attic with one room that clearly hadn't been used for a long time, and an area where spare furniture was stored.

"You can have this room," she said to Nellie. "Wait until I bring you some hot water bottles. Let me get the sheets and make the fire."

"I can do that," Nellie said. She followed Clara into the room.

Clara set an oil lamp on the table next to the unused bed. She pulled some neatly-folded sheets out of the wardrobe.

"You look after your father's bed," Nellie said. "I can manage."

Clara left the room again, and Nellie busied herself lighting the fire and putting the sheets on the bed while Clara went downstairs to get some blankets.

Henrik came into the room, leaning against the door-post. "Are you comfortable here?"

"It's very kind of your daughter to put up with us," Nellie said. "I hope this is isn't going to be risky for them."

"That is what you do for family. But we're safe. If it were really as bad as Gus says, Master Thiele would have warned us."

"He did say to be careful."

Clara came back, and a moment later the bed was made.

It was now starting to get warmer in the attic, and Nellie invited Henrik to sit by the fire in the attic room for a little while.

"Bring your blankets," she said. "You can warm them by the fire and they will be nice and warm when you go to sleep."

"I'm pretty tired," Henrik said. "I'm not used to all this travelling anymore." But he brought his blanket anyway, and he sat on the hard wooden chair with the cushions that stood next to the hearth.

"I'm sorry if I embarrass you," Nellie said.

"You don't."

"But your family doesn't know what to think about me."

"That's because I don't know what to tell them. *A friend* doesn't sound very satisfactory, does it?"

Nellie looked down. Blood rushed to her cheeks. "I don't know that this is a good time to discuss . . ."

"Why not? We're about to start something dangerous tomorrow. I don't know that you understand how danger-ous. It's a mutiny. This whole town is eating out of the shepherd's hand, and we're wanted people. There are few people in town who will protect us, and we've spoken to those already. Everyone else in this town is hostile to us."

"I understand."

"But then surely you understand not wanting to do this alone?"

Nellie wasn't quite sure what he expected her to say. Martha had died a few years ago, and sometimes noblemen took a new wife very soon after their previous wife had died. But obviously Henrik and Martha had been very much in love, and she didn't think that it would be appropriate to push Henrik on the matter.

She didn't even dare hope that he was interested in her.

The attic was under the sloping roof of the house, and there was a small window in one of the sloping sides. From where she sat, Nellie could see the dark sky.

"You're avoiding me," he said.

"I'm not."

"Why are you looking out the window, then?"

"Because I've just noticed there is a window."

"I still think you're avoiding me."

"What do you want me to say to that? It seems that whatever I say, you will never believe me."

"Not when it's about you. I can see the look in your eyes. You're wondering if it's appropriate for me to be up here with you."

"Well, I do wonder that, especially because of your daughter. What is she going to think?"

"Stop thinking about what people think. This is my house, so I have the final say over whether something is appropriate."

He met her eyes. "You're so guarded, I couldn't possibly do a better job guarding the palace with all my colleagues. Why are you scared?"

"I'm not scared."

"Yes, you are." He rose, and crossed the room. The bed wobbled when he sat next to her.

"Whatever should I be scared of?" But her heart was hammering.

"Precisely." His look was very intense. "Have you ever been with a man?"

"I've had suitors."

"Anyone you favoured? Anyone who kissed you?"

"Of course." There had been some young men, and she had taken some walks by the river holding hands, and one or two had kissed her, but it was all a very long time ago, and working for the queen had been a life she didn't want to give up. Mostly because Mistress Johanna had never wanted to marry. She always said that the life went out of a woman's eyes once she married and there were children to look after. Of course not being married for a noblewoman like Mistress Johanna was out of the question, but most maids didn't marry, and if they did, they gave up being a maid, and that, more than anything, frightened Nellie: sitting at home by herself in a prison of her own making would be insanely boring. As maid, she had travelled, she had been the queen's closest friend, she had influence without responsibilities and the citizens of the city didn't even realise that she, and not the queen, had a major hand in raising those two children.

"So who was it? Tell me about it."

"I can't see why. It was a long time ago. The men are happily married as far as I know, and I don't need to blot their reputation."

"That's just it: you are always concerned with other people first. Is there going to be a time you'll think about yourself?"

Nellie started laughing. Her hands were sweaty with nerves, and she could do nothing else.

"What?" Henrik asked.

"Men are so transparent. Henrik, if you really want to kiss me in my unattractive old age, I suggest that you shut up and do it."

He laughed, too. "Practical, down-to-earth Nellie."

If she'd been wondering about kissing, the next moment he did just that. It turned out she didn't really know anything about kissing at all, or about any of the things that might follow from it. But, as they said, you were never too old to learn.

CHAPTER 17

NELLIE WOKE UP the next morning because faint light filtered onto her face. Through the window above the bed the sky was dull grey. Something warm and heavy lay by her side.

By the Triune, Henrik.

Nellie pushed herself out of the bed, her heart thudding. It was already light, and he'd been here all night. She remembered how he had rested his head saying that he should really go downstairs.

The ice-cold air bit into her skin. Shivering, she found her overdress and stockings and pulled them on.

Henrik opened his eyes.

"Don't look."

He smiled. "Is there anything I haven't seen?"

"Not in the daylight. This is so embarrassing. What is your family going to think?"

"Nothing they haven't thought from the moment we came to the house together."

And those looks had been uncomfortable and questioning. They would be even more uncomfortable now.

Not only that, it was late and they needed to start

looking for Bruno. "We were supposed to be at Master Thiele's already."

He pushed the blanket off. "First breakfast. You can't walk around the city all day on an empty stomach."

Clara was in the kitchen cooking porridge for the children. A maid had also turned up, and she was warming water for washing.

The young girl's presence was probably why there were no uncomfortable questions over breakfast. And Nellie knew Henrik was right: she did worry far too much about what other people thought of her, but that was a hard habit to break. She happened to think it was important, because the way you treated other people influenced what people said about you, and that said a lot about whether people would trust you, or whether you could trust another person.

Nellie and Henrik ate quickly and then went back to the guild's hideout. Four men and one woman were already in the room downstairs.

The air was bitterly cold. A servant had just lit the fire but, as yet, it did little to warm the room.

Nellie didn't know any of the other people except for August, but she had seen their faces while they stood guard at the palace gates or in the streets. The woman was a cousin of the mayor's. She had no husband or children, but she was extraordinarily good with numbers and Saardam's bookkeepers would pay her to check their accounts. The men were the guards who protected the palace, but they would spank a little apple thief across his eight-year-old bottom rather than put him in jail. They would trust the mayor's cousin with the accounts.

Master Thiele had spread out a number of documents on the table, maps mostly, from what Nellie could see.

On one paper, she could make out the streets of the city, with the church and the palace clearly marked.

Someone had divided the city into four parts, each a different colour.

Two more men came in to be greeted with solemn nods, and then Master Thiele judged that everyone had arrived.

"Welcome here at this early hour. You are my most trusted people. I realise I'm asking a lot from you, and I may ask you to act against your orders. I'm definitely asking you to face great danger. It has come to the point that we are the protectors of fair Saardam. Everyone else, including your colleagues, is the enemy. They are unaware, but they have been corrupted with magic through the food they eat. We are gathered because we need to secure the safety of a young boy who is the key to all our efforts to restore fairness and peace in Saardam. We're asking you to protect Prince Bruno."

In a few sentences, he explained the situation as Nellie had explained it to him yesterday. The five men and one woman listened, their faces displaying nothing except the fullest attention.

"Obviously we can't just walk into the palace and demand to be taken to the ballroom," Master Thiele continued. "First we need to make sure that we have enough people to push the palace guards aside and get into the room. Exactly how we act depends on the number of people we can recruit. Please note that I'm not looking for a violent struggle unless we meet violence. Our faces are familiar to many of the guards, and I hope that violence will not necessary. I'm also not looking to usurp power, merely to instate a council that will take action and solve the succession problem considering all the facts, not just some people's agendas."

He put his hands on the table, on top of one of the maps.

"We need to find support. To this extent, I have

brought this map. Some of you will be very familiar with it, but to explain to others"—he looked at Nellie—"this is the map the guard commanders use to allocate parts of the city to different patrols. The coloured sections are called quadrants. We will be using the same boundaries, because it's easy; and we don't have to explain to our members because they will be familiar with where the boundaries are. You will divide into groups. Each group will be given the names of potential supporters. We will visit them and ask for their support. Explain to them what I have just said and that time is of the essence."

But what about the magic? Nellie grew increasingly frustrated. Again, these people pretended magic didn't exist even while warning about it.

"This would be so much better if we could give these people a remedy against magic first," she said when Master Thiele had finished speaking. Right now, with most of the people members of the guards, it was a matter of chance whether they struck someone who hadn't been eating the shepherd's handed-out food. Even then, the person could go back to the palace, eat there and betray the group.

"There is no time for that," Master Thiele said.

Nellie disagreed, not because she thought time unimportant, but because she knew that, without a remedy against magic, the plan was doomed to fail.

Nellie and Henrik ended up in a group with a young man called Adrian whom Henrik knew through the palace guards. Henrik explained that Adrian had a delicate stomach and never ate the palace food because it made him ill.

Next, they all spent time dressing up. They were to look like ordinary citizens, but also wanted to be unrecognisable, especially Henrik. To this end, they went into a very cold, musty room next to the main living area that was full of wardrobes with various types of clothing.

Henrik chose a dark cloak and hat. The fact that he'd grown a beard since leaving the palace helped his disguise as a well-off citizen.

Then it was Nellie's turn. "Hmm, I think you should dress as his wife."

He gave her a long woollen coat that was much nicer than anything she had ever owned. It smelled a bit musty, but the moment she slipped it over her shoulders, it felt warm and comfortable. He also found her a pair of nice shoes with metal buckles, and replaced the tatty shawl she wore over her head with a very fashionable hat.

Adrian, who was young enough to be their son, got a slightly more flamboyant outfit such as a young merchant's son would wear.

They went out into the misty morning, mingling with the citizens on their daily business and listening for gossip.

Since Nellie had been here last, even more shops in the artisan quarter had been boarded over, their owners gone from the city. The only shops that seemed to be doing a good trade were those selling second-hand items. Plenty of things were for sale, since people leaving the city didn't want to take all their things with them: the most exquisite tableware and furniture were available in big quantities, and so was luxurious clothing in the latest fashions. The elaborate dresses hung in rows on racks, and the prices were low.

Nellie almost wished that she were young and careless and just married, and had a house to furnish. There was so much for sale.

Slowly, they made their way through the main street towards the market square.

When they came to an address on the list, Henrik and Adrian would talk to the person named by Master Thiele. Sometimes Henrik would go alone and sometimes Nellie would come. They would ask to speak with the person on

Master Thiele's list, and when this person came to the door they would ask a few questions to establish their loyalty.

Half the time, this was enough to know that it was probably not a good idea to continue. They ended up getting confirmations from only fourteen people. Enough to continue with Master Thiele's plan, if the other groups found an equal number of people, but too few for Nellie to believe they would succeed.

The main street through the artisan quarter joined the square at the north side of the church. The block behind the church consisted of buildings related to the church: the shepherd's residence, the old, no-longer-used seminary where monks visiting from out of town would stay, and the chapel of the Holy Mother that was a relic from the Belaman church but used for private services, mainly baptisms and funerals. There was also a school where young boys would learn the Verses if they were interested in joining the ranks of the monks or becoming a shepherd.

As Nellie, Henrik and Adrian walked past the complex, a tall man in a flapping robe crossed the courtyard. Nellie had assumed that Shepherd Wilfridus was in hiding, based on what Master Thiele had told her last night, but the figure she spotted walking across the courtyard looked very much like him. Because of his height, he always walked bent over. He held his robes at the front with one hand to shield himself from the cold. He held his head bowed and walked with deliberate strides in the direction of the chapel.

Nellie stopped walking and turned to Henrik. "Do you see that? I wonder where he is going in such a hurry."

"Only one way to find out," Henrik said.

The area behind the church was open to the public so citizens could pray in the chapel when no services were held.

The three of them walked across the courtyard and up the steps of the chapel.

It was a simple but elegant building with a domed roof. Pillars lined the front, where two marble steps led up to the entrance. The door stood open, but it was dark and cold inside.

From the steps, you could see across the entire courtyard.

"There," Adrian said.

Shepherd Wilfridus had met a monk at the entrance to the seminary. The monk spread his hands as if in apology, and the shepherd pointed his finger at the man's chest. His voice carried across the courtyard, but the men were too far to hear what was being said.

Henrik pulled something out of the pocket of his coat and gave it to Adrian. "Your ears are better than mine."

Adrian unfolded the thing into a funnel-shaped contraption made from whalebone and fabric, not unlike a corset. There was a thin tube on one end which he put to his ear, and directed the wide mouth of the funnel at the seminary.

They stood in silence.

The shepherd yelled and the poor monk barely got a word in.

Adrian listened. Nellie didn't dare say anything because he might miss important information.

Eventually, the shepherd went down the steps, strode across the courtyard to his residence, went in and slammed the door behind him.

The monk wiped his face and went into the seminary.

"What was all that about?" Henrik asked.

Adrian packed the funnel away and gave it back to Henrik. "Come. We need to tell the others."

He didn't speak again until they were in the street.

"Something has happened in the palace," he said in a

low voice. "I didn't get all of it, but the shepherd blamed the monks for allowing it to happen. He said that Casper is now out of their control and it was all the monks' fault and that his only option is to kill them all. The monk felt it was against the spirit of the church and the Shepherd asked if he would like to be ruled by evil magic instead."

Nellie felt cold. What was the bet that it had something to do with the dragon?

Maybe Bruno had shown Casper his dragon and maybe Casper, being desperate, had invited Bruno to do whatever necessary to get rid of the palace guards outside the door.

They walked back to Master Thiele's house.

The other groups returned shortly after.

The group whose area had included the harbour district had picked up rumours in the taverns. One rumour that repeated a few times was that the youngsters had a ceremony where they placed a boy on the throne that had been untouched for ten years.

Several people gasped at this news. Not even Regent Bernard had dared sit on the throne, even if he had declared his intention to become king. According to several people, Casper was an insolent lout who needed a strong father.

None of Master Thiele's people had seen Casper's letters to Adalbert Verdonck. To them, he was just a lout.

"He has gone and declared his own successor to the throne," Henrik said in a low voice to Nellie while outraged protests rang through the room. "Would Casper hand the leadership to a rival?"

Nellie said, "Is Casper really Bruno's rival? They're both young men badly let down by those around them. They realise they need to be smart, because otherwise neither of them will survive. They're stronger when they work together. If Casper is smart, and I think he has become smart in a hurry, he knows he will never be king. The next best thing is to be a king's friend."

While she spoke, the people in the room had fallen quiet, and all listened to her.

Master Thiele said, "If that is true, we have a dragon king."

"And Shepherd Wilfridus is going to kill them both."

Everyone in the room was silent.

Into this silence, Nellie said, "We need to get into the palace and we need to show the people what is really happening."

Master Thiele nodded. "That's why we're here. But it's easier said than done. We are not terribly many, and the entire citizenship of the city is controlled by the shepherd."

"So we do what Lord Verdonck has done all these years: we eat food that contains remedies against magic. We hand it out to the people. Then we go to the palace."

"We'd need an army that we don't have. We're not poor but we can't afford to hire an army."

"No, we don't need an army. We need a circus, and we're going to have the biggest party to end all parties."

CHAPTER 18

ALL THE SECTIONS of the most daring plan she had ever come up with had come together in Nellie's mind. She explained her thoughts.

"If Bruno is with Casper in the palace, and the guards are intent on keeping the boys there, those guards are controlled by the shepherd, and he is stepping out of the shadows to take control. I doubt he planned to do that just yet. He might have wanted to wait until Casper did something that made him so disliked that the people would support the shepherd in removing him from the palace. But Bruno is a snag in his plan, because the shepherd doesn't know what Bruno will do. Bruno can tell the people a story about his imprisonment, and it is all true. One thing the shepherd hasn't been able to erase from the citizens of Saardam is the love for the king and queen. Bruno will not play nicely and he will never do what the shepherd says. And Bruno is a magician—not a very good one, but he has magic. So things are likely to get nasty. As I said, we will have to get into the palace."

"Have you seen how many guards are at the gate?" a man said.

"We're not going to use an army or weapons, because we don't have an army and we can't pay for one, and if we could find someone who said he would, we couldn't trust him. Ever since I've been old enough to remember, powerful men have fought over the throne in the palace. No one rich enough who's prepared to buy us an army is going to give up a victory for a fourteen-year-old boy; he's going to grab the throne for himself."

Master Thiele said, "That describes Adalbert Verdonck."

"I doubt he's the only one," Henrik said.

"It's not about the person with the most weapons or power," Nellie continued. "Weapons are no use against magic. It's about who controls the citizens. Shepherd Wilfridus does that. He gives out magic food from the stores. He has been giving out magic food to the guests who come to the palace and to the Regent and now his sons. We can't be successful unless we break the magic and we can't do that with weapons."

"You're suggesting we need a magician?" Master Thiele said.

"No; besides, we don't have one. We need to give the people a remedy that stops magic. The type of magic that's used on the food is not very strong and a concoction of common herbs will do it. Lord Verdonck used it."

"I don't know if you noticed that Ronald Verdonck is dead. Didn't work so well on him."

"Yes, but the magic only poisoned him when it was strong. For years, when he ate at the Regent's table, he was not affected by the magic that made everyone agree with the Regent and think he was wonderful."

"I never ate much at the palace either," Henrik said. "My family preferred that I came home as much as possible."

"And I never ate much at the palace because of my

stomach," Adrian said. "I noticed how some of the other guards would raise questions about the Regent, only to say those questions weren't important later."

Master Thiele said, "So what are these remedies and how would we get them to people? Forgive me, but I'm a man of arms."

"There are herbs we can use, many of which are commonly grown in this area."

"But it's winter and nothing grows."

"We can get dried versions. A number of shops in the city sell the things we need."

"And how are you going to get them to the people?"

"By giving them something they like. Do you remember Yolande's sweet shop?"

"The one that used to be in the artisan quarter?"

"Yes, that one. Yolande was one of the people we rescued from the harbour. She has not been well, but is recovering. However, our group also has a number of women who are good at cooking and I'm sure Yolande would be happy to tell us how to make sweets if we can get enough sugar."

"I can get sugar," someone said in the back of the room.

"And how would you get the sweets to everyone?"

"We will drop them from a balloon."

He frowned. "A—what?"

"Madame Sabine is also with us. She used to be with the balloon division of the Lurezian army. She has a balloon in Lord Verdonck's shed." At least Nellie hoped it was still there.

"You're just going to drift randomly over the city to drop sweets from a balloon?"

"No, we're going to come into the city with a parade. A circus parade with exotic animals. And the balloon will be tied to the elephant. All the people will come out to watch, and we'll give the sweets to them. Then, when we get to the palace, we ask for an audience with the Regent and promise a private show. Madame Sabine says her son is very fond of sweets. We'll all be dressed up. Who is going to refuse entry to a circus troupe? Especially with the promise of a feast and a private parade of animals?"

Master Thiele gave her a wide-eyed look.

"They won't let you in the palace with weapons," Adrian said.

"We won't have weapons. The enemy is magic. Weapons are useless."

"There *will* be weapons," Henrik said. "Maybe not in the main party, but as long as I live, no expedition like this will take place without armed support. Anyone who is capable and can carry a weapon will accompany the troupe in the shadows. I don't know how it will work, but we will be there."

"I can provide some men as well," Master Thiele said. "It's the most ridiculous scheme I've heard, but it might just work. All I know is that a straight attack will not only be treason against the state but is likely to get us all killed. Just enlighten me on what is going to happen once we're inside the palace."

"We'll have a feast. We bring the food and the wine and the palace kitchen staff will not have to do a single thing. We invite all the nobles because Casper will want to impress them. The food will contain the magic antidote. Shepherd Wilfridus will not be invited. If he invites himself, there will be lots of questions for him, because the people are no longer under his control."

"He's still a magician."

"Yes, but we have a dragon."

Somehow, there would be a confrontation when Shepherd Wilfridus turned up, and she wasn't sure that the dragon could win it, or that Bruno had enough control over him to make sure that he didn't flee like he had done previously. She supposed she could talk to the dragon sternly, but would it be enough? The shepherd wasn't going to give up, not until he was dead.

And would it be sufficient to put a fourteen-year-old boy on the throne to settle a ten-year-old succession dispute, especially since the boy wasn't ready for the task?

Henrik continued, "We, the armed men, will be outside waiting for signs of trouble and informing the citizens of what they need to know if there are curious masses, and I'm sure there will be plenty, once the sweets start doing their work."

"Especially if we leave the elephant in the forecourt," Nellie said. "And the promise of more sweets."

Master Thiele looked from one to the other. "How long have you two been planning this?"

Nellie said, "I don't plan, I make use of the things I have."

Henrik said, "I do as she says."

The men all laughed.

Because the secret guard guild was small and had no power, Master Thiele had few resources. Many of the members had worked for the guards but were not guards anymore, although some still had contacts with their former colleagues. Master Thiele assured Henrik that there would be a small but experienced and well-informed group of armed men available.

But first many other things needed to be done. To start, the required herbs against magic had to be obtained. Nellie agreed that she would take care of that.

And then, if the women and whoever wanted to come were to enter the city disguised as a circus troupe, they needed to have suitably flamboyant clothing. They needed things to make sure people didn't recognise them: hats, scarves, face paint, masks, things like that. Nellie agreed that she would also take care of that. Others would be in charge of finding another cart and horses, and bringing weapons.

Nellie went to the artisan quarter, but the shops that normally sold local herbs of the sort she would need were no longer there. Yolande's shop of sweets and knickknacks had been boarded over. Another shop with little trinkets and magical items was completely empty, the windows broken, the door smashed in.

In despair, she went to Mistress Julianna's shop, only to find it burned out.

That made her feel cold. What had happened to its occupant? Nellie didn't like Mistress Julianna, but she didn't wish any ill on her either.

A new shop sat on the corner at the start of the street, opposite the church. It was open, and a steady stream of people went in and out the door.

Nellie stopped to have a look.

She was sure the shop hadn't been here in the short time when she lived in the artisan quarter. It sold fresh bread, hams and sausages, spices, sugars and jars of pickles, salted fish and many things. A wonderful smell came from within, and because Nellie wanted to look like she was shopping, she went inside. At least twenty people were inside the shop, all of them waiting at the counter to be served.

Then she recognised a woman behind the counter. It was one of the wayfarers in Zelda's group.

By the Triune.

Nellie couldn't leave quickly enough. Spies were everywhere.

Where could she find the herbs?

Last time when she had looked for juniper berries, Els had suggested she go to Mistress Julianna. Maybe the two sisters would know where everyone was getting their remedies now that Mistress Julianna was gone. So she went to the unfinished warehouse to ask Els

Els seemed genuinely pleased to see her. She was very keen to hear that Gisele was safe, and that they would be coming back to the city. She said, "To be honest, I was afraid that I would have to run the gin business by myself, and Gisele is so much better at it than I am. But I can't go back to the palace, not with what I know now. I've often said that I don't want to end up like my mother, and I truly don't. I want to have a proper business that I don't have to hide."

"So do we all. We're working hard at making this a fair place again."

"I want to help."

"Well, I need a number of things. I know how to find most of them, but I do need to buy some herbs, and it seems that all of the herb sellers have disappeared. Not even Mistress Julianna's shop still exists. I thought she was in with Zelda and would be protected by the palace guards but apparently that's not so."

"Mistress Julianna was always a strange one. She doesn't really want to work with anyone, and that was her biggest problem. She just isn't a very nice person."

"Where can I buy the herbs I need?"

"People buy them from Zelda."

"You mean Zelda's shop on the corner? I can't go in there. Zelda has already betrayed us once. She would betray us to the guards again if she thought she could make money out of it. I don't think the shop sells what I need anyway. It seems to be for fancy cakes and bread."

"They have the herbs, but you need to ask for them."

"And then someone records what you buy and passes the information to the guards?"

Els looked like she was going to say something. She

opened her mouth, but closed it again. Her eyes grew wide.

"I bought some juniper berries," she said, her voice soft. "The next day, a man came in here, demanding that I pay him so much or he'd go to the guards."

"Did you pay?"

Els shook her head. "I don't have that much money. I expect the guards to turn up any day. Without Gisele, there's not much point in carrying on with this business. I can't do it all by myself, and they know this when they threaten me. Maybe I should follow Mistress Julianna's example."

"Where is she?"

"Word is that she fled town, but no one knows if that's true."

People believed that those who had fled town were somewhere in the surrounding cities, but Nellie knew that wasn't true. The mercenaries outside the city had the grisly task of killing everyone who tried to leave.

The full horror of the situation depressed her. Every time she thought things were improving, they got worse. They couldn't rely on any help from outside, because anyone who left the city never came back.

How could they break the spell of magic? All the herb sellers were gone; all the shops that sold non-magical food were gone. If the palace banquets took care of the nobles, Zelda did the same for the rest of the people: the merchants with her special tea, and the citizens with her cakes. And the church looked after the poor with the food given out from the stores.

She asked Els, "Could someone from the Science Guild possibly help me?"

Els shook her head. "They aren't meeting any more. After the raid where Madame Sabine was arrested, they thought it was too risky. I've heard that some of the merchants have left town, but I don't know all of them, because I never went there very often."

So it seemed like the secret guard guild was one of the very few places where the truth still held out. Nellie didn't know where else she might buy the herbs that she needed, and with dread she realised that the only place left to get them was the nunnery next to Lord Verdonck's estate.

She realised it was a risk to speak to Els about getting these herbs, in case Els was captured for her illegal gin making and questioned. So she asked about where to buy the best clothing and where to buy some of the other items they needed.

Els told her that the shops in the street that sold second-hand clothing were far too expensive. "Really, those things are worth very little any more, because there are no people who want to buy fancy clothes. Most of the clothing is not very practical, and would be more useful if you wanted to start a circus."

Well, then, wasn't that a coincidence?

Els sent Nellie to visit a family who had collected a lot of the nobles' abandoned wardrobes and were preparing to export them.

They lived in a dingy old house with paint peeling off the door and the window frames. The windows were grimy, the curtains dusty and faded.

After her knock, she heard sounds on the other side, but the door remained closed.

"Please open the door. Els send me."

The bolt was driven back, and slowly the door opened.

For some reason, Nellie expected an old woman like Juliana, but the person who opened the door was a handsome young man who was quite well dressed.

He lifted his eyebrows. "Can I help you with anything?"

"Els sent me here. I would like to buy some nice

clothes, but I don't have a lot of money. Someone told me that you could help me."

"Come with me."

He took her through the hallway to a room at the back of the house that was packed with clothes racks, crates and boxes.

They held all sorts of luxurious clothing: ruffled dresses in the latest fashions and colours, including ones with scandalously low necks, and garishly coloured men's trousers and jackets and shirts with ruffles of lace.

"Wow." It was cold in the room, and Nellie's breath steamed in the pale light.

He explained. "These clothes all came from houses of families who have left. I'm not sure how much you'll find that's practical, but you're free to have a look."

Nellie wasn't looking for practical clothing. In fact, she was looking for the most garish and outrageous outfits she could find, the type of clothing that turned heads, and there was plenty in this room.

It seemed like the young family had emptied the wardrobes of all the noble ladies and their families. The room was full of beautiful dresses as well as servants' clothing.

Nellie chose a stack of glamorous dresses in different sizes. She picked out ridiculous hats and veils. She found some masks in the shape of bird faces, with long beaks. And she selected men's outfits: long trousers, cloaks and hats.

A big box in the corner contained all manner of powders and lip paints, so she selected the most ridiculous colours from that.

All the while the young man watched from the door. Once, a toddler boy came for a curious look, half-hiding behind his father's legs.

"It looks like you're dressing a crowd for a noble ball,"

he said, when Nellie dropped another dress onto the pile, this one for Koby.

"We're staging a play," she said, because that was what they had agreed to say if someone asked.

"That's a brave thing to do in this hard time."

"It will be free, and we hope to cheer up the citizens."

"An admirable goal. I might have something else you like." And then he climbed on a ladder and pulled some hatboxes off the top of a wardrobe. They contained the most outlandish hats, with ruffles and huge bright-red feathers.

"Yeah, I like those."

He then pulled out all manner of things, from belts made of leopard skin to bright yellow shirts and long sheer veils and gloves with so many beads that the wearer couldn't possibly pick up anything while wearing them. And corsets that were supposed to be worn on the outside of the dress, with little bells that tinkled when the woman walked.

Quite coquettish, Nellie thought. All of those things went into the pile.

Then the moment came that she had to ask how much he wanted to be paid, and he didn't want anything.

"All these things are just a burden to us. They take up space, but no one wants them. We get the occasional merchant lady wanting to buy a dress, but it has to be something that she can wear in the street without creating a scandal. That's why we're preparing to take all of this to Burovia, where hopefully the mindset allows women to wear these things. But we can't take everything, so I'm happy to be rid of the most outrageous items. I wish you good luck with your play. Do tell me when it's on."

"I will, and thank you so much."

CHAPTER 19

NELLIE ARRANGED FOR the items to be packed up—she would send someone around with the cart later in the day—and then made her way back to Master Thiele's house through the misty streets. Some people were out, but it wasn't very busy.

Nellie crossed the markets and passed the palace gates, which were still closed. A number of bored guards stood in the guard box.

After she went into the street that led from the market to the harbour, she had the feeling that someone was following her. It was as if a dark spot moved in the corner of her eye. She stopped walking and looked over her shoulder.

It was a dog, a mangy beast with a dark grey coat of matted hair. Once she stopped walking, it came closer, sat on its haunches and whined.

It wore a collar.

Poor thing. It looked like it had been abandoned. She wondered who looked after it now.

But at the same time, she realised: Bruno and the dragon were under siege in the palace. That was why the gates were closed, after all. But if she'd doubted those rumours, here was her proof. The dragon's presence attracted animals, and this poor scruffy dog was one of them. Being a dog, with a dog's nose, it might even be able to smell the dragon on her. She held out her hand to the dog, but that was too much. It got up and scooted away.

In Master Thiele's back yard, the men had brought in the cart and Nellie and Henrik's two horses, so she asked them to pick up the purchases.

Inside the house, Master Thiele's men had collected packs and weapons from their homes and stacked them in the corner of the large downstairs living room.

Nellie went to make tea and found a large kitchen that reminded her of the palace. She filled a kettle from the pump and set it on the stove.

"What disguise did you get for me?" Henrik had come into the kitchen after her.

"Oh, you gave me a fright. I was just thinking that this kitchen looks like the one in the palace."

"This used to be a guesthouse," he said. "Master Thiele retired from the guards when he became injured and started a series of ventures for retired or wrongfully dismissed guards. He tried to clear their names. He was head of the King's Guard when they existed. Their job was guarding the guards to make sure that they behaved according to the king's law. When the king died, he was forced to go into hiding, and that's when he opened the guesthouse. It was for ordinary travellers, but anyone in the guards knew that if you ever got into trouble for standing up for the right thing, the doors here were always open. Still are, even if the guesthouse has closed."

"A man of extreme honour," Nellie said.

"Definitely. More honour than me."

"Don't talk yourself down. You acted with a lot of courage."

He sat down on one of the chairs at the table. "I remained loyal to the Regent for too long, even if I knew how much he took from the citizens. I couldn't kill the magician and had to settle for leaving two boys orphaned. I was dumb. I was rash. I was too keen to make it up to you."

The kettle produced clouds of steam. Nellie took it off the stove and poured the hot water into the teapot.

"I got you a nice suit," she said.

"Some silly colour?"

"No, it's black, and there is a hat as well. You can be the circus magician, with a pink silk handkerchief."

"*That's* a silly colour."

They both laughed.

"You should clip your beard."

"I should shave."

"No, I like it. And you didn't have a beard when you were in the guards so it's a disguise."

She found a pair of scissors, and a comb, and proceeded to cut the straggly hairs on his chin all the one length.

It was very stiff, a lot of it was white and some of it still sandy-coloured. Having his beard neat made him look much younger.

When she finished, he looked at the reflection in the window.

"I'm almost handsome man again. It's funny how we don't appreciate when we're young how good we look."

"I always thought you looked good."

"I thought you looked good, too."

"I did not. I was a horribly skinny mousey thing, and I acted like a mouse, too."

"I thought you were pretty. Not too loud. You didn't too obviously try to get my attention just because I wore a uniform."

"So why did you never talk to me?"

"I was the oldest son. I had to set the right examples."

"And my father was not the right example, I'm guessing."

He blew out a breath. "I don't like to speak ill of people, but he was so . . . severe."

"Scary?"

"Yeah." He chuckled. "He was like: if you want my daughter, you better be worth it."

"And you didn't think you were?"

"I think he just didn't want to lose you."

And he reached up to her and pulled her onto his knees.

"Nellie, I think you are the craziest woman I have ever met. I never thought that in my grumpy old age I would ever find someone like you."

"You're making me all embarrassed now."

"Listen to me, Nellie. When all of this is over. I want to share what's left of my life with you."

Nellie giggled. "Henrik, are you really asking me to marry you?"

"I guess I am. Once we're safely through this time. Will you?"

"Do you think you're going to get away with such a lame effort? I want to be asked on your knees."

"All right." Henrik rose, took off his coat. Then he knelt on one knee and took her hand.

At that moment, the kitchen door opened and a group of people came in. Someone said, "I'm hungry."

Someone else said, "Whoa."

They were Master Thiele's men, and they stopped at the door and fell silent.

Henrik said, "With these good folk as our witnesses, will you answer the question: will you marry me?" He looked up at her with his clear grey eyes, utterly sincere.

Nellie said, "I will." Her mouth felt dry and her hands clammy.

Was this really what it felt like to decide about the rest of her life? Yet she wanted to do this, because she was sick of being alone.

The people at the door cheered.

Master Thiele came in, wondering what was going on.

"We'll celebrate!" Adrian said.

"Not until everything is ready and packed. There are many spies in the city and we need to be out of here by tomorrow morning." That was Master Thiele, focused on the job. He had never been married, Nellie heard when he had left the kitchen, and probably cared less about these things than everyone else.

So they packed up the clothes and hats when they arrived. Someone had gone into Yolande's old shop and had retrieved some of the equipment from the back: two big blackened cooking pots and jars and trays and utensils for making sweets. The man who had promised the sugar had brought it, big heavy bags stashed away under oiled cloth. All those things were loaded on the cart and the cart went into the shed. The men brought a second cart and loaded an array of weapons and packs onto it.

When it got dark, it was time for the promised celebration, and Nellie was ashamed to say that she drank a bit too much gin and almost fell asleep at the table.

Henrik helped her up the stairs, because they had decided to stay in the former guesthouse corridor upstairs rather than endangering Henrik's daughter any further.

They were not the only people staying overnight, as the small band of ex-guards who would travel to the Lord Verdonck's estate were there, too. All the others were men, so Nellie had a small and very dark room in the upstairs corridor to herself. It was cold and smelled musty, and the mattress had seen better days.

On top of that, Nellie found it hard to sleep. The house was full of strange noises, and the gin churned in her stomach. Also, she worried about not having gotten the herbs. There were so many people involved in this plan, and it was up to her to get the most vital ingredients. What if she couldn't get them at the nunnery either?

Somewhere in the middle of the night, she must have fallen asleep because a sharp sound woke her.

She thought everyone in the house was upstairs, but it seemed as if the sound had come from the kitchen. Was it time to leave already?

She lay still, listening. Somewhere in one of the other rooms a man was snoring loudly.

The sound came again, as if someone was walking around and tripped over a chair in the kitchen. That meant either they hadn't lit a light or were unfamiliar with the room.

That couldn't be any good, could it?

Nellie pushed herself up, found her shoes by the side of the mattress, pulled on her coat over her underclothes and slowly opened the door to her room. The floor in the hallway creaked something terrible, and she had to walk at a snail's pace to keep it from making too much noise.

Very slowly, she crept down the stairs.

It was completely dark downstairs. She could hear someone breathing.

"Master Thiele?" she called out.

There was a huff of breath as the man got a fright. He knocked over or threw down a bottle that shattered on the floor and at the same time burst into flames. By the light, she could see a young man, not part of their group.

Nellie froze for a moment, deciding whether to run after the man or to start putting out the flames, and then decided in favour of the second, and then decided that maybe she should go and warn the others first so that the could come down and help her.

She ran into the hall, almost tripping over one of the chairs, and yelled, "Fire, fire, please help!"

There were some stumblings and a door opened upstairs. Someone said, "What's going on?"

"There's a fire down here," Nellie said. "Get the others."

The glow from the kitchen was getting stronger.

She ran back into the kitchen, and found somebody's cloak and tried to throw it over the burning flames. But the fire was too big now, eating into the floorboards, and the fluid from the bottle was spreading over the floor.

Someone came into the room after her, coughing with the smoke. "Get out," he said.

It was Master Thiele. He carried a big square box made from dark wood.

"But your shop will burn down," Nellie protested.

"Go outside to the cart. We're leaving." He gently pushed Nellie into the hallway with the box. "Outside. Save yourself."

A few other people were coming down the stairs, and Nellie ran after them out the back door to where the cart stood.

Master Thiele came a moment later, with a thick fur cloak draped over his box. He set the box on the cart and pulled the cloak over his shoulders.

Nellie wondered what was in the box. It looked very heavy.

"I'll get the horses," Henrik said. He went to the stable and came back with the horses, both of them quite nervous. The fire had spread through the kitchen and was coming into the hall.

Master Thiele's people were all in the yard, some carrying items out the back gate.

"Don't we need to help put it out?" Nellie asked Henrik when he came with the horses. Her teeth chattered.

Henrik said, "The guild can't afford the attention they'll get. Yesterday's activity must have given the guild's locality away."

He strapped one horse in the harness and held the other by the reins. Then he climbed into the driver's seat of the cart.

"Come." He held out his hand.

Nellie grabbed it and pulled herself next to him.

He flicked the reins and the horse walked out of the yard.

Master Thiele stood at the gate, holding up a hand as the cart went past.

"Isn't he coming?" Nellie asked.

"He'll organise his people for when we come back. They'll take the other cart to another location."

Nellie wondered again what was in the heavy wooden box. Weapons, she guessed. She wondered if Master Thiele realised he had accidentally put it on the wrong cart.

And so the cart and two horses traversed the streets in pitch darkness, leaving behind the burning building.

Most guild members had fled the scene, but other people were arriving to have a look. Shouts of "Fire!" rang through the streets.

Henrik said, "There are elements in the city and palace guards who really don't like Master Thiele. He rarely goes out during the day, and even at night he usually goes with others. If his enemies can't challenge him directly, they pay street urchins to sneak in and cause damage."

"But what if I hadn't woken up in time?"

"Believe me, that has happened before. Master Thiele has badly scarred skin on his arm from a fire. He was the only one who made it out of the house alive. The guild lost all their records in that fire. Ever since, he makes sure that everyone only brings into the guild headquarters what they can carry."

"Do you know who orders these fires?"

"It could be anyone, from corrupt officials to a man wanting to hide a dark past in order to purchase a business licence, all the way up to major officials who know that secret guild members have information they don't want revealed."

"It's amazing what some people will do to hide the truth."

"That's because the truth shows them in a bad light. The uglier the truth, the more desperate the measures to hide it."

CHAPTER 20

THE MORNING WAS MISTY, and it didn't get properly light until after the cart had left the city.

They travelled through the dreary countryside, avoiding the muddy puddles in the road. A few farmers headed into the city, but otherwise it was quiet.

The horse plodded along, droplets of moisture lacing its back.

Neither of them spoke very much, and Henrik kept checking over his shoulder. What for, he didn't say. Not until they were well out of the city, and had passed the levee bank of the river, did he begin to relax.

They were riding through fields of orchards with bare branches. "Most of this land is Adalbert Verdonck's," Henrik said. "It's the main food supply of the city, because this side of the river is higher than the other and there is no contamination by salt water. It's important land that Saardam needs to control or the people will starve."

"We won't get anywhere without his support."

"No." Henrik shook his head. "Fortunately, he doesn't think much of the Regent and his family, or the shepherd."

"Is that why he'll never be king?"

"There are other reasons. I'll show you when we get a bit further."

"Now you've made me curious."

When they came to the rolling meadows—now all brown—surrounding the Verdonck house, Henrik turned into a side road leading to a little grove surrounded by pine trees. Because pine trees remained green in winter, the row made a shelter against the wind.

Henrik let the horses rest for a bit and led Nellie into the grove.

The meadow surrounded by the trees was well-tended, with neatly-clipped bushes and clean paths surrounding a stone basin containing water and a statue of an angel looking at the sky. In the grass stood a number of moss-covered gravestones.

Henrik led her along a gravel path.

The first grave was new, the stone as yet untouched by the weather. The inscription said, *Ronald Adalbert Verdonck. He hoped when there was no hope and fell when he spoke the truth*.

Nellie stopped briefly, pushing her shawl down, and said a brief prayer, unsure if that was appropriate for someone who had found so much fault with the church.

But, she reminded herself, Lord Verdonck had been a fair person, and had no beef with the divine, just with the power-hungry shepherd.

Henrik waited a bit further down the path.

Nellie joined him at a spot where eight older gravestones stood, all quite close together and all with small headstones.

The inscriptions on the stone were simple, and all were for children, ranging in age from one day to six months, who had died over a period of about ten years, the latest three years ago.

She met Henrik's eyes and frowned.

"The Verdonck curse," he said, his voice low. "This is why the family is unsuited to the throne. Adalbert is the last child in the family to have been born healthy. They needed an heir to the estate, so they married him at seventeen. His first wife gave him a son who lived five days, before dying of illness herself not much later. His second wife gave him two children; neither lived to their first year. She then had a third child but it was clear the child wasn't his, so she fled. His third wife gave him five children who all died soon after birth, before she threw herself off the tower. He loved her and he was heartbroken. When you come to the house today, you'll see there is no tower. That's because Adalbert had it torn down."

"What a sad story." She remembered that Madame Sabine had just told her that Adalbert's wife *couldn't give him children so he was looking for a new one*. She also remembered thinking that she was glad she wasn't a noble because of the anguish caused by the issue of having a suitable heir. Did Madame Sabine know about this? On second thoughts, had Madame Sabine tried to worm herself into the Verdonck family tree by offering to give Ronald Verdonck another child, seeing as the family line looked like it would stop with Adalbert? All of a sudden she saw Adalbert Verdonck's dislike of her in another light.

Henrik nodded.

"What is Adalbert going to do?"

Henrik shrugged. "All I know is that the family was considered for the throne. This is why they were not suitable, and since that time, they've distanced themselves from the church and have missed their opportunity."

"Unless Adalbert takes it by force."

"Well, that's always a possibility."

And if that happened, many of the city's nobles would object, and there would be struggles; and when the city was divided, Burovia or Aroden or Gelre would make a move.

Nellie clamped her arms around herself. "It frightens me. Sometimes I don't even know what's good or bad anymore."

"That comes with being older," he said, taking her hand. "You see that good can be bad and bad can be good, and sometimes good can be so good that it becomes bad, and bad can be so bad that it becomes good."

Nellie chuckled. "Now you're making no sense."

"It makes sense," he said. "You'll see when you're a few years older."

"Don't be silly."

"Then let's go and prepare for our highly sensible circus parade so that we can put a fourteen-year-old boy on the throne, or at least stop him from getting himself killed or using his dragon to kill others."

They both laughed, but the sound fell flat.

They would enter the city disguised as a circus. They would hand out sweets that they hoped would counter the effects of the shepherd's magic so that the people would, somehow, see how the church forced people to leave and was taking over the city. And they would magically have the courage to stand up against their fellow citizens, with magic being forced out of the city, and would put a boy with foreign blood on the throne.

Yeah, it was a strange plan.

It was the only plan they had.

They continued on their way. The mist had grown thinner, but now it started snowing, even if the snowflakes melted as soon as they hit the ground.

Henrik remarked that the only good thing about the snow was that fewer people would take notice of them.

They turned into the estate's main drive. Someone was

at home in the main house. Smoke curled from the chimneys and the smell of burning wood hung over the fields.

When they passed the house, the sound of an axe hitting wood echoed over the empty fields. Wim was outside the barn, chopping wood. Two children were gathering the pieces and taking them inside.

"There they are!" Mina yelled.

Nellie slid from the cart and hugged her friend.

"Did you find Bruno?"

"We know where he is. We have to go back to get him. I'll tell you all about it when we're with the others."

"We were so worried about you."

"We weren't gone that long."

"No, but yesterday afternoon those men turned up." She glanced at a spot over Nellie's shoulder.

Nellie turned around. The far part of the horse paddock outside the barn had changed into a camp of at least ten tents. A couple of horses nosed around in a pile of hay. Smoke rose from a fire in the middle of the camp.

"They're mercenaries," Wim said, joining them with the axe on his shoulder. "Those are retired war horses. We think Adalbert Verdonck has hired them to take the city."

"Have you seen him around at all?" Henrik asked.

"Only at a distance," Wim said.

"Is Madame Sabine still here?" Nellie asked.

"As far as I know, yes," Mina said. "She moved to the other shed, because I suggested that she might want to help us do the cooking. Agatha seems to like her, though."

It was warm and comfortable inside the barn. In the camp kitchen, Agatha was stirring a pot from which wonderful smells spread through the air. "You're just in time for soup," she said, without commenting on Nellie's return or asking how she was.

When everyone squished together, the fruit-pickers' kitchen was just big enough to hold the entire group.

"Where is Boots?" a little voice next to her asked.

Anneke had wriggled herself in between Nellie and Mina.

"He's still with Bruno," Nellie said.

"I don't understand why Bruno didn't come back with you."

"We couldn't take him. We need to rescue him."

"Can I help, please?"

"We'll see." But Nellie had no intention of taking children on the parade. That would be too dangerous.

When everyone finished eating and the bowls were collected, Nellie and Henrik got to tell their story. Nellie had to explain her plan.

In case some people didn't quite understand what was going on, she explained from the beginning: The citizens of Saardam were controlled through the food they ate; the Shepherd controlled the food supply and was a good magician; and remedies could be taken against magic. They were going to give those remedies to the people in the city, so they would see the misdeeds against the crown prince, and would not believe the lies of the shepherd when he denied wrongdoing.

Also, because Casper and Bruno were both in the palace and the shepherd had closed the gates, they needed to be creative to get in.

Agatha's reaction was disbelieving. "So then what are we going to do? Rock up to the palace and simply invite ourselves to dinner?"

"We are going to do exactly that. We are going to invite ourselves to a grand welcome in the palace, and we're going to bring our own food. The shepherd won't be able to do anything without outing himself as being just as bad as the Fire Wizard, and risking the anger of the surrounding countries. Lord Verdonck has told me that Burovia and Estland are concerned about what is happening, but because no one gets out across the borders, they have no news, and so they mind their own problems. Everything the shepherd has done so far is to disguise his grab for power—putting the Regent in the palace, and letting the Regent make the declarations that magic is not allowed. But they are all the shepherd's decisions. Casper, for all his foolishness, does not want to listen to the shepherd. I think the shepherd allowed Casper to behave as he wants because he hopes that one of the nobles will get so frustrated with the boy that he'll kill him. And when that happens, then the shepherd has a reason to step up and seize control of the city, and all the citizens will be happy that the shepherd saved them from this horrible mess, and then the shepherd will have total control of Saardam, like the Fire Wizard did. That is what we don't want to happen. But we need support from the people in the city, and we can't get that as long as they are still influenced by the food they eat."

Agatha said, "And you want to have a feast to stop this?"

"Yes, because that's what people do at a feast: they eat. It's our best chance. We must get the entire city looking at the palace for the magnificent parade, and enjoying the sweets we're going to give them. We're all going to disguise ourselves as part of the royal party."

Mina said, "But I am no royal. And I have no royal clothes."

"The clothes are all in the cart," Nellie said. "Everything we need, I got while I was there. I used to work for Queen Johanna, so I know what's involved in dressing people up."

They all wanted to have a look, and Nellie showed them the chests with the dresses. They marvelled over the frills and the extravagant hats.

"Do people really wear this?" Koby asked.

"They do, to banquets and balls," Nellie said.

"I really like this dress. Come on, Gisele, have a look at these dresses."

"I'd rather be a monk."

But Nellie had considered Gisele. "You don't seem the type to wear dresses, so I brought you this." She held up a dark-green velvet men's suit. "You just need to cut your hair a bit and you can make a fine young man."

Gisele grinned.

"Oh, look, there's a box we haven't opened," Koby said, pointing at Master Thiele's wooden box.

"That one needs a key to open," Hilde said, holding a pink dress over her arm.

"There are no clothes in this one." Henrik picked up the box and put it aside.

Nellie wondered what was in it. She could ask later. First there were things to do.

Apart from the outrageous dresses, Nellie had brought one that was a bit more civilised for herself. It was dark red, quite modest and, most importantly, suitable for winter.

She dressed herself, made an attempt to do her hair, and went up to the house.

She found Adalbert Verdonck in his study, where he sat at his big wooden desk, writing with a feather pen on piece of paper.

When the servant knocked on the open door to announce he had a visitor, he looked up.

"Come in." He pushed aside a piece of paper Nellie recognised: the letter from Casper. Was he replying to it? Was he still considering what to do?

Nellie went into the room and sat on one of the richly covered chairs.

He looked her over from top to bottom. "It seems I was mistaken. I thought you were a maid."

"I have been everything in my life. Once, longer ago than you may remember, I was a member of the court of Queen Johanna. I'm not of noble descent, but my family are honourable people. Cornelius Dreessen was my father."

His eyes widened briefly.

"You knew my father?"

"Everyone in the Science Guild does."

"Are you a member?"

"My father was. I am, too, but I haven't attended any meetings for a long time. There have been some . . . differences in opinion. I need not bore you with the details. Why have you come?"

"I have a plan, and was hoping you would be able to help."

"And what sort of assistance? I presume you want money?"

That was something only a noble would say. "No, actually, I would like to borrow a coach. And some horses to go with the coach."

He raised his eyebrows. "Would you know how to handle a coach?"

"If you have any doubt about it, I would gladly borrow a coachman, too. As long as he's not afraid of anything."

Adalbert laughed. "Here are you—what?—old enough to be someone's grandmother, telling men of arms not to be afraid?"

"Afraid of magic."

His face closed.

"I am not a witch, as I'm sure you know already. But there is great magic in the city, and there is no other way to fight magic other than with magic."

He laughed again and let an uncomfortably long silence lapse. After a while, he said, "My father dabbled in magic. I'm sure you saw the scar on his calf."

"I did, and madame Sabine also explained to me how he received it. It was not through magic, but through wanting to use the dragon with the balloons."

He snorted. "It's all magic to me. It's unnatural for people to want to fly."

"But surely you recognise the value of being able to fly over a city, even to arouse the curiosity of the people?"

"I want none of it here, and I need the barn. I have told my father's mistress that she should leave. Any time now, people will arrive to take all her stuff off my land."

"As far as I know, yes, although all her balloon stuff may have been taken off. Frankly I would've wanted to burn it."

"I think that would be unwise."

He looked at her curiously.

Nellie continued. "For all the time that I worked for the royal family, all the time I've been in the palace, and all the time I've gone to the church and attended services, I have seen people who wanted to pretend that magic doesn't exist, and that ignoring it will make it go away. I have seen how young children who have magic get ignored and end up harming themselves and those around them because they were never taught properly how to deal with magic. This is what happened to Princess Celine. I have seen how the church became so afraid of magic that they drove from the city a huge number of people who are useful. Our city has become a ghost town. And now we have in the city a magician who wants to rule all of it, and cannot be challenged, because we have no one left who is able to challenge him. This is what we are about. This is why I want to use every new thing possible. And I want to do it not through arms but through convincing the people. We know about the magic. We know that much if it comes through food. Your father knew this. We know that the shepherd wants to rule the city by himself and that it would be a terrible thing once he pushes aside poor Casper who is just caught in his plan. Now Casper and Prince Bruno have holed themselves up in the palace, and what do you think the shepherd will do? He will starve them, and then he will move in and kill both of them, and we will have lost the only chance we have of getting our old city back. You do a lot of business with the city. What would you do if they stopped buying your food?"

"They won't, because there is no other place to buy it close by."

"They will stop buying it, because there will not be as many people in the city."

His face worked. In his eyes Nellie thought she could see the warring emotions of wanting to come to the city as a saviour and being crowned the king or simply surviving and getting praise and money without the crown. She didn't really understand what he wanted, but although he was not very pleasant, she didn't think he was a bad man.

He agreed that she could borrow a coach. He also agreed to send a group of capable men.

She asked whether those guards were the men camped in the horse paddock.

He said those were mercenaries returning from a mission. What they had done, he didn't say and she didn't feel it appropriate to ask. He stressed that the men did *not* work for him.

Somehow, Nellie didn't believe him.

Back at the barn, Henrik told Nellie that they might be a danger more than a blessing, but there was no option other than to accept his help, because they couldn't do it alone and because without Lord Verdonck's support, Saardam was nothing.

"I'm sure the nobles will have a lot of bad things to say about allowing him back into the city," he said.

This was all very much more complicated than Nellie

had assumed, and it was turning into a game she wasn't well equipped to play.

"I meant to ask you before: do you know what's in that box Master Thiele put on the cart?"

"I think I might, but he hasn't told me so I can't be certain."

"Do you have the key?"

"I know where it is." Which wasn't an answer.

"Do you think they're weapons?"

"Of a kind, but without opening it, I can't tell, and I don't want to start rumours."

"Don't you know I hate it when you're mysterious like this?"

"I do, but if the box contains what I think it contains, then the fewer people who see what's inside, the better."

CHAPTER 21

NELLIE WENT TO SEE what Madame Sabine had been up to. The door to the shed was locked from inside, but she could hear Madame Sabine's voice inside. She knocked.

The voice fell quiet and then said, "Who's there?"

"It's Nellie. I need your help."

A moment later, the door opened. Madame Sabine peeked out. She wore a man's outfit, a pair of overalls belted at the waist. She had her hair tied up in a ponytail and wore a shawl around her head to keep it warm.

"Yes, what do you want?" She didn't sound terribly friendly.

"I have a plan, and I would like your involvement, because this is about your sons."

Madame Sabine gave her a suspicious look. "What do you know about my sons?"

"They're holed up in the palace. Don't you want to help them?"

Madame Sabine said nothing, just stared at Nellie as if she had said something dumb.

Nellie's frustration boiled over. "I don't understand

you. Do you care nothing for your sons? I understand that you don't like the way their father raised them, but I'm sure you must care *something* for them? They need you now."

"They don't need me. I just get in the way of their parties. I'm just a boring woman."

"Did they tell you that? Did you see their faces in the upstairs window in the harbour when your husband was going to drown you? Did you read the letter they sent to Adalbert Verdonck?"

Madame Sabine said nothing, which, Nellie was sure, meant that she hadn't seen the letter.

"Casper wrote a letter asking Adalbert Verdonck for men to help him secure his position as Regent."

"Him? That's ridiculous."

"Tell me: what should he have done instead?"

"He should have done what I have told him to do many times: go to his aunt's estate in Burovia and learn some civility and manners before attempting to do such ridiculous things as seize the throne of a foreign country at the age of sixteen."

"Then why didn't you order a coach and tell both of them to get in?"

"You know how many times I've tried that already? They don't listen to me. I don't know how many times I have to explain. They don't listen. Their father fills their heads with nonsense."

"Their father is dead. They're in the ballroom surrounded by guards. They need you."

A flicker of concern crossed her face. "They don't. They told me they don't need me or want me. They never listened to me when I was with them. Why would they listen to me now?"

"Because they know everyone else is out to get them?

Because they might think you're brave, doing your own work and not pandering to the shepherd or the nobles?"

She snorted. "I'm not brave." But Nellie could see the thoughts whirling behind her eyes. Then she added, "And you come here just to tell me that I should tell my sons to behave?"

"No, but I would appreciate if you could tell them that as well. I'm planning a parade into the city, and it would mean a great deal for me if you were to be there."

"What? To be laughed at?"

"No, to be marvelled at, because of your balloons. I presume you have one here that we can use?"

She frowned. Then she opened the door further. "Come in, so you can explain what this is all about."

Nellie went into the shed, where she noticed that Madame Sabine had unpacked all the crates with the balloons again. Obviously, finding transport out of the area in the winter was not so easy.

Maybe it was just an empty threat she was making. After all, a Burovian noble receiving her letter with request for a coach to take her elsewhere might just laugh and throw it in the fire.

As Nellie had already known, Agatha was also in the shed. She was sitting at a table, sewing together two lengths of fabric. She gave Nellie a defiant look.

If the situation weren't so dire, Nellie might have asked why the two of them seemed to think that the world conspired against them. The fact that they worked together was a strange development, because they had seemed so hostile to each other, but Agatha had not survived on her own with the children by being dumb.

Being a fly on the wall in this shed might reveal some interesting conversations, though. Both women were all prickles.

In the uncomfortable atmosphere, Nellie went on to

explain her plan, and how she thought Madame Sabine's balloon would help distribute the sweets and draw attention to the parade.

Madame Sabine listened with interest. She asked questions, ones Nellie couldn't answer because she didn't know whether any of the nobles Madame Sabine asked about were involved. She thought not, but she didn't know what Master Thiele was doing in the city and who he had involved in this. She thought his contacts were mainly guards. She didn't know if Adalbert Verdonck planned to send any of the men camped outside in the horse paddock along with them.

"It's a big plan and it involves all the people in the city. It involves trusting that they will see what the shepherd is doing and that they don't him to become another Fire Wizard. I can't control what individuals will say or do."

"There are too many points of danger in this plan of yours," Madame Sabine said.

"Does that mean you won't be involved?"

"Not necessarily, because I would love to teach that stupid priest a lesson, but in order for my commitment, I want to command my own group of people. You understand that with my history, I am not exactly well loved in the city, and several of the powerful people would rather see me dead. I have to protect myself."

Nellie agreed that she could keep working with Agatha, and that she could select a number of other people to look after the balloon. Nellie suspected she would ask for Gisele and maybe Wim or Floris the fisherman.

Fortunately, getting Mustafa's cooperation was a lot of easier. He wanted to return to the city, because it was his only source of income. Getting money from visitors to his animal park would allow him to have more animals, which was what he really wanted.

"What is the use of having the talkative parrots if the children can't come to laugh about their bad language?" he said over a couple of cups of far-too-strong tea in his barn. "I need visitors because I need money to pay for food for the animals."

He was happy to bring his animals for the parade. He would bring his wagon, too.

"I don't know that Esme would be happy to have something tied to her collar, but we could tie the balloon to the wagon. It's big and heavy. There are metal cages in the back. Maybe you can dress some children as gnomes and put them inside. People love looking at gnomes. I can put Lila on top of the cage, so it looks like she has caught the gnomes." He stroked the leopard over her soft head while he said this.

And that left just getting the herbs.

Nellie and Henrik had come to Mustafa's place together, but had decided that just Henrik would go down to see the nuns, because they had not seen him before, and his plea to buy herbs to cure someone who was ill at Lord Verdonck's estate would probably sound plausible.

Dandelion, blackberry and anise could be used. If they didn't have those, he might have to ask for more outlandish ingredients like amaranth, and that might arouse suspicion, but Nellie hoped he wouldn't have to go that far down the list she had given him.

Nellie waited with the cart at the top of the driveway and watched him go to the buildings.

It took Henrik quite a long time to return. But finally she saw him coming up the driveway. He walked a bit faster than she thought was good, but he did appear to be carrying something.

"Come on, let's go," was the first thing he said when he reached Nellie with the cart and the horses.

"What's going on?"

"A group of soldiers are staying at the nunnery. They're all mercenaries hired by the Regent. I served with some of them. Word has gotten around that the Regent is dead, and they're scouting for paid work. Apparently, they came to the nunnery because the nunnery posted a notice in town stating that the church needed armed men to *defend the honour of the shepherds*. They didn't see me, but it was a near thing."

By the Triune, no. Did Shepherd Wilfridus want to start a war? "Did you get the herbs?"

"I did, because I wasn't game to show my face back here without them." He grinned. "But I hope no one recognised me and they don't know that we're here."

"They'll know that we're here very soon if they don't already," Nellie said. "But Lord Verdonck has his own army, and they won't want to come here to risk confrontation."

Henrik nodded. "Though I'm not sure how long that's going to last. I have a feeling that from now on, time is going to be essential. We have to move as quickly as possible."

In the barn, the women helped Yolande make the sweets. The messy process involved cooking lots of sugar in cauldrons and stirring the herb mixture into it. Then they added a powder that turned the mixture red, and spread the thick, sticky paste out on oiled paper before cutting it into cubes while still warm.

They also went into a cooking frenzy. They made cakes and biscuits. Mina oversaw the cooking, helped by most of the other women, while Wim walked in and out of the kitchen carrying water, firewood and whatever else they needed.

Mustafa arrived with his troupe of animals late in the afternoon. Everyone in the barn came outside to watch Esme the elephant, who led Mustafa's column, with Mustafa himself holding a rope attached to a colourful collar around her neck. He also held a stick that he occasionally used to poke the top of her leg when she became too interested in the dead grass or a stick by the side of the path.

Behind him was the wagon, pulled by two horses, that contained a metal cage with the zebra horse and the goats and cow. Lila the leopard lay on top, her tail dangling into the cage.

The two foul-mouthed parrots flew from the top of the cage to sit on the elephant's back, making their loud screeching noises.

When they arrived at the barn, Koby ran out with a handful of carrots, which she proceeded to feed to the elephant under the wide-eyed looks of Anneke, Bas and Jantien's children.

The women opened the barn doors, allowing the menagerie to come inside. All the animals were alert.

Lila jumped off the wagon with a graceful leap and trotted into the stable, sniffing the hay where the dragon used to sleep.

Then, when everyone was inside, they had tea and ate some of the cakes still warm from baking, and some non-human creatures got carrots. Mustafa had also brought some skinned rabbits, which went onto the spit.

Over a meal in the kitchen, they decided they would leave the next day, because Mustafa said the soldiers Henrik had seen at the nunnery would likely come to the Verdonck estate. They should not find anyone there.

Someone in the corner said, "What about me?"

Brother Martinus rarely spoke up. He seemed to have resigned himself to being an unwelcome guest, even if he'd offered to leave a few times.

Henrik said, "We'll leave you here. You can take the ship back, or up the river, or you can go to the nunnery, but only after we're gone."

Brother Martinus' face showed no emotion, not even when everyone continued talking. Nellie wondered if he was so worried the decision to let him go might be reversed that he didn't want to give anyone the impression he was happy. When she finished eating, she went to sit next to him.

He didn't look at her or acknowledge her presence.

"The Triune will guide you," she said. "The Triune is good, even if the flesh of some in the congregation is weak."

He must have heard their stories about Shepherd Wilfridus, although he had never shown any emotion that betrayed what he thought about it.

"I'm . . . going to stay here," he finally said.

"You don't have to."

"I don't . . . like travelling alone."

"You can come with us."

He shook his head. "It's best I don't. The Triune will guide you and He will decide my fate."

He looked sad.

She had so much still to do and no time to sit and talk. She rose and placed a hand on his shoulder. "The Triune will welcome you back into His house. I, too, never forget the teachings of the Book. I read it to myself every night."

"I believe that, sister. I don't believe you are bad." He hesitated. "I know some of these people are heathens, but if you trust them, then I trust that they are good people at heart. You have my blessing."

"Thank you."

And then Nellie left the kitchen. What a strange conversation.

After having eaten, Madame Sabine took Agatha, Koby and Floris out to the shed with the balloons. They brought back a huge bundle of fabric carried between them and then took the cart to get the basket with the ropes.

Madame Sabine stoked a giant fire outside the barn and used a frame of metal to suspend the mouth of the balloon high enough above it that it didn't catch fire.

The four of them were out all night because, apparently, it took a very long time to fill a balloon with hot air.

When Nellie got up before dawn, the yard in front of the barn was quiet, but the massive cloth bag floated in the air with the basket attached to it. The assembly was tied to the horse paddock fence with a thick rope. The fire was still going, the cart stood next to it, and Madame Sabine, Koby and Floris were asleep in the tray.

Inside the barn, preparations were in full swing. Mina was cooking breakfast, people were gathering their possessions to be taken on the cart and an atmosphere of excitement hung in the air. Some people, like Gisele, had already eaten and were in their costume.

Nellie was happy with how Gisele looked in her green suit: just like a handsome young man.

"I wish Els could be here," Gisele said. "Do you think she'll come to watch the parade?"

"Maybe," Nellie said, although the warehouse was in a different part of town.

"You're not dressed yet," Henrik said. He looked very handsome in his black suit and top hat.

Gertie helped Nellie do up the strings to her red dress. She then piled her hair into a tower on the top of her head. It was quite knotted and there were plenty of spaces to put pins to hold it up. Then she put on a heavy coat made of long fur and as a finishing touch a mask that covered most of her face, which had a protuberance like a bird's long curved beak over her nose.

Agatha and Josie also wore masks, but Koby painted her face, and Floris donned a bright red cape and a hat with a ridiculous feather.

Madame Sabine painted her face white and her lips

bright red, and she wore a pink dress with so many frills it was hard to see the fabric underneath. Over top of that, she wore a cloak of white fur.

Everyone looked splendid.

Mustafa put the colourful saddle on the elephant. His horses wore headpieces with bells that tinkled with every step they took. The balloon was tied to his wagon. Mustafa hauled in the rope, and Madame Sabine made sure the bag was full and that the burner in the basket had enough oil. Then Koby climbed in. Henrik and Gisele handed her bags of sweets.

Slowly, they let go of the rope, sending the balloon with Koby into the air.

Agatha, Mina and most of the rescued women took Adalbert Verdonck's cart and horses. It also held all their packs with their normal clothes and other possessions. Before they left, Henrik came out of the barn carrying Master Thiele's locked chest and set it on the tray of the cart before pushing it as far forward as possible, so there was absolutely no chance of it falling off.

Then the column set in motion.

Nellie travelled in the coach with Wim, the children, Jantien and Yolande. The plan was to let Jantien and the children out once they got to the edge of the city. Henrik had given her a list of places where they might find safe shelter. Jantien wanted to help hand out sweets, but it would be safer for her to hide.

The long column snaked through the fields. Mustafa and his elephant went first, followed by the zebra horses and the leopard on a leash. The parrots sat in their cage on the wagon, screeching their heads off. They seemed to enjoy themselves.

Then came the coach with Nellie and the others. Henrik sat with Adalbert Verdonck's coachman in the driver's seat. Nellie could hear their voices talking and laughing.

The day was nice and the sky pale blue. The sun hung low over the fields.

Sections of the road were muddy, but once they came to the small villages, most of the roads were paved with cobbles. That made the journey quicker but the clatter of hooves and wheels over the cobbles was very noisy.

They could see the city in the distance.

Soon, they were between the small farms that grew vegetables and kept chickens, pigs and cows. Here and there, people were working in the fields, feeding their sheep or cows or mending fences. The balloon got a lot of attention. Farmer's wives and families came out of their houses to stare at it. They walked along with Esme, who didn't once stray from her path.

Mustafa had climbed onto her back, and continued to feed her carrots from a bag attached to the saddle.

They came to the outskirts of the city, where the poor people lived in rows of little houses, sometimes with very small plots of land. People ran to the side of the road to have a look at the passing column and marvel at the balloon.

Mustafa produced a metal funnel that made his voice louder when he spoke into it. They were a travelling group of artistes, he said. They were coming to bring cheer to the city. Everyone would get free sweets.

Soon, a horde of children—and older people—followed along. Those at the back of the crowd got their sweets from Koby, who threw handfuls of them into the audience from her position high above the street.

The crowd swelled and swelled.

People came running out of side streets. Koby was throwing sweets down from her perch, and the people were putting them in their mouths. Children came with grubby little hands; young men came with eager looks on their faces; young women danced with dainty moves, as if afraid that so-and-so from next door would notice; and grandmothers followed with half-closed eyes that could only see the good times of years past, when for half a cent you could buy a bag of sweets so big that you could eat one every day for a month and still not run out.

Many people followed the parade, asking for more sweets. Nellie had told Koby and the others that it was important that enough sweets remained to hand out in the market place, because the people there were the most likely to visit the main church and be influenced by Shepherd Wilfridus.

They came past the council building where a queue stood for people to receive their food rations. Henrik tossed a handful of sweets onto the desk where the officials asked for names and other details. Several men leaned forward to grab the treats. They put them in their mouths.

"We're going to see the fair Regent of this town," Mustafa called. "Come along and tell him you want to see our animals and parade. Come along if you want to go for a ride in the balloon! If she likes you, Esme might let you feed her carrots."

And many people came and followed. They cheered.

CHAPTER 22

FINALLY, THE PARADE with the elephant, the wagon and balloon, the horses, goats and parrots, the carts with beautifully dressed-up people and all the citizens tagging along, keen to get more sweets, arrived in the middle of the city. They crossed the marketplace and went through the palace gates. There was a short holdup at the gate when Mustafa held his talk about bringing fun to the city for the benefit of the palace guards. Nellie couldn't hear what was said, but a lot of guards came to the gate, and after protests and pleading from Mustafa and promises of sweets, the palace gates opened.

Madame Sabine had said several times that Casper loved sweets.

The coach rattled across the cobbles of the forecourt. Nellie sat on the side facing away from the palace. The crowd of citizens had to stay at the gates because only the parade of colourful people and animals were allowed inside. Against the dreary grey buildings of the city, they looked very colourful indeed.

The coach stopped and the coachman jumped off the

driver's seat to open the door. Nellie felt like she had stepped back in time to when she would travel with Mistress Johanna like this.

It had not been warm inside the coach, but the air outside was positively freezing. Nellie pulled the sides of her coat closer around her. Her legs were stiff. They had only been underway for half a day—not long at all compared to how far some people travelled—but Nellie rarely sat still for that long.

The steps to the coach were narrow and hard to navigate in a dress where one couldn't see one's feet.

Looking up at the majestic building where she had spent a substantial part of her life, a wave of nerves overcame Nellie. Certainly at least one of these guards would recognise Lord Verdonck's coach or his coachman. Then again, Adalbert Verdonck never used the hospitality of the palace when he came with his father.

Floris and Gisele were pulling in the rope to bring Koby and the balloon down. She was shivering with cold, but her eyes shone.

"You can see so much from up there!" she said to Gisele.

They gathered the people who were going inside. Not everyone was, because Floris and some of the women didn't want to risk being questioned by anyone. Agatha, however, said several times she had nothing left to lose. She had left her children with Jantien, who was taking them to one of Henrik's safe addresses. The risqué low-cut dress had transformed her from a frumpy peasant to an elegant dame. She didn't look half as old as Nellie had previously guessed her to be. She walked next to Madame Sabine—an unlikely friendship—who covered her face with a veil.

Nellie shivered. She was uncomfortable in this dress. She was really not made for this type of clothing.

Finally, the party started up the palace steps. Mustafa led, dressed in a bright purple jacket, a red- and black-striped top hat and blue trousers. He had twirled his moustache into curls and carried a walking stick which he threw into the air and caught deftly. The giant snake hung draped over his shoulders. Lila walked next to him on a leash, and Koby took the leash with the zebra horse. One of the parrots sat on her shoulder and the other fluttered over the party, screeching. Esme climbed the steps with her master, but because only the small doors were open, she didn't fit through. Koby offered to stay outside.

The remaining party went into the palace foyer, with the rear end of the column carrying the many baskets and boxes of food they had brought for the celebration.

Two servants were scrubbing the floors, but Nellie tried not to look at them, for fear they would recognise her. If she felt nervous, she could only imagine what Madame Sabine must feel like.

They went into the ballroom, passing through a guard consisting of two teenage boys in too-big guard uniforms.

Nellie had expected chaos, with food on the floor and broken furniture and other things that came with wild orgies, but the first thing that struck her was how orderly and clean the room was. The tables stood in straight rows. While it was clear that people slept here, the row of mattresses lay against the outer walls of the room, and all the blankets were neatly folded. The floor was swept, the tables clean.

The places on the dais that would normally be taken up by the venerable old advisers of the king or the Regent were now taken up by younger people. Nellie recognised quite a few of them, and noticed how they looked much older and quite well presented.

She saw Bruno at the table. He sat with a straight back, his chin up. He wore a cloak that resembled the king's carmine cloak but it was a different garment, because Nellie remembered seeing the Regent wear it. His sleek black hair hung like curtains on both sides of his narrow face. On his lap, he held the dragon box.

Behind them, up two further steps, stood the king's throne.

In years past, it was the only piece of furniture no one had moved from its original position, in the hope that one day the succession problem would be solved. No one had touched it or attempted to sit in it.

Mustafa walked forward leading the leopard by the leash. He stopped in front of the dais and bowed. The gathered youngsters moved aside so that a path opened to the throne. The leopard sat down, its tail twitching.

"We present to you the animal extravaganza." He turned around and waved his hand at the group of people behind him. Nellie stood next to Madame Sabine. The sweat ran down her back, even though it wasn't very warm in this room. "We bring you exquisite food, sweets, cakes, and sausages. We would have brought the elephant, but she doesn't fit through the door."

There was a bit of laughter at this, and some of the noble sons and daughters started to relax.

"What is your business in this town?" asked a clear voice, old enough to have obtained a man's dark tones, but still young enough to sound like a child, and Madame Sabine took in a sharp breath.

It was Casper, and for Nellie, the first sign she'd seen that Madame Sabine felt anything towards her children. Nellie could see Frederick at the edge of the group, next to a noble daughter who looked barely older than twelve.

Again, Mustafa bowed. "We have come here for a celebration and hopefully to solicit custom of the well-off citizens of this town. We arrange parties, we entertain, we show exotic animals and we cook." He held out a box of sweets to Casper, and the boy took one, popped it into his mouth and chewed.

He nodded. "Tastes good." He took another.

Nellie let out a breath that she hadn't realised she was holding. It might just be that this plan would work.

"Make sure you give the guards some sweets as well," she whispered to Hilde next to her.

At this moment one of the parrots at the back said loudly, "You idiot."

Sniggers broke out among the noble sons and daughters.

"We truly mean no harm," Mustafa said. "We are a band of travellers in need of shelter, and funds to feed our animals. The countryside is very poor indeed, and not many people are happy to have us. They spread rumours that the animals are dangerous. Can you imagine it? Look at her." He bent down and patted the leopard on the head.

While he was speaking, Bruno's eyes met Nellie's. She was sure he recognised her. He gave a tiny smile.

"Well then, what are you waiting for," Casper said. "Bring out the tables. Let's have a feast."

"We have brought a variety of exotic foods that we would like you to try," Mustafa said. "We have sausages and wines and exotic spices and sweets. We would like to share these things with you as our gratitude for hosting us in your city."

He was doing an amazing job as entertainer. Nellie remembered how he would take groups of people around his animal park and delight them with his strange accent and funny stories.

Servants drew the tables across the room.

Nellie was sure that one or two of them recognised some of the people in the party. No disguise was foolproof. But they said nothing and did as was ordered. Most importantly, people in the party offered them sweets.

Food was brought up, and the women shared the sausages and cakes they had made. For a while everyone was happy, and the talk was about animals and where they had come from.

Mustafa walked the leopard and the zebra horse around the hall so that everyone could look at it. The youngsters could pat the leopard, but the zebra horse was a cranky creature, likely to kick or bite. Casper needed to demonstrate that, to the great hilarity of his friends. Just to prove that he hadn't quite grown as serious as events suggested.

The youngsters were not as reckless as Nellie had expected, but they'd arrived at this situation because they were stuck for ideas of how to get out.

So they partied.

It was all they could do. While the city was hungry, they partied. When they didn't know what to do, they partied. Banquets and plenty of wine solved everything. In this case, it really would.

Nellie took one of the sausages, cut small slices and made sure that everyone had a piece and that she spoke with everyone. She asked the noble girls their names and who their families were, and she made compliments about their dresses and their hair.

In between the levity, she heard that most of the girls were in the palace because they'd had disagreements with their parents, who thought Casper was a menace to the city, and the girls considered Casper a friend.

One girl confided in Nellie that she couldn't see how Casper's behaviour was any worse than that of his father, and that none of the older generation objected to the Regent's banquets. "Just because they're not invited, that's why."

Nellie badly wanted to ask why the girl thought the doors were shut and they couldn't go to their homes, but that would give away that these "travellers" were more knowledgeable about the city than they should be, although the whole plan was probably about to fall apart anyway.

Another girl added, "It's just horrible what they did to Prince Bruno. Our parents are ashamed, and that's why they don't like us here, because we hear his stories of how the church locked him up for years, and they know we will blame our parents for allowing it to happen. I was only five when the king and queen died, but my parents were adults, and they should have asked about Prince Bruno, but they didn't. They were cowards and they believed the church."

The first girl said, "Shhh, Amalia, why do you think these visitors want to know about this? You're going to get us all into trouble."

Nellie bowed and backed away. "I'm sorry. I don't want to cause trouble for you." She resumed her course around the hall.

When people asked, she would tell stories about her travels, mostly exaggerated from the time she travelled with Mistress Johanna. If you had a long life, you could find quite a few things to use as embellishments.

She made up how she was a servant at the court of the Red Baron, and told them about the forbidding castle, and she could do a reasonably good job because she had actually been inside the castle. She told them about the magical forest and, for a while, everyone was happy.

Nellie went to serve Prince Bruno as well. She asked him quietly if he was all right, to which he said that he was. She didn't dare ask anything else, like whether the dragon was in the box, and whether he had indeed fought the shepherd and lost.

From close up, he looked even more fragile than he had when they first came in. He knew his position was dangerous. He knew he wasn't ready to fight.

She gently touched his hand when he took a piece of the sausage she offered. It was all she could do to reassure him. She remembered him as four-year-old boy, but the adolescent Bruno was still too disturbed to confide in her. Yet she must help him, even as he rejected or ignored her. He was not ready to face this.

She couldn't ask him what he was doing here, and whether this meant that he was Casper's friend or was trying to use Casper, or whether Casper had wanted to take the throne for himself. In the end, it was not relevant, because they were all prisoners in this magnificent palace.

And then came a commotion at the door.

Someone shouted, and the two guards posted there were trying to keep a person from coming in.

A man called out, "Let me through, you imbeciles."

It was Shepherd Wilfridus.

Show time.

CHAPTER 23

SHEPHERD **WILFRIDUS** strode through the hall, his robes flying, sidestepping the guards who tried to stand in his way. The guards themselves were young boys, no match for the shepherd.

He walked straight through the gathered circus troupe party.

He did not stop in front of the dais, but climbed the steps in a single jump, belying his age, and grabbed Casper by the arm.

"What do you think you're doing, boy?" His voice was like a snarl.

"Take your hands off me." Casper pulled his arm out of the shepherd's grip.

The shepherd clearly hadn't expected that, and gave Casper an angry look. "What's wrong with you? Can't you ever listen to what a superior tells you?"

"I am not your servant," Casper said. "I am the legal successor to the Regentship." His face was pale, but he sat straight.

"You wish."

"I have more claim on the position than anyone else. You don't have the right to bully me about."

The shepherd took in a sharp breath.

No, he had definitely not expected that.

"You will do as I say. I am through with this ridiculous behaviour of yours. I have left you free rein since your father died because I took pity on you. It's finished now, and it's time you start listening to me."

"I don't need to listen to you. My father was appointed Regent, and I have assumed that position."

"I did not appoint you to that position. You're a brat."

"I'm sixteen. I'm an adult."

"I did *not* appoint you."

"Well, in that case, I may just have to ask the king's advice."

And everybody turned around to Bruno, who looked very small and skinny.

In the tense silence, he rose from his seat, walked across the dais, up the two steps and sat down in the empty throne where nobody had sat for over ten years.

The shepherd's eyes widened. His mouth opened and closed as if he were a dying fish. He glanced at the guests and the food on the tables, much of which had not been produced in the kitchens.

Perhaps he realised what the group had done and that he no longer controlled the people in the hall.

He stammered, "You can't . . ." And then he found his voice. "A king has no right to rule without the crown and sceptre."

Everyone in the hall knew that was right, and also that the location of the crown and sceptre was unknown. People whispered that the church had them, and certainly Nellie had seen the cabinet that held the crown in the crypt . . . but *without* the crown on the dusty velvet.

A tense silence followed, in which Nellie expected the

shepherd to drag Bruno out of the chair, or conjure the fire dog and attack the young nobles on the dais.

But none of that happened, and she didn't notice that Henrik had left the safety of the group until he was halfway up the dais.

He carried the heavy wooden box that Master Thiele had given them. Nellie held her breath. She suddenly thought she knew what was in the box.

In the tense silence, Henrik set it on the table, then dug in his pocket for the key. He opened the lid with a creak.

From inside the box, he lifted an ornate staff with a golden lion at its end. He gave it to Bruno. Then he lifted out the king's crown, gold and so heavy that he needed to hold it in both hands.

The shepherd looked on with wide eyes.

Henrik gave the crown to Bruno, but Bruno kept it on his lap, on top of the dragon box. Nellie didn't know if was aware that the king couldn't wear the crown until properly ordained, or whether Casper had told him.

"This is the man who locked me up in the crypt," Bruno said, pointing at the shepherd. His voice sounded thin and nervous. "This is the man whose monks would make me work until I was so tired that I couldn't keep my eyes open, who would then beat me for not paying attention, never quite badly enough to cause permanent harm. They kept me like an animal, telling me stories about how all hope was dead, and how the only thing I could do that made any sense was to cooperate with their wishes. This is the man who wanted to take the throne for himself. He wanted to declare himself the undisputed leader of the city, the undisputed leader of the church, and he wanted to banish all other churches and all other people from the country. He wanted to rule your world. He wanted to rule your minds."

Shepherd Wilfridus' face was white. "You filthy liar. Why do you disgrace our throne like that? You can't even prove that you're the queen's son. You're nothing but an impostor, a poor whore woman's child who thinks he's a prince."

"I have seen plenty of evidence that he speaks the truth," said a noble boy who Nellie recognised as the son of one of the Regent's former advisors.

The shepherd turned to him, the look on his face disturbed. "And who do you think you are?"

"My name is Ruben Demeer," the boy said, in a voice so young it hadn't yet broken. "I have seen plenty of evidence that Bruno is indeed the prince who was supposed to have died, according to some of your sermons."

"Yes," a girl said. "And you knew back then that he was alive. You must have, because he told us everything."

"He is a liar,"

"I don't think so," Ruben said. "The things he says, he couldn't make up. He knows the names of all your monks that mistreated him. How else would he know all these things?"

"You're just a bunch of impertinent kids," the Shepherd said. His face was red.

"No, they are not," said a female voice.

Madame Sabine strode up to the dais, lifting the veil from her face. Casper's eyes widened.

She walked around the table until she stood behind her son, placing both her hands on his shoulders and facing the shepherd.

"My sons are no angels," she said. "I am no holy mother. My husband spoilt them rotten and they picked up many bad habits. However, it seems that life is a great selector of good people. I thought I'd lost hope for my sons, but they have behaved themselves honourably here today."

"We are the future of the city," young Frederick said. He looked terrified but his back was straight. He rose from his seat and, in his hideous red suit, went to stand next to Bruno.

Casper also got up and went to stand next to Bruno. Madame Sabine positioned herself behind all three.

Nellie wiped her sweaty hands on her dress. Her anti-magic concoction was working. Maybe it was working just a little bit too well. Who was to stop the shepherd from harming all these kids who had disagreed with him?

"Shepherd, kindly remove yourself from this room," Casper said. "I know you were my father's closest advisor, and my father always did what you said. However, I am not my father, I don't really like what you're doing to all my friends, and I don't like your having banished so many people from the city. I shall sign a document that the Church of the Triune is no longer the sole state church of Saarland, that the Belaman church is allowed to come back, and that we will have a new book of laws that are written by people from all groups in the city, not just the church. I am thankful that you helped my father, but I think it's time to move on. Kindly leave. This is a private function, and I am entertaining my friends."

The shepherd pressed his lips together, whirled around and strode in the direction of the door.

He didn't take any notice of the people in the circus troupe who were still standing there. For moment, Nellie wondered if he was actually going to do as they'd asked. Would it really be so easy to get rid of him?

But when he approached the door to the foyer, the shepherd turned around again. "You insolent boy. Feel the full force of my power."

He stretched out his hands. A ball of flames burst from

them. While it rolled over the carpet, limbs unfolded, a head formed. The parrots started screeching, a few people screamed. A number of the noble youngsters jumped from their seats and retreated to the back of the hall.

Someone opened the door to the garden room, sending in a waft of cold air.

Bruno remained in his seat, straight-backed and with a face that showed no emotion. On his lap he held the crown and the dragon box.

The fire dog landed on all four paws in front of the dais. Head held close to the ground, it stood poised to spring.

It was not more than a few steps away from where Nellie stood. She could feel the heat radiating from its body.

From close up, the creature was even more terrifying than from a distance. It looked more like a wolf than a dog, with a big head, powerful jaws and huge paws. Its body looked solid. Fire trailed off its pelt.

The shepherd still stood on the other side of the hall, his eyes closed as he poured magic into his creation.

People screamed, scrambling away from the area, but the dog only showed interest in Prince Bruno.

Slowly, the prince leaned the sceptre against the side of the throne. Then he lifted the crown so that he could take the dragon box from underneath. He opened the lid.

The dragon erupted in a shower of sparks, taking only a few heartbeats to fully form into a solid creature. He had grown so much.

He jumped into the air and landed in front of the throne, facing the dog with his head bowed low and trails of smoke curling from his nostrils.

The dog sprang, and at the same time, the dragon jumped from the dais. The two met at the bottom of the steps in a ball of flames and claws and fire.

It was almost impossible to see what was going on, both the dog and dragon moved so fast. Several times the two creatures fell apart, scrabbled up and went back into the fight.

Even though the dog was much smaller, it never gave up. It ripped at the dragon's neck, paws and wings. The dragon howled and screeched. He was not fast enough to catch the dreadful creature.

He was losing the fight. And if the dog defeated the dragon, that would be the end.

"Call him back," Nellie called to Bruno. "Before it's too late."

Bruno held the box open on outstretched arms, but the dragon kept fighting and snarling after the dog. He blew fire, setting the carpet alight. Acrid smoke spread across the hall. It was hard to see what was happening.

Bruno called out, "He's not listening to me!"

Nellie ran up the dais snatched the dragon box from Bruno lap. She opened it.

"Come here," she yelled. "Come here."

The dragon turned his head. He looked terrible. His sides were marked with gashes and trails of sparks were oozing out.

He noticed her and made a run for her. Nellie expected him to go back into the box, but instead he grabbed her dress.

"What are you doing?" she yelled.

But the dragon ignored her. He ran through the hall dragging her by her dress. Nellie managed to grab hold of the dragon's neck and hung on.

He jumped and flew a couple of paces and then ran again. He was making for the door of the hall, but that was closed.

"Stop, stop!" Nellie called.

But the dragon burst through the door, scattering wood everywhere.

She expected him to take off through the foyer and fly out the front door, but the foyer was full of people and animals. The elephant had come into the hall by ripping the door off its hinges and pushing aide part of the wood panelling that surrounded the door. Dogs barked and horses neighed and people shouted.

The way to safety was barred.

CHAPTER 24

THE DRAGON SKIDDED to a halt. Too many people and animals were in the hall for him to jump over them. The pillars were too close together for him to fly.

Nellie managed to get her feet under her.

The noise in the hall was deafening. Dogs barked, horses neighed, a rooster crowed, the parrots screeched.

The dragon cared about animals, and all these animals from outside on the forecourt had come in here because of him. A number of guards had driven Esme the elephant into a corner of the foyer, where she stood, flapping her ears and swaying her long nose from side to side. She was unhappy and Nellie had no doubt that those guards couldn't stop her for a second if she really wanted to get out of that corner.

People shouted, "Down with the magician," and "All hail the Dragonspeaker."

Nellie wanted to shout, "Do you know the magician is in the hall behind you?" One who was very much not defeated yet and who would soon come out here.

But the people cheered.

They wanted to come into the hall, and heavens, there were even a good number of armed men securing the doors against an attack from outside. She thought she spotted Master Emmel with them. They were Lord Verdonck's men, helping her, as he had promised.

Except the threat was inside the hall.

Nellie looked desperately over the heads of the crowd in the hall, which included horses, cows, goats and sheep, wherever they had come from. It included citizens from all different groups of the city. She recognised the mayor, shopkeepers, people from the markets and people from the street. She even saw poor Bert, who looked worse than ever. He gave her a gap-toothed grin.

She looked for something, anything, that could defeat the shepherd, or, failing that, anything that would give her a chance of defeating him.

A flock of birds swooped over the heads of the people. They included crows, pigeons, sparrows and seagulls. A couple of ducks perched on the banisters of the stairwell.

Clouds of smoke billowed from the hall behind her. The fire dog would come out very soon, and it would defeat the dragon for a second time. Bruno, who controlled the dragon poorly anyway, was nowhere to be seen.

There was only one chance, and she held that chance.

She ran her hand over the dragon's side. "I hate to ask you this," she said. "But this is the third, perhaps the fourth time you have faced the dog. It's smaller than you, and certainly together with Bruno's magic we should be able to defeat it. If you don't fight, we are all going to die. I can fight, too. We should all fight together, but I want you to understand that there is no fleeing from this fight. I should never have called you away. We win or we die, and if we die, a lot of other people die as well. They're all good people who don't deserve to die, but who risk their lives in hopes of stopping a second Fire Wizard. We won't get another chance."

The dragon looked at her.

Nellie never knew whether he understood what she said. "The shepherd is a magician. I have no magic at all and have no chance against him. I can't defeat him alone. No one can. We must defeat him together."

It was too late. The fire dog had come to the entrance of the hall. It stood in the doorway, head low to the ground, with flames licking its luminous fur.

People screamed and pushed away from the door.

In the panic, Esme in the corner made a loud noise. She held her nose right up into the air. Mustafa had made his way out of the dining hall and was trying to keep her quiet. The dogs barked and the sheep bleated. The horses neighed. A couple of palace guards were trying to take them back outside, but the horses were nervous and kept rearing, especially a white-maned horse, which was one of Madame Sabine's animals.

Nellie understood. The dragon wanted help, but it didn't want that help from people.

She yelled at Mustafa, "Let her go!"

Mustafa used the side of the fountain to climb onto the saddle on Esme's back.

Esme charged forward, moving surprisingly quickly for an animal of her size.

People pushed out of her way.

The dragon turned around slowly. He held his head high and faced the door to the hall.

The fire dog still stood at the entrance, because it had nowhere to go. It seemed smaller than before—of course, so did the dragon—but Nellie couldn't be certain. She put her hand on the dragon's flank, feeling the heat under the skin.

"Go, you have our blessing. May the Triune be with you."

The dragon jumped forward. He met the fire dog in the doorway, and the force of the impact sent the two rolling back into the hall.

Nellie ran to the door looking in. The dragon had flown off with the fire dog in its claws. The creature was wriggling, trying to bite the dragon's claws. It sank its teeth into the dragon's leg.

The dragon flew to the other side of the hall, and bashed the dog into the wall. A rain of plaster came down.

It took off across the hall again, and bashed the fire dog into the other wall.

The fire dog struggled and howled.

Nellie was looking around for the shepherd, because without him the dog would be weakened.

The dragon flew low over the tables and chairs in the hall. He dragged the fire dog across the surface of the tables, pushing the tableware off the sides. The shattering of plates on tile floor drowned out the dog's yelps.

A normal dog had managed to get into the hall. It was a large black-and-brown animal with short hair and a strong square head. It sprinted across the tables, snapping at the fire dog and barking when it wasn't snapping.

Two more dogs entered the hall, following the first one.

With a loud fluttering, a large bird flew over Nellie's head. It was a goose, and it soared over the tables after the dragon that flew with the fire dog hanging from its claws.

The black dog snapped at the fire dog. The goose bit its tail. Bits of fur floated to the ground, trailing smoke on the way down.

Then Nellie saw the shepherd.

He stood with his hands above his head, chanting

words that Nellie couldn't make out. His eyes had gone luminous white.

Despite her fear, she scouted for a weapon, finding a coat stand.

Oof, it was heavy.

The dragon had turned around again.

A trail of sparks dropped from the dog's pelt. Where the sparks hit the table, the abandoned food on the plates came to life.

No, not all of it. The sausages that the circus party had brought remained where they were. But slices of bread, legs of ham, wine and tea flew into the air, turning into sparks of magic as they did so.

A flock of little furry creatures flew over, gathering the sparks as they went.

Nellie knew bats lived in the palace towers, but had never seen any about during the day, before.

A shout came from the doorway as a guard tried to stop a group of geese coming in. They ran waddling, flat-footed, into the hall while honking indignantly.

And when had the pigs come in from the kitchen yard? Nellie recognised the old cranky sow with the black ear.

While a servant ran in to chase after the pigs, two horses came into the hall, and they shied away from the leopard, which sprinted across at tremendous speed, leash trailing over the ground.

The dragon still flew around, but his wingbeats were slower, and once or twice he bumped into a table or chair.

"Come on, we have to help him!" Nellie called out.

She started towards the shepherd carrying the coat stand. Gisele and Koby followed. Henrik came as well, brandishing a lance that he appeared to have "borrowed" from a guard.

The fire dog managed to free itself and dropped to the

ground. The dragon landed on a table, scattering plates and glasses.

The food that the palace had provided had all disintegrated, but Agatha's biscuits were still intact. Nellie rushed to the table. The dragon looked terrible. She put the coat stand down and held out a biscuit to the dragon.

"Here, eat a biscuit."

The dragon took it out of her hand. His lips were wet with moisture. Snot or sweat?

He crunched on the biscuits and then lifted his head, more alert than before.

She hadn't expected the biscuit to help *that* much, but . . . Anneke had helped make them, and she had magic.

Nellie rubbed the dragon's neck. "Come on, we've almost defeated the fire dog. You attack the dog. I'll look after the prince. When we win, you can have all the carrots in the world."

The dragon took off again. He picked the fire dog off the floor. The creature snarled at the dragon.

Nellie ran across the hall. She heaved the coat stand above her head. She had lost sight of Gisele and Koby, but Henrik was a few paces ahead of her, still making his way to where the shepherd stood against the stream of people who were fleeing the hall.

Several things happened at the same time. A loud crash came from the doorway as Esme made her way into the hall, ripping the doors from the frame. Mustafa hung onto the back of the saddle. Several horses burst in. The dragon flew towards the dais.

Bruno cowered in his seat, covering his face with his arms.

"Come on, help us!" called Nellie.

Casper grabbed a carving knife and jumped onto the table. He lunged for the fire dog when the dragon flew over.

Nellie approached the shepherd from behind. He held his hands raised, chanting evil words at the top of his voice.

Nellie swung the coat stand.

She didn't think about him being the leader of the church she loved. She didn't think about the beauty and serenity of the big church with its arched ceiling, scent of candle wax and incense and rows of pews full of friends and trusted people.

She only thought, *This evil needs to be cut from the church.*

She brought down the coat stand.

At the same time the shepherd turned around.

The coat stand came down. Nellie couldn't stop it anymore. Henrik yelled behind her, but she couldn't hear his words.

The shepherd held up his hands to protect himself from the blow. Magic burst from his hands and engulfed the metal stand. Nellie had to let go of it.

But when this happened, the shepherd lost control of the fire dog. It stopped biting and scratching the dragon.

"You insignificant little woman," snarled the shepherd. "How dare you attack me!"

Nellie was so scared she felt numb. And the numbness reduced her fear. While standing there, facing this terrible man with the skull-like face and the blood of people on his hands, she felt serene. He could kill her if he wanted, but for that moment she didn't care, because he was wrong and the Triune would punish him.

"You worry about wrong and right, and about the real church," she said, her mouth stiff with nerves. "We are the real church, because the Triune loves us all and dislikes cruelty. In fact, it took cruelty into itself and suffered on our behalf so that we didn't have to. We are the church, and you're just a selfish tyrant."

He was going to reply. He was going to smite her with

the magic that was flowing from his hands like smoke, but the dragon was flying up the middle of the hall, coming straight for the shepherd with a ball of flames in its paws.

He must have seen the shock in Nellie's eyes, and noticed how she stumbled back. He turned around.

Too late.

The dragon dropped the flaming ball—the magical essence of the fire dog—on top of the shepherd. It exploded in a big ball of fire.

Nellie ducked. For a moment, she could see nothing in the brightness of the magical fire.

The flames crept up the dais, consuming the carpet and licking at the table that stood there. Strands of magic encased the inferno, dousing the flames, but some of it still leaked out.

Esme trotted across the hall, with Mustafa still trying to climb into the saddle. She stuck her nose into a bowl that contained water for washing one's hands. She then spurted the water onto the burning carpet. The fire went out in a cloud of smoke.

And when the smoke cleared, Bruno sat straight-backed on his throne, as if nothing had happened.

"All hail the king," someone yelled.

Someone repeated the acclamation, and it went all around the dining hall. People from the foyer rushed into the hall. In their hurry, they trampled the dust—all that was left of Shepherd Wilfridus—into the carpet.

A little spark of gold flew across the devastation and settled on Nellie's hand. The dragon had shrunk so much containing the fire that he was barely bigger than a mouse. Nellie used her index finger to stroke his back.

"Thank you," she said, because you always had to be nice, even to a dragon.

Amid the chaos and cheering, Bruno came down the dais. When he stood next to Nellie, he again was the little fragile boy she rescued from the crypt. He had left the crown on the seat of the throne and the sceptre leaning against the armrest.

"I'm sorry," he said, his voice soft.

"It all ended up fine," Nellie said.

"Yes, but that wasn't because of anything I did. I was silly and impatient. I'm only alive because people helped me, and you helped me most of all."

He held the dragon box out to her.

Nellie took it, opened it and let the dragon flutter inside. Then she shut the box and handed it back to Bruno.

He shook his head. "It's yours."

"It is your dragon. Your father gave it to you."

"I don't know how to use it. It won't listen to me anyway. I thought I knew how to control it, but I don't."

"Then you should learn."

CHAPTER 25

WHILE EVERYONE WAS celebrating victory—or merely confused—Master Thiele's men moved into the palace.

The master himself was not there, but Nellie recognised several of the dark-clad men who came into the hall. They sealed the entrances. They made sure the servants went back downstairs and all the people who had streamed into the palace left again.

Master Thiele himself came in later, in the company of three heavily armed guards. By this time, Casper and the noble youngsters had already cleaned up a good deal of the mess: the broken plates, the spilled food, the remains of burnt items. Wet carpets were replaced with dry ones, and the tables put back in orderly fashion.

Nellie helped with this, although her dress made the work uncomfortable because one side kept slipping off her shoulder.

But when Master Thiele came in, the table was ready. He sat down and gestured for everyone in the hall to do the same.

"Us, too?" Nellie asked.

"Especially you," he said.

Nellie felt nervous. She had to remind herself that she was no longer Nellie the maid, and that hiding in the kitchen was such an easy thing to do.

When everyone was seated, Master Thiele gave a quick explanation of who he was. He told the gathered young nobles that in the chaos following the king and queen's deaths, he had taken care of the crown and sceptre, planning to bring them out when a rightful heir to the throne appeared or was appointed with the approval of the citizens.

But since Bruno was too young, and not properly prepared, a temporary solution must be found. "We need to resolve the regency quickly and peacefully."

Everyone looked at Bruno, whose face was pale and who appeared very small.

He spoke only a few stammering words, his cheeks red. Ten years locked up in a dungeon was no way to prepare a young boy for a task as important as this.

"He will need our help," Master Thiele continued. "He is alone and too young. Until he is older, we need a strong leader—a group of leaders. Ideally, we need to write a council of advisors into the laws."

Casper said, "I can help."

"You're too young, too. For the stability of the city, we need someone older and more experienced to establish proper procedures."

"The mayor," Henrik said.

"Someone whose honesty is not compromised by ties either with the Regent's family or any of the competing noble houses or countries."

According to the law, the Regent was appointed by the church, and none of the Regent's powers transferred to the Regent's family after his death. The church assumed the power instead, but the law said nothing about what happened in the absence of the leader of the church. This was why Master Thiele had sealed the palace off and insisted that no one leave the hall until they found a temporary solution.

The discussions went on well into the night. Instead of allowing the influential families to come in together and argue, Master Thiele invited them one by one and asked them very specific questions. He explained, in between interviews, that he was looking for people who were willing to consider the welfare of the city over their own or that of their business.

From these visits, he produced a list of names of candidates for council positions, which the attendees in the room approved.

By now, it was very late, and the young people in the hall looked worn out. To be sure, Nellie felt worn out. It had been a long day.

But Master Thiele insisted the younger generation be included in the meetings, because the carrying out of the agreement would rest on their shoulders.

They agreed that over the next few days, they would put together a governing council that would take control of the city until a more permanent solution could be negotiated.

The council would include representatives from each industry, as well as elected officials, such as the mayor, and the heads of the major organisations. Surprise suggestions were Master Beck from the Science Guild and the leaders of the Baker's Guild and Tailor's Guild. No noble representatives were to be included solely on the basis that they were noble. Many names from the nobility were on the list of possibilities, but it was clear why each person was there: because of their trade or their knowledge. There would be a position for the church, but Master Thiele would let the church find a candidate to fill it. That would take some time.

After this, Master Thiele ordered the doors opened. A guard carried a copy of the agreement across the palace forecourt, and attached it, as traditional, to the door of the church.

When everyone was leaving the room, going back home or finding places to sleep, Nellie felt a deep sense of fatigue come over her.

"I guess it's time I find that little cottage and start my vegetable garden," she said.

"Bruno has asked us to stay," Henrik told her.

"Stay here?" Nellie looked around.

She had spent a good deal of her life in the palace, both as servant and queen's confidante. The place was full of memories, good and bad.

"He says that he doesn't have parents. We can be his parents."

"He has his father."

"Who know where he is or when he's coming back?"

"Please, I want all of you to stay," Casper said from behind her. He looked taller than he had seemed the last time she met him, and the blue suit didn't look as ridiculous on him as it had looked before. His younger brother was with him. "We don't have anywhere to go."

"What about your mother?"

"She wants to go back to Lurezia."

"But she said she was proud of you."

Frederick said, "She did, but she doesn't want to live here anymore."

Casper looked down. "I want to have a real business, with ships and captains and . . . people who can look me in the eye and tell me I'm a respectable person. People who would defend me and the business because they believe it's a good business. Not because they like my banquets. I want a wife whose family thinks I'm a good person. Can you help me with that?"

"Of course." Heavens, poor young man.

The story of what had happened here over the past few days would no doubt be told later, but it had a profound effect on these young people.

And the idea of staying in the palace appealed to Nellie.

After spending the night at Henrik daughter's house, she returned to the palace the next day to oversee cleaning up the royal family's living areas. She took great pleasure in removing the Regent's dreadful furniture and dusting off Queen Johanna's elegant furnishings and restoring them to their former positions. She made sure that all the rooms were well-furnished and welcoming.

In the evening, she and Henrik shared a meal with the three boys. From not having a family, Nellie had gone to being a favourite auntie for three lost boys.

Nellie didn't venture into the kitchen until a few days later. To her sadness, Dora was gone. Apparently the Duke of Aroden had needed a cook. Nellie intended to write to Dora, but in a way, she was afraid to find out just how much her friend had been involved with the shepherd and whether she had betrayed Nellie, and if so whether it had been by choice or because she was scared. Maybe it was best to leave things as they were.

Almost everyone else was back working there, including Maartje, who looked like she had received a significant promotion out of the scullery and into the main kitchen. She was, she said, training to be a baker.

Nellie asked about Els, when she noticed that Maartje's older sister was not there.

After his unwitting involvement in the poisoning of citizens for the shepherd had become clear, Mr Oliver had declared he had enough of ruling the shop. Who better to take over his legal gin distillery than someone who already knew everything about making gin?

Nellie had to smile when she heard people talk about "the handsome young Lurezian man" who now ran the distillery with his "fair-haired Scandian lady." Gisele was more comfortable facing the world as Gerard.

Madame Sabine left the palace without further ado. After having boasted that she would go back to Burovia and her influential friends, or to Lurezia and her family who was related to the king, she chose to stay in town, moving into a stately house in the noble quarter. She was a strange woman.

The two boys continued to live in the palace and take lessons with Bruno. The council also wrote to neighbouring countries to find a magic teacher for the young prince.

Mistress Luisa came all the way from Senoza and arrived in town in the middle of a wave of people returning to the city after having fled on the shepherd's strong "suggestion". Her skin was as dark as Mustafa's too-strong tea and her hair black and bushy. She spent long days with Bruno in a room in the palace cellar and he was always very tired after those sessions. He had so much to practice, and a lot looked like training the dragon like a dog: walk behind the prince, sit still when waiting, don't frighten visitors.

Mistress Luisa assured Nellie that flying on the dragon's back was a long time away, a feat reserved for only the strongest magicians.

Nellie had to smile at hearing that.

Other people who returned to town included Jantien's husband. He brought stories of having fled murderous mercenaries. He'd been very lucky to survive. Many of the other refugees had never made it to their intended destinations.

After the death of Shepherd Wilfridus, two of the church's senior deacons fled the city, leaving the church in the hands of a junior deacon and a couple of visiting monks. The church was in disarray.

Nellie went to the main church every day. She helped to clean and to pack up all of Shepherd Wilfridus' possessions. In his house, at the back of the church, they found many books on magic.

A few days later, when she came to the church, a familiar figure greeted her.

"Shepherd Adrianus!" She ran to him and hugged him.

He told her he'd been taken to one of the monasteries and had seen with his own eyes how the Regent's men stopped people leaving or entering the city. "They said it was because they wanted to stop magic, but that did not justify the cruelty I saw. I'm deeply ashamed that I ever supported such a man. I will need to beg the town for forgiveness."

He did just that a week later, when during the ceremony that saw him elevated to head of the Church of the Triune, he sank to his knees facing the audience—and the church was full to bursting—and pleaded with them to forgive him and not to hesitate to tell him if he ever strayed from the path again.

Nellie and Henrik sat in the front row with Bruno, and after the service, they went to the shepherd's house to ask him for a favour.

The following spring, everyone returned to the church for a service of a very different kind.

Before the eyes of the town elders and the packed congregation which included the young king, Nellie and Henrik exchanged their vows of marriage.

As recently instated head of the palace guards, Henrik wore his uniform. He'd decided that his beard was going to stay.

Nellie wore a pretty and elegant dress in pale blue, with hundreds of little beads adorning the skirt.

Henrik's daughters and Master Thiele were witnesses. Casper and Frederick led the parade. Having just turned fifteen, Bruno signed the document.

He was fast turning into a knowledgeable young man, and rarely went anywhere without Mistress Luisa, who was about to start teaching other children. Nellie had been happy to hear that Anneke was one of them.

Their troubles were far from over. For one, where there were nobles and priests, there were scandals and scheming. That would never change.

The church had received a letter from The Most Holy Father of the Belaman Church, demanding that reparations be paid for the damage to the recently reopened church building in Saardam.

Madame Sabine had taken off suddenly. Rumours went that she had gone to make reparations with the Burovian king's brother, whose new young wife Baroness Hestia had unexpectedly given birth not three months after their wedding. The nobles were outraged.

And people continued to be outraged at the newfangled exploits of the Science Guild.

But Mustafa reopened his animal garden and many people came through the gates to see and hear the foul-mouthed parrots. He even bought a plot of land opposite the entrance, where he built a house especially for Esme. At all times—except when she was taking children on rides through the city—she could be seen through the windows, and she would stick her trunk through the gaps to beg for carrots. And, in a happy ending for her, Mustafa hired Koby to help him.

The river traders started to return to the harbour.

And in summer, a letter arrived at the palace that spoke of an upcoming visit from a ship of the Eastern

Trader office. The letter was short on detail, but Bruno was sure his father would be on board.

Saardam once more took its place as a hub where the world met and occasionally disagreed, but mostly got along just fine.

Thanks for reading

THANK you for reading the Dragonspeaker Chronicles. Have you read the *Ghostspeaker Chronicles* yet? That series covers the story of Queen Johanna and King Roald.

ABOUT THE AUTHOR

Patty Jansen lives in Sydney, Australia, where she spends most of her time writing Science Fiction and Fantasy.

Her story *This Peaceful State of War* placed first in the second quarter of the Writers of the Future contest and was published in their 27th anthology. She has also sold fiction to genre magazines such as Analog Science Fiction and Fact, Redstone SF and Aurealis.

Patty has written over twenty novels in both Science Fiction and Fantasy, including the *Icefire Trilogy* and the *Ambassador* series.

pattyjansen.com

BOOKS BY PATTY JANSEN

www.ingramcontent.com/pod-product-compliance
Lightning Source LLC
Chambersburg PA
CBHW051652180726
48284CB00006B/1964